THE OLD ASIAN WAS STILL ATTACKING THE SEAL

But now plastic shards had begun to fly like string confetti in a homecoming parade.

Impossible! He was using his fingernails to whittle away at the supposedly invulnerable polymer.

Hahn glanced at the monitors. He was watching two screens at once. The young one was across the room while the old one and the girl stood under the door overhang. Hahn zoomed in on the roof.

Yes. There it was. The acid was rotting the securing bracket away. No sooner had he focused the camera than the metal twisted and snapped. The roof lurched and collapsed.

Two dead, one left. Hahn reached for the control panel. There was no protection, no way out.

Hahn flipped the last switch. Gripping tight to the edge of the control panel, he threw his attention back to the monitors. To watch the younger man finally do as he was supposed to.

Melt into a pile of steaming flesh and bone.

Other titles in this series:

Created by Murphy & Sapir

THE Destroyer™

AIR RAID

A GOLD EAGLE BOOK FROM

W RLDWIDE®

TORONTO • NEW YORK • LONDON
AMSTERDAM • PARIS • SYDNEY • HAMBURG
STOCKHOLM • ATHENS • TOKYO • MILAN
MADRID • WARSAW • BUDAPEST • AUCKLAND

First edition January 2002

ISBN 0-373-63241-X

AIR RAID

Special thanks and acknowledgment to
James Mullaney for his contribution to this work.

To Kath,
who renamed him the much more appropriate "Sage Carlin."

To the Glorious House of Sinanju.
e-mail: housinan@aol.com

And to everyone who has taken time
to write letters of encouragement to the above address.
If the author hasn't made clear his thanks
for all of your kind words, he's dong so now.

1

It was only three-quarters of an inch long, but it was more destructive than a billion atomic bombs the size of the one dropped on Hiroshima. At least that's what the scientist sitting before him claimed. But if there was one thing he'd learned in life, it was that a lot of times scientists said things that weren't exactly the unvarnished truth.

"Are you sure? Are you absolutely, positively, one hundred percent *sure?*" Hubert St. Clair asked.

"I wouldn't say it if it wasn't true, Dr. St. Clair," replied the young scientist. The precious object was clamped snugly between the slender steel tips of a small pair of medical forceps.

When he saw the sudden withering look on Hubert St. Clair's face, the scientist suddenly remembered whom he was talking to.

Dr. Hubert St. Clair was the head of the Congress of Concerned Scientists, a group of pseudoscience worshipers that specialized in issuing dire predictions on epic, global scales, none of which ever seemed to actually come true.

"Oh," said the young scientist, offering a weak apologetic smile.

Dr. Brice Schumar was still holding his tight smile as St. Clair wordlessly pulled the forceps from the embarrassed scientist's hand. Lifting his glasses up to his forehead, he brought the tiny object close to his nearsighted eyes.

It looked like an ordinary plant seed.

The seed was a bluish purple. The two halves of its perfectly symmetrical bifurcated body were separated by a deep groove. One end was round; the other terminated in a blunted point. At the rounded end sat a fat blob of perfect azure.

St. Clair had never seen a more beautiful blue. His sour expression slowly melted back to joy. He stared, captivated by the little blue seed and all it represented.

"It's magnificent," Dr. St. Clair said softly.

Squinting his right eye, he held the seed up to his left. It was just small enough to blot out his pupil. His reddish-brown iris and bloodshot white were still visible.

"It was a lot of work," Dr. Schumar replied.

The tiny seed shifted, and Hubert St. Clair's pupil reappeared. "I wasn't talking to you," he said, his look of intense displeasure returning. "And this seed coat looks tough. You better not have the same coumartling problem you had a couple of years ago."

The scientist shook his head. *"Coumarin,"* Schumar corrected. "And there are virtually no antiauxins present at all. Didn't you, um, read my report?"

"No time," St. Clair said with a dismissive wave

of the seed-gripping forceps. "We in the governing body of the CCS can't be bothered with dusty old reports. We're out there in the scientific trenches, verbally engaging the Katie Courics and Oprah Winfreys of the world. And ever since the tragic, untimely end of our latest and greatest member, we've all been pulling double duty."

Of course Dr. Schumar knew precisely whom St. Clair was talking about. None other than the legend himself, Sage Carlin. At one time the most famous scientist in the entire world. The deceased CCS elder had been an outspoken member of the scientific community and a celebrity mouthpiece for the Congress of Concerned Scientists since the 1960s. Carlin had also—to Dr. Brice Schumar's knowledge—never once let his passion for environmental issues be clouded by a single fact. His version of science was all conjecture and hope masquerading as truth.

When he was alive, Carlin had wagged a hectoring finger at the world about everything from ocean warming to dumping toxic waste to deforestation. His had been a life of easily digestible factoids and buzzwords, embraced by the ruling cultural class and fast-food, quick-fix Americans with MTV attention spans.

In his darkest heart, which he dared not reveal to anyone else within the CCS, Dr. Brice Schumar had hoped that with the passing of Sage Carlin five years earlier, the congress would abandon its former leader's love of sloppy science and turn to a more reasoned approach of addressing the ills of the world. Even though Carlin's showy claims garnered much attention, they were ultimately very destructive to the credibility of real scientists. After all, a mile-wide asteroid hadn't destroyed Atlantic City, cow flatulence wasn't depleting the mesosphere and the sun hadn't exploded. Schumar knew that this last claim of Carlin's had relied on particularly sloppy science, seeing as how it was made after he'd watched a screening of the film *Superman* in the CCS theater.

When he learned Carlin had died, Dr. Schumar was ashamed of the quiet relief the news gave him. His hopes for a return of serious scientific thought in the world headquarters of the CCS in Geneva were short-lived.

He couldn't exactly remember when he first noticed the trend, or who started it. He only realized what was happening one afternoon at the Swiss headquarters when he spotted a fellow scientist sporting a dusty corduroy jacket with wide lapels. In the ensuing weeks, a handful of similarly clothed men became a dozen. Then a multitude. Until nearly everyone in the Geneva labs and offices was wearing the same uniform.

It was the curse of Sage Carlin.

The world-famous scientist and activist had a unique sense of style. Dr. Schumar had always thought of it as a sort of antifashion. In addition to an omnipresent corduroy jacket, Carlin wore a thick turtleneck sweater, always in the darker shades of green or earth tones. He wore powder-blue jeans that were always hopelessly out of fashion. They were tight in the thighs and rump and wide as church bells around his sandals. The 1970s lived on into the nineties, at least sartorially, on the body of Sage Carlin. In homage to their fallen leader, his troops at the CCS adopted Sage Carlin's mode of dress.

Dr. Hubert St. Clair was no exception.

As head of the CCS, St. Clair ensured his lapels were always the widest, his bell-bottoms the biggest. To preserve some sense of scholarship, his jackets always seemed to smell vaguely of chalk dust, even though it had been a long time since the former professor had seen an actual blackboard.

In Brice Schumar's lab, Hubert St. Clair was still studying the single blue seed.

"I see," Dr. Schumar said, clearing his throat. "If you haven't read my report, then there's something that you might be interested in seeing." An anxious smile flickered at the corners of his lips.

"What?" St. Clair asked.

"Trust me," Dr. Schumar insisted, a flush of excitement rising in his cheeks. "You have to see this."

St. Clair reluctantly put down the forceps and the beautiful blue seed. He allowed Dr. Schumar to lead him out into the hall.

They traveled deep into the bowels of the CCS complex, stopping outside the sealed double doors to the greenhouse.

"We know absolutely now that the problem with the last batch was overproduction of antiauxins," Dr. Schumar said as he punched the code into the keypad of the greenhouse doors. "The growth hormones couldn't be released. So while the plants we engineered grew to maturity, they couldn't reproduce without monumental help from us. In effect, they were sterile.''

"No kidding," St. Clair muttered.

There seemed something more behind his words.

St. Clair kept far from the door as Schumar entered the code. He eyed the panel with mistrust.

A red light above the door winked out and a green light clicked on. There was a hiss as the hermetic seal on the door popped. The two thick plastic panels parted.

"Those early trees were a learning experience," Schumar stressed as they stepped inside.

The double doors shut automatically behind them. St. Clair almost jumped out of his skin when they did. They were in a small control room. A second set of doors—this one of thicker plastic composite—blocked their path.

"Learning is overrated in science these days," St. Clair said as Dr. Schumar entered a second code into the next security pad. "The smartest people I've ever known are complete morons."

Another hiss and the main greenhouse doors whooshed open.

The first thing that hit Hubert St. Clair was the smell. It burned his nostrils and seared his eyes.

"Sweet Georgia Brown, what is that?" St. Clair demanded, gagging on the fumes. His eyes watered.

"Ammonia with a touch of methane," Schumar explained.

The burning air didn't seem to bother the young

scientist. He had spent too many hours in the green-house to even notice it any longer. He ducked inside. Dr. St. Clair trailed reluctantly.

"Smells like my grandma's bathroom closet," St. Clair complained, pulling a handkerchief from the pocket of his corduroy coat. He stuffed the hankie over his nose and mouth.

"She stored cleaning materials there, I imagine," Schumar said. "The skylights and fans can clear most of the air in here in less than a minute, but the ammonia lingers. We might have made this greenhouse unusable for future projects."

St. Clair merely grunted beneath his handkerchief.

The CCS greenhouse was colossal. Sunlight sparkled off the angled roof far above. Fans, sprinklers and sensory equipment were attached to the fat girders that spanned the massive structure. All helped to carefully control and maintain the artificial environment.

The skylights were all open, a necessity given the unique danger the greenhouse presented.

At the center of the huge greenhouse, hundreds of trees were lined up like patient soldiers. Schumar led St. Clair into the meticulously maintained forest.

The trees in the CCS greenhouse were unlike any seen in nature. Although the shapes of leaf and trunk were familiar, the color was all wrong.

The leaves were the thin blue of a cloudless late-afternoon summer sky. The trunks were a dark midnight blue.

"You haven't been here since before the most recent growth cycle, have you?" Dr. Schumar asked.

"No," St. Clair replied.

He hadn't been to the greenhouse in months. The trees stretched up from a series of squat rectangular boxes filled with chemically treated soil. The tallest was now almost thirty feet high. The last time St. Clair had seen them, the biggest was less than ten feet.

St. Clair was struck by the beauty of the trees.

"Only God can make one of these, my ass," he said under his breath.

They were breathtaking. Absolutely breathtaking.

The instant the word formed in his brain he realized how true it was. On every level.

"They're growing faster with each passing cycle," Schumar was saying. "Frankly, the growth spurts in a tree this age are incredible. And even a little disconcerting when you think about it." As he looked up at the soft blue leaves of the trees, his face was grave. "I'm glad we have them under lock and key. There's no telling what might—"

"Wait a minute," Hubert St. Clair interrupted all at once. "What the hell is that?"

Even as he pointed up under a tightly bundled knot of leaves, he was scrambling onto the edge of a planting box.

It became more difficult to breathe the closer he got to the trees. He had been told they needed to be spaced far apart in the beds. If they were any closer together, it would be impossible to breathe while standing between them.

Head tipped back, St. Clair examined the underside of the leaf cluster.

Some kind of blue growths had sprouted up on the branches. Hidden beneath the leaves, they looked almost like bumpy beehives. He didn't see any insects.

"Dammit, you've got some kind of infestation here," St. Clair snapped. "Get some DDT before we lose these blasted things altogether."

Brice Schumar didn't move. He just stood there on the greenhouse floor, an idiot's grin plastered across his face.

"Look closer," he suggested.

Nose crinkling, St. Clair peered more carefully at the cluster of abandoned hives clinging together on the underside of an overhanging branch. When he realized what he was looking at, he nearly fell off the raised plant bed.

It was the sheer number of them that had thrown him. But he saw now that they were all identical to the one he'd seen just a few minutes before in Schumar's lab. Seeds. Tons of them.

"Are these *all* seeds?" Hubert St. Clair croaked.

"They came with the latest growth spurt," Schumar said. "Thousands on each tree. It was in my report."

St. Clair slipped around the far side of the tree.

Another cluster of seeds clutched a branch on the other side. Still others were visible higher up.

A second tree grew a few feet away in the same

bed. St. Clair saw more of the teardrop-shaped blue seedlets clinging all over the branches.

Numbly, he climbed down from the bed. His mind was reeling.

"What about the seed coats?" St. Clair asked. "They look like leather."

"Not a problem," Schumar said excitedly. "They're tough-looking but easily penetrated by water. We had a lingering of some chemical inhibitors prior to germination, but that's been eliminated. Now the growth inhibitors are easily bleached away by the introduction of water."

"Just regular water?" St. Clair asked.

"Tap water, rainwater. It's all the same," Schumar said. "Of course, that's not going to be good enough for all alien climates. And at this point it wouldn't even work for some of Jupiter's moons or Mars, since we've got ice to contend with there. The next generations of the plants will have to be weaned from water."

"Weaned?" St. Clair asked, coming back around. "Why?"

"Well, that was the whole point of growing them," Schumar said. "Eventually developing an oxygen-producing strain that could help terraform an alien world."

"Yes, yes. Of course," St. Clair said gruffly. He stabbed a finger at a seed cluster. "Get me a bunch of these. I want to dissect them in my office."

Schumar was surprised and relieved by St. Clair's sudden interest in legitimate scientific inquiry. Maybe with this one, great project the Congress of Concerned Scientists could return to its founding principles and finally put to eternal rest the destructive ghost of Sage Carlin.

"Yes, Doctor," Schumar said. He scurried obediently onto the nearest raised plant bed.

As he happily picked seeds, he saw Hubert St. Clair hurry out the open door of the greenhouse.

Probably the ammonia smell. Most people couldn't take it for very long. Even the little seeds he was slipping into the pocket of his white lab coat smelled vaguely of the stuff.

His hand was snaking for another clutch of tiny seeds when he was startled by the sound of the overhead alarm.

Dr. Schumar thrust his face out through a bundle of blue leaves. The red light was flashing a warning even as the greenhouse doors were sliding slowly shut.

Of all the people on the face of the planet, Dr. Brice Schumar understood best what it meant to be on the wrong side of those closing doors.

The seeds in his hands slipped from his terrified fingers. Jumping down from the plant bed, he ran for the door, lungs burning from the ammonia in the air.

The thick plastic doors clicked shut just as he reached them. There was a hiss as the automatic seal inflated to prevent vapor from seeping out of the greenhouse to where Hubert St. Clair sat uncomfortably.

The warning alarm switched off.

"Dr. St. Clair!" Schumar shouted, pounding on the door.

There was an environmental control panel in the alcove between the two sets of double doors. As Schumar watched helplessly, Hubert St. Clair began picking at the buttons. The very act of touching them seemed to bring him pain.

Schumar heard a rumble from above. Spinning, wild-eyed, he saw the skylights begin to slide remorselessly shut. Like the thick greenhouse doors, they clicked then hissed, becoming airtight. Even as the skylights were sealing, St. Clair was switching on the interior speakers.

"You've done a good job," St. Clair said, his voice distorted by the speaker next to the door.

"Let me out," Schumar begged. *"Please."* The air was already growing thin. Panic flooded his chest as he struggled to breathe.

Carlin shook his head. "Can't," he said. "I know you've done a lot of tests, but there's really only one we're interested in. And you're the perfect subject. You never really fit in around here, Schumar. You and your scientific method and your facts this and facts that. Always looking down your nose at the rest of us like we weren't real scientists." His expression suddenly grew as cold as ice. "Do I look like a real scientist to you now, Dr. Schumar?"

There was touch of madness deep in his red eyes.

Brice Schumar began beating his fists against the plastic door. His lungs were on fire, his throat raw.

The air was evaporating.

His hands and wrists ached. He stopped hitting the door.

"Please," Brice wept. The word was inaudible.

Beyond the pane, Hubert St. Clair watched, growing more disinterested with each passing minute. He seemed more concerned with the equipment he was using. As if there were some infection he could get just by touching it. He wrapped his finger tightly in his handkerchief to avoid direct contact with the buttons.

Brice Schumar didn't know how long it took him to die. With each labored breath he felt the air grow thinner. Slipping out until the last oxygen was gone. Until all that was left was poison.

The air was thick with ammonia and methane. The worst was the carbon dioxide. The colorless, odorless gas flooded the interior of the greenhouse.

His lungs were lead as he sank slowly to the floor. A crimson rash decorated his face around his nose and mouth. With dying eyes, Dr. Brice Schumar gazed over at the small grove of trees. Trees he had helped create.

Amazing that so few could do so much damage. In a lucid part of his rapidly clouding brain, he felt relief that he hadn't grown more. Obviously, Hubert St. Clair was a maniac. With more trees he could—

Schumar suddenly caught sight of a cluster of seeds.

The seeds. St. Clair had thousands of seeds.

Dr. Brice Schumar's lungs pulled one last time at

the oxygen that was no longer there, and he tipped over onto the plain dirt floor of the CCS greenhouse.

IN THE SAFETY of the control room, Hubert St. Clair looked at the digital clock buried in the console. He kept his distance from the device. He liked clocks about as much as he trusted the buttons on the control panel.

"Precisely thirty-one minutes," he announced to himself. "*Now* who's the real scientist?" His proud smile evaporated. "Oh. Wait." He scrunched up his face as he examined the clock. "Or was it forty-one? Oh, damn, I lost count."

He pulled his eyes away from the clock. Like most digital devices, looking at it made him extremely uncomfortable.

With an angry frown he wrapped his finger in his hankie once more. Reaching for the control panel, he began to vent the alien atmosphere from the greenhouse.

2

His name was Remo and he was trying to do his good deed of the day. But, to his increasing annoyance, the day was stubbornly refusing to cooperate.

The sidewalks of New York were packed with people. A steady stream filled the slushy walkways and flooded the crosswalks. Cars clogged the streets, all spewing smoke and honking horns and cursing drivers. Unlike the people, the cars never seemed to move. They were part of the backdrop, like the towering buildings or the glimpses of grimy gray sky that lurked above the entire scene like the billowing cape of some wintry phantom.

Remo wasn't watching the sky or the buildings or the cars. As he strolled along the sidewalk, he was watching the people. Few pedestrians returned his gaze. Most were too wrapped up in the holiday bustle to give a stranger a second glance. Not that there was anything extraordinary about Remo to warrant more than a single quick look.

Remo was a thin man of indeterminate age. He was of average height with short, dark hair and a face that regularly skirted the line between ordinary and cruel.

The only two things outwardly odd about him were his abnormally thick wrists—which he rotated absently as he walked—and his clothes. In spite of the fact that it was mid-December, Remo wore a thin black cotton T-shirt and matching chinos. Odd, yes, but in New York City, odd was fairly easily accepted. After all, there was a lot worse than Remo.

And so the man in the T-shirt was either seen and dismissed or not seen at all as he glided alone up the packed sidewalk.

As a general rule Remo didn't like Manhattan. Worse was Manhattan at Christmastime. The whole holiday rush was a nightmare he would have just as soon avoided altogether. But the circumstances of his life had conspired to plop him down into the busiest city in the world at the absolute worst time of the year.

Remo was a Master of Sinanju. On the verge of becoming the *Reigning* Master of Sinanju, the titular head of the most ancient house of assassins in the history of mankind.

He thought he had already become Reigning Master two months ago. After all, the time had felt right. And he had been told that every Master knew instinctively when the time was right. So that should have been that. But things never worked out so easily for Remo Williams.

He soon learned that he was technically the Transitional Reigning Master. There were obligations prior to his ascension that would have to be met before he could officially assume the title of Reigning Master and all of the awesome responsibilities the position entailed. One of those things, which had brought him to Manhattan this day, seemed to be at odds with everything he had been taught.

Sinanju assassins were the pinnacle of the profession. Only two existed per generation—Master and pupil—and the training regimen they endured endowed them with abilities that seemed superhuman to the average man. The fear and mystery that surrounded the very thought of the Sinanju Master had been carefully cultivated over five millennia. Remo sometimes thought the perception had as much to do with marketing hype as it did with the truth.

The one constant that had persisted throughout the ages was that Masters of Sinanju were consummate professionals. They were paid handsomely for their services, since only fools and amateurs worked free. And yet, here was Remo Williams, professional assassin, looking this day to deliver a freebie.

Just what he had to do, he had no idea. But according to his teacher, he had to do something nice for someone. Of course, his teacher didn't come right out and say that. No. That would have been easy. Instead, he had prattled on for three hours about honor and obligation, duty and commitment, before finally getting around to the point. And so after three hours— 180 of the longest, most painful minutes he had endured in years—Remo had culled the word *nice*.

Maybe it was something simple. As he walked along, face drawn in a deep frown, he noticed a woman struggling near the curb. In her arms she balanced a stack of boxes wrapped in shining green-and-red Rudolph paper. A cab was parked near her. The driver sat at the wheel, refusing to help.

Remo trotted up to the sweating woman.

"Can I give you a hand, ma'am?"

He was amazed at how fast she moved.

The woman wheeled like a street fighter. "This is *my* cab," she snarled, even as she flung her precious packages to the snow. From her pocket she whipped out a can of pepper spray which she proceeded to squirt at Remo's eyes.

Remo ducked away from the spray. "Geez, lady, I was only offering to help," he complained.

Behind him, the squirted stream struck a hapless pedestrian square in the face. Screaming in pain, the unlucky businessman dropped to the ground in the fetal position. The moving crowd didn't even see him. People stepped right over him and continued down the sidewalk.

Before Remo, the woman scowled. She wasn't used to missing a target. "Stand still," she commanded.

Another squirt hit a superthin, impeccably dressed female pedestrian in the side of the face. Yelping in pain, the injured woman whipped out her own can of pepper spray. The two women proceeded to spritz each other like gunslingers at the OK Corral.

Remo danced lightly between them. Other pedestrians caught in the cross fire weren't so lucky.

"Mine, mine, mine!" the first woman screamed.

Half-blinded now, she whipped the door open and began flinging packages inside the back of the cab.

The second woman hadn't even wanted a taxi, but the unprovoked attack, as well as the first woman's loud proclamations, had triggered some base territorial urge. She suddenly decided that she wanted the cab, too. When Remo turned away, the second woman had the first in a bear hug around her ample middle while the first whacked her over the head with a roll of infant-Jesus Christmas paper.

"Try to do something nice for someone," Remo muttered.

Shaking his head in disgust, he headed down the street.

On the corner, a man dressed as Santa rang a bell for charitable donations. As Remo approached, he saw a scruffy-looking pedestrian grab Santa's donation bucket from the metal tripod where it hung. The man took off.

As Father Christmas yelled obscenities, the mugger ran down a nearby alley.

Remo was off like a shot. The crowd seemed suddenly charged with some electrical current that repelled them from Remo's path. They split instinctively up the middle as he raced down the sidewalk. Remo flew past the still screaming Saint Nick and ducked down the open end of the dark alley.

He caught up with Santa's mugger twenty yards in. The man was still running full-out.

"You know," Remo said as he grabbed the startled man by the scruff of the neck, flinging him into a grimy wall, ''as stupid crimes go, it's pretty dumb to rob a guy who keeps a list of who's been naughty or nice.''

The mugger spun on Remo, a demented gleam in his eye. Dropping the bucket he'd pinched from Santa, he clicked open a switchblade.

''I'd say assault with intent to commit bodily harm falls into the naughty category, too,'' Remo advised him. ''You're bucking for a lump of coal in your stocking, pal.''

The mugger lunged at Remo's belly with the knife. Dodging the blade, Remo snagged the man's wrist between two fingers, guiding the thrusting hand toward the alley wall.

In a twinkling, the solid brick seemed to go soft. To the mugger's amazement, the blade of the knife somehow managed to penetrate deep into brick before coming to a stop at the hilt. When he tried to pull it free, he found it stuck more firmly than Excalibur in the stone.

With a look of fear washing over his pale face, the mugger backed away from Remo. He bumped the wall behind.

''Not that *nice* is all it's cracked up to be,'' Remo grumbled. ''Here I am, supposed to do something nice, and I don't even know the what or the who.'' He shook his head. ''It's always the same thing. Always about tradition. First he says I've become Reigning Master just because I say I'm Reigning Master, then he pulls all this traditional rite-of-passage crapola out of his pocket. And not even right away. Oh, no. That'd be too painless. He eases into it during the month of hell I spend recovering from third degree burns. That's what he's like. Korean water torture. Drip, drip, drip.''

"He who?'' Santa's mugger asked anxiously. His eyes darted to the mouth of the alley. It seemed very far away.

"The pain in the ass who taught me,'' Remo said. "And don't think I haven't spent the last I-don't-know-how-many years of my life trying to figure out if he's an okay guy who's also a pain the ass or if he's a pain in the ass who just happens to sometimes be okay. On days like this, I just think he's a plain old everyday run-of-the-mill pain in the ass, and that's that. End of story.''

"Yeah. Wow. That's too bad,'' the mugger commiserated. He would have begun inching to the street, but this wacko with the flashing hands and the fingers that could stick steel through brick was standing right in his path.

"It is, isn't it?'' Remo agreed. "So I'm supposed to be Reigning Master, right? Wrong. Now I've got this whole Master Nik tradition to deal with.''

The mugger's face brightened hopefully. "Nick?'' he asked. "That's my name.'' He smiled, hoping to establish some kind of a connection with this crazy man.

"And if I was your parole officer or the guy who used the free needles after you, I just might give a fat flying Kringle,'' Remo assured him. "This Nik lived about twenty-seven hundred years ago. Didn't do anything to distinguish himself as Master, except establish one tradition.'' His voice grew mocking as he repeated the words passed down from Master Nik. '''No disciple of Sinanju shall attain the title of Reigning Master without he first deliver the proper act of kindness.'''

The mugger blinked, sensing opportunity. ''Kindness?'' he asked.

''Yeah, can you believe it?'' Remo asked, shaking his head. ''Vague as all get out. And what's with that 'without he first'? Is that even proper English?''

The mugger didn't hear. ''So you've got to, like, do a good deed?'' he pressed.

Remo nodded. ''All of a sudden now I'm a freaking Boy Scout,'' he said. ''As a kid I was a Cub Scout for barely one day. Mrs. Callahan was the den mother. She smoked cigars, had fifteen mooching Callahan kids running all over the place and her kitchen floor had more sand on it than Pismo Beach at low tide. I quit after the first meeting.''

''So this good deed you gotta do,'' Santa's mugger said, steering Remo back to the topic at hand. ''You sure you don't know what it is?''

Remo scowled, annoyed at the interruption. ''No.''

The man's face was hopeful. ''Maybe it's that you should let me go,'' he offered brightly.

Remo considered for a long moment. As he mulled over the man's words, the mugger grew increasingly optimistic. His hopes were dashed the instant Remo opened his mouth once more.

"Nah," Remo concluded firmly. "I'm pretty sure that isn't it. Besides, it's time for Santa's revenge."

Even as the mugger's face fell, Remo was reaching out.

The mugger didn't have time to run.

Remo spun the man, tapping a spot at the top of his fifth vertebra. The mugger's arms went slack.

"I hope you got all your Christmas stealing done for the next five years, because that's how long it'll be before you get back use of your hands," Remo announced as he deposited Santa's mugger headfirst into a garbage can.

Scooping up the small donation pail the mugger had stolen, Remo headed back out the alley.

Someone had run into a nearby store to call the police, but a cruiser had yet to arrive. Santa was standing anxiously near his tripod. He was cautiously relieved when he saw Remo appear with his bucket. Relief became amazement when he found it still full of coins and bills.

"You're a real lifesaver, buddy," Santa said, pawing a green mitten through the bucket of money. "Here, have a five-spot. Hell, it's Christmas. Take ten."

"Isn't that for the poor?" Remo frowned.

"Yeah, and reindeer can fly," Santa said with a broad wink. He stuffed some of the bills in his pocket. Remo saw the pocket was already bulging with Christmas cash.

Realizing that there was little hope that this was the good deed he was after, Remo let out a frustrated sigh before sticking the bucket firmly onto Santa's head.

Loose change rained onto the sidewalk. Pedestrians promptly prostrated themselves on the pavement, their grabbing hands scooping up wayward coins. The last Remo saw of Saint Nick, the portly man was stumbling blindly into traffic, his belly jiggling like a bowlful of panicked jelly.

By the time Remo heard a squeal of tires and a Santa-size thump, he wasn't even looking. Chin in his hand, he sat morosely on the curb.

"Maybe it's something even simpler," he muttered.

He noticed a nearby stray dachshund on the sidewalk. He tried to pet the dog. With snapping fangs, the little dog tried to take his finger off. When the owner of the dog—which was apparently not so stray after all—saw someone near her precious Poopsie, she started screaming "Dognapper!" at the top of her lungs while simultaneously attempting to strangle Remo with her Gucci dog leash.

Remo snapped the leash in two and, resisting the urge to kick both dog and owner, slouched off down the street.

He wandered the city for another two hours. He was ready to call it quits and head back home when he came upon a crowd outside the theater on Seventh Avenue.

The men and women heading into the building looked exceptionally affluent, even by New York standards. Remo was surprised to find that he recognized quite a few of them.

There were pop music performers and movie stars. He spotted a fat woman from a popular television legal drama who was allegedly proud of her gross obesity and whose mouth he would have liked to fill with cement if it would have had time to harden around all the moistened pizza crusts.

Falling in with the crowd, he melted through the open theater doors. A sign in the lobby advertised the event as a fund-raiser for something called Primeval Society.

Tables had been set in a great hall before the stage. A lot more celebrities were packed inside. Remo saw many people who had been successfully annoying him for decades.

He wondered briefly if the nice thing he was supposed to do was to tie everyone to their chairs and set the building on fire. Deciding that the attendant risk to the theater staff and fire department made this unlikely, he wandered the hall, eventually finding his way backstage.

In the wings he found performers hurrying in every direction as they got ready for the night's entertainment.

For some reason two tiny barefoot men in loincloths lurked sullenly in the shadows. They looked as if they'd be happier spearing fish in some South American jungle.

A table was piled high with hair tonics, mousse, curling irons, crimping tongs, coloring agents and a hundred different plastic bottles filled with scented salon products. Fighting for both bottles and mirror space were ten young men whose attention to the intricacies of personal grooming would have made a primping Liberace look like a rugged lumberjack.

A theater employee with a radio headset was walking by. Remo collared the man.

"Hey, don't I know them?" he asked.

"Are you kidding?" scoffed the harried stage director. "Those are the two most famous boy bands in the world."

Remo blinked. That's where he'd seen them before. Prancing on television and preening on magazine covers. Although Remo couldn't fathom why, the bands Glory Whole and But Me No Butz were American cultural phenomena.

He nodded as he recognized the poodle-haired one with the mushed-up face and the doughy bleached one with the granny glasses and the muscle shirt.

"What are they doing here?" Remo asked.

"For one night only they're forming a supergroup called Harmonic Convergence to raise money for the rain forest."

"Oh," Remo said. "Haven't we paved over that yet?"

But the stage director was no longer listening. Barking orders into his headset, he hurried off into the darker recesses of the wings. The two natives exchanged a few words in some guttural language before trailing after him. They each carried spears in their hands.

For a moment, Remo watched the ten young men preparing for their act. And in a moment of sheer maliciousness, Remo suddenly decided that he'd had enough of trying to figure out what this nice thing he was supposed to do was. He decided to do something nice for himself.

The two bands suddenly got into a scuffle over a can of particularly heavy-duty Vidal Sassoon mousse. The instant they were distracted, Remo fell in with them.

There was a lot of pinching and slapping as the fight escalated to include other hair-care products. So bitchy did it become that they failed to notice the tap just behind the right ear Remo gave each one of them in turn. Once he finished with them he slipped away. He took up a sentry post in the wings, a contented smile on his face.

Ten minutes later the concert began with polite applause when a thin woman in a long black gown took center stage. She was apparently the wife of the benefit's organizer. In a British accent that was obviously phony, she droned on and on about the importance of trees and rocks and butterflies and fluffy clouds and Mother Earth. Only when some of the crowd began to nod off into their soup did she finally introduce Harmonic Convergence.

The boys from But Me No Butz pranced in from stage left. Those from Glory Whole minced from stage right. When they met in the middle of the stage, it was less a harmonious convergence than it was a postpubescent pileup.

They couldn't seem to find their equilibrium. Every time they tried to dance, they stumbled into one another. After a few vain, bumbling tries, their frustration and embarrassment changed to anger. The boys from the bands redirected their energies toward one another. The fight from backstage erupted anew, this time with biting, kicking and hair pulling. By the time the nipple twisters started, the crowd was already breaking up.

As he turned from the pile of goatees and leather writhing on the stage, Remo was nodding in satisfaction.

"If that doesn't get me honorable mention in the annals of good deeddom, I don't know what will."

Whistling happily to himself, he ducked out the stage door and into the dimly lit alley.

3

The traffic out of Manhattan was worse than it had been going in. Still, Remo didn't mind.

The highway was a crawl to Rye, where he took a clogged off-ramp. The traffic situation in town wasn't much better than it had been on I-95, yet Remo remained unbothered.

He soon broke away from the mass of humanity that was heading home for the day. A lonely road that snaked alongside the black waters of Long Island Sound eventually brought him to a sedate, ivy-covered brick building. Humming happily to himself, he steered his car through the gate and up the great gravel drive of Folcroft Sanitarium.

Folcroft was cover to CURE, the supersecret government organization for which Remo functioned as enforcement arm. Folcroft had also been Remo's home for the past year.

Remo parked his car in the employee lot and headed for the building's side door. He was whistling as he danced down the stairwell to the basement.

The quarters he shared with the Master of Sinanju were tucked away from the rest of the sanitarium. As he pushed open the door, Remo didn't sense a heart-beat or breathing from the rooms beyond.

He stuck his head in the Master of Sinanju's bed-room. An unused sleeping mat was rolled tight in the middle of the room. Aside from a bureau, the room was otherwise empty.

"Hmm," Remo said.

He headed back out into the hall. He took the stairs up to the top floor of the sanitarium, coming out into a dusty hallway that looked as if it hadn't seen a living human being in fifty years. At the far dark cor-ner, an enclosed wooden staircase led to a warped door. The ancient steps made not a single creak as Remo mounted them. The door opened silently.

Folcroft's attic was a time capsule to another age. Medical equipment that had been modern seventy years ago looked like medieval torture devices. Metal had rusted and leather straps were rotting from age. A single bare overhead bulb hung from a low lintel.

At the far end of the long room, three tall windows looked out over the black night. Through the trees, Long Island Sound washed the frozen shore. Above, stars like shards of cold ice twinkled in the winter sky.

As Remo had expected, a familiar figure sat before the ceiling-to-floor windows.

The wizened Asian seemed as old as stars or sea.

At the roof of the house Remo had lived in for ten years, there had been a glass-enclosed cupola that the Master of Sinanju often used as a meditation room. The house and its tower sun room were now gone.

Lately, the Folcroft attic had been a poor substitute for his teacher's beloved retreat.

Dried flesh speckled with age was pulled tight over a skull of fragile bone. Twin tufts of yellowing white hair jutted from above shell-like ears. On the back of the old Korean's flaming orange kimono, coiling green dragons framed a bamboo pagoda. The body that moved beneath the shimmering silk kimono was reed-thin and frail.

The old Asian was writing again. He'd been doing a lot of that lately.

Over the past few months the Master of Sinanju had been carting a stack of ornate gold envelopes around wherever he went. He had been writing letter after letter. He didn't have to worry about secrecy, since most times he was writing in languages Remo didn't understand. But at one point when he was peeking, Remo swore one of the envelopes was addressed to the queen of England. The envelope had been quickly pulled away and hidden from his prying eyes.

From what he had managed to see, it almost looked to Remo like the Sinanju version of a résumé.

There was a stack of the envelopes on the floor now. A pile of smaller silver envelopes sat beside it. The Master of Sinanju had been including one of the silver envelopes with each of his carefully inscribed letters.

This evening it was not the mysterious letters that held the old man's attention.

The Master of Sinanju seemed oblivious to Remo's

approach. Yet when the younger man was nearly upon him, he shook his aged head. His soft hair quivered at the motion.

"You are white," said Chiun, Reigning Master of the House of Sinanju. He spoke the words with sadness, not malice. He did not turn to face his pupil.

"Guilty as charged," Remo replied.

He saw his teacher's face now. A thread of beard quivered at the tip of Chiun's pointed chin. Hazel eyes that still appeared young, despite the Korean's advanced age, stared solemnly out the dirty windowpanes.

Chiun offered a forlorn sigh. "Long have I danced around the subject of your rampaging whiteness."

"What dance?" Remo asked. "You've been griping about me being white for as long as I've known you. You called me an albino at breakfast this morning and a snowman on my way out the door. I should have known something was up. Even for you, that seemed a bit much for one day." He nodded to a parchment on the floor. "This has something to do with my place in the Sinanju Scrolls, I assume."

Chiun was no longer writing letters. A sheet of plain rice paper was rolled open at the Master of Sinanju's crossed knees. Near it was an open bottle of ink. The old man held a quill in one bony hand. Although he'd dipped pen to ink hours ago, he'd yet to make a single mark on the paper. The ink had long dried to the quill's tip.

"White," Chiun lamented. "You are not 'fair' or

'pale' or any of the others things I have said you are to avoid stating the absolute truth. You are white.''

"White as Michael Jackson," Remo agreed. "And I thought we were over this. Once we found out my family had a Master of Sinanju in the woodpile, I thought you'd finally given all that junk a rest.''

"A drop of good in an ocean of you can only offer small comfort. It cannot dissipate the rest of the youness which—it pains me to admit—is white. Yes, white, Remo. There, I have said it. You are white. White, white, white.''

"Big whoop, I'm white," Remo said. His face was slowly drooping into a scowl. "Why are you so worked up about this all of a sudden?''

"Because I have reached a turning point in my recording of Sinanju history," Chiun replied. "I must finally address your sad condition in the Sacred Scrolls.''

"What's so different about today?" Remo asked. "You've been lying in those scrolls for years. Who'd know the difference if you just pulled one of your usual cover-ups?''

Chiun's face and tone grew cold. "I do not lie," he said. "Yes, on occasion I have left a fact unrepresented. But that is not the same as lying. Avoiding the absolute, unvarnished truth is sometimes necessary, Remo, and is not automatically or necessarily a lie.''

"All depends on what your meaning of *is* is, I suppose," Remo said dryly.

"Precisely. And I can no longer not tell the full

truth. I must record for future Masters of Sinanju the
truth of the *is* that is you, lest some blabbermouth tell
it after me and cast a shadow on my entire Master-
hood. For the scandal of deceit could taint my reputation posthumously. Therefore, I must divulge your
secret now. Woe is me.'' Releasing another long sigh,
his shoulders sank pitifully.

Remo's eyes narrowed. ''Wait a second,'' he said.
''I'm the guy who takes over the scrolls next. You're
afraid *I* might spill the beans, aren't you?''

Chiun gave him a baleful look. ''Wouldn't you?''

Remo considered. ''Maybe,'' he admitted. ''Since
I'm not the Korean version of Al Sharpton like you
are, I doubt the subject of race will come up for me
as much as it did for you, but if it's relevant I'd say
so. I don't have any reason to be ashamed of who
and what I am.''

''A distinctly white thing to say,'' Chiun said, crinkling his nose in displeasure. ''I knew this would be
your feeling because you have never seen your white
skin as the social disease that it is. And so I am left
with my great dilemma.''

''The truth will set you free, Little Father.''

The lightness had returned to his tone. The Master
of Sinanju glanced up in suspicion at his pupil.

''Where were you all day?'' he asked, eyes narrowing.

''Drove into the city,'' Remo replied. ''It's a real
zoo this time of year.'' He squatted, picking up one
of the gold envelopes. The scrawl of a foreign language looked familiar. ''Is that Russian?'' he asked.

Chiun snatched the envelope from his hands. On the back Remo saw briefly the symbol of Sinanju. A trapezoid bisected by a vertical line. It had been formed in a single drop of melted wax that sealed the envelope.

"None of your business," Chiun snapped, sweeping a hand across the pile of envelopes. The entire stack vanished up the broad sleeve of his kimono.

Remo didn't seem very bothered by the old man's harsh tone. He was thinking of the benefit concert he'd just left. Without knowing it, a smile stretched across his face.

Chiun's eyes narrowed. "You seem very pleased with yourself," he said slowly. "Have you fulfilled the tradition of Master Nik?"

"Nah," Remo said. "I just did something nice for me and I'm happy."

The Master of Sinanju's eyes grew flat. "I am glad that you are happy, Remo," he said.

"Me, too."

"It is important that you are happy."

"Here it comes," said Remo.

"Whether or not *I* am happy is unimportant."

Remo was relieved at that moment to hear the sound of footsteps on the stairs leading to the attic.

"Saved by the bell," he muttered.

Across the cluttered attic, the ancient door opened. While it had opened silently for Remo, it creaked now on its rusty old hinges. A familiar face peered into the attic.

"There you are. I saw your car in the parking lot, but you weren't in your quarters."

Remo wasn't a big fan of Mark Howard, the new assistant director of CURE, but at the moment the young man was a welcome sight.

"Just got in," Remo said. "What's up?"

"Dr. Smith said you might be up here," Howard said. "He'd like to see you both in his office as soon as possible." Still at the door, he was looking around the dingy attic. "I thought I'd taken a complete tour of the building, but I somehow missed up here. Some of the corridors in the older wing are like mazes."

Remo wasn't interested in the assistant CURE director's architectural observations. From what he'd seen of the young man in action, he wouldn't be surprised if Howard got lost every time he tried to pull on a sweater.

"Tell Smitty we'll be right down," Remo said.

With a nod, Howard backed from the attic. The stairs groaned as he descended.

"We better see what he wants," Remo said to Chiun.

"Of course," Chiun sniffed, gathering up his ink bottle and blank parchment. "Jump the moment a member of your own race calls, but do nothing for the one who has given you everything."

"I can't be anything but white, Little Father," Remo said, shaking his head. "Not even for you."

The Master of Sinanju rose to his feet in one fluid motion. "Yet another example of white ingratitude."

In a flurry of orange robes, the old man headed across the attic floor and swept out the open door.

DR. HAROLD W. SMITH sat rigid in his comfortable leather chair behind his familiar black desk in his Spartan office in Folcroft's administrative wing. A canted monitor just below the desk's onyx surface displayed lines of tidy text.

The monitor couldn't be seen except from Smith's vantage point. As long as they stayed on the far side of the desk, visitors to the office would not even know it was there. The big picture window at Smith's back was made of one-way glass, preventing anyone from sneaking a peek from behind.

The shadows of night hugged his gaunt frame as he studied the data on his computer. Every now and then as he read, a low hum of concern rolled from deep in his throat.

Smith was a gray man with a face like a squeezed lemon marinated in grapefruit juice. To match his natural disposition, he dressed exclusively in suits of gray, most of which had been lurking among the mothballs in his closet since somewhere near the middle of the previous century. The only dash of color that had been allowed to creep into his wardrobe was his green-striped Dartmouth tie. Although it was late in the evening and all of the regular Folcroft staff had gone home, the tie remained knotted tightly at his neck.

His rimless glasses were clean of dust, the flint gray eyes behind them sharp and piercing. When the knock sounded at his door, the director of the supersecret agency known as CURE did not raise his head.

"Come in," Smith called.

Only when the door opened did Smith lift his eyes. His thin lips pursed in annoyance when he saw that the young man entering his office was alone.

"They'll be here in a minute," Mark Howard promised when he saw the expression on his employer's face. He crossed the room and took a seat before the desk.

Even before he had sat on the hard wooden chair the office door was swinging open again.

"Why you couldn't make life easier for me and just be born Korean I will never know," the Master of Sinanju was saying as he breezed into the room.

Remo came in behind him. "For the same reason I wasn't born a schnauzer," he said, peeved. "My folks weren't Korean. And in case you haven't heard, only Koreans can make Korean babies."

Chiun's weathered face grew thoughtful. "Emperor Smith, perhaps your experts can do something about this problem," he said as he padded up before the desk.

For countless centuries Masters of Sinanju had hired out to thrones around the world. Even though he did not want it, Smith was awarded the title of emperor, for the simple reason that Chiun refused to work for anything less.

"What problem is that, Master Chiun?" Smith asked.

Chiun stroked his thread of beard wisely between

tapered fingers. ''This terrible and pervasive lack of Koreanness among your subjects. I have heard on the television how women may go to a place where they are made to be with child without lying with a man.''·

''Fertility clinics, yes,'' Smith said.

The old Korean nodded. ''That is the name they go by. I have also heard that mistakes have been made causing white women to give birth to black babies and hapless black women to bear ugly screeching whites.''

''Yes, I have heard of such mix-ups,'' Smith said slowly.

''Then your course is clear. Issue a decree for the workers at these places to throw out the inferior white and black bottles and save only the one that makes babies Korean. Within a generation you may begin to wring the whiteness from this land so that future Masters of Sinanju need not be vexed as I have.''

Smith cleared his throat. ''That is simply not possible, Master Chiun,'' he insisted.

Chiun's voice lowered. ''In that case, is there a procedure by which Remo could be made more Korean?''

Beside him, Remo shook his head. ''Doesn't matter if there is, because Remo ain't volunteering.''

''Hush,'' Chiun snapped under his breath. ''You will become Korean if I tell you to become Korean. What's more, you will thank me afterward.''

''I'm not going to become some freaky *Tan like Me* sociology experiment just because you don't like having a white pupil," Remo said. "Tell him, Smitty."

Smith was shaking his head firmly. "I am sorry, Master Chiun, but that is simply not possible, either," the CURE director replied.

The old man's face crinkled in displeasure. "You can put a man on the moon, but you cannot turn a white man right. Why bother to have all your science if you are not going to give priority to the things people actually want?"

Still frowning, the wizened Korean sank to a lotus position on the threadbare rug.

Grateful for the silence, Smith quickly turned his attention to Remo.

"Remo, are you aware of an organization called the Congress of Concerned Scientists?" Smith asked.

"Not that I know of," Remo replied. He settled cross-legged to the floor next to his teacher.

"It is a politically active group whose membership includes scientists from around the world. They are concerned with global and national environmental policies, in addition to having a political component."

Remo shrugged. "Sounds like the kinds of nits who tell freezing old ladies in Vermont to turn the thermostat down to zero and put on a sweater 'cause the squirrels in the chimney might not like the soot."

"They are oftentimes extreme in their positions," Smith admitted. "Until now, however, they had remained harmless enough. Some of the personnel at the CCS headquarters in Geneva have recently fallen victim to misfortune. There have been several deaths, as well as a number of disappearances.''

''Let's all rev up our SUVs to celebrate,'' Remo said.

''There is no cause for celebration,'' the CURE director said, his voice deadly serious. ''The victims were all involved in the same project. Apparently, the CCS has spent the past few years developing a genetically altered tree called the *C. dioxa*. Unlike its counterparts in nature, this plant produces carbon dioxide.''

Remo scrunched up his face. ''That's a twist,'' he said. ''Plants are supposed to make oxygen, right?''

Smith nodded. ''What's more, they *clean* carbon dioxide from the air. The CCS has turned nature on its head. In addition to carbon dioxide, their tree also produces ammonia and some methane.''

''That's bad?'' Remo asked.

''The potential for destruction is unimaginable,'' Mark Howard interjected.

Howard had read a lot of the material the CURE director had forwarded to him on the CCS and the *C. dioxa* project. He couldn't pretend to understand all that was said about covalent hydrogen compounds or methane and ammonia-producing organisms, but that wasn't necessary. He understood enough to know why Smith was concerned.

For his part, Remo kept his irritation in check. Howard was a change to CURE that Remo had not yet accepted. These days he was doing his best to acclimate himself to the young man's presence by ignoring him as much as possible. The same could not be said for the Master of Sinanju.

"How grave must be the danger to crown and country for the Emperor's young Prince to speak with such passion," Chiun intoned. "Yet even with talk of peril, the sweetness of your voice fills my soul to overflowing."

Remo had been putting up with a lot of kissing-up these past few months. Too much, in fact.

"Can you ratchet that down, Little Father?" he griped.

"Just pretend to care about whatever idiocy they are babbling about," Chiun said in Korean. "Look. The old fidget has made the young one a worrywart like him."

Remo glanced at Howard. Chiun was right. The young man was looking a little frayed around the edges. There were dark bags under his greenish-brown eyes that weren't there when he started at CURE almost one year ago.

"You okay, kid?" Remo asked, brow drooping.

Mark seemed surprised at the attention. "Yes," he said cautiously, expecting a punch line to Remo's setup.

There was none. Remo only nodded. He returned his attention to the CURE director.

"Mark's assessment of the *C. dioxa* is correct," Smith said. "Unleashed on the world, it could disrupt or even destroy the oxygen cycle.

Sitting, bored, on the floor, Chiun asked Remo what that was. Remo told him he thought it was one of those stationary bikes fat people pedaled at health clubs.

"You join a gym, Smitty?" Remo asked.

"Actually," Smith said thinly, "the oxygen cycle is the name for the process by which photosynthetic organisms synthesize carbohydrates from water and carbon dioxide and release oxygen into the atmosphere as a byproduct. At the same time, aerobic organisms—mankind included—use up oxygen and give off carbon dioxide and water through a variety of complex metabolic processes. The one feeds the other on a planetary scale."

"So you're saying you didn't join a gym," Remo said.

Smith took a deep breath. "Animals breathe out carbon dioxide," he explained slowly. "Plants clean the carbon dioxide from the air and release the oxygen that the animals breathe. If the plants didn't do this, we would all die."

"Hey, I think I got that," Remo said.

"Good," Smith said seriously. "Because we are facing something that could reverse part of that process. If that happens, we cannot begin to contemplate the damage."

Remo waved a dismissive hand. "Aw, I've been hearing stuff about the world imploding for years, and we're still here. It can't be that bad, Smitty."

"Yes, Remo, it can. The threat to the environment this plant represents is incalculable. If released into the wild, it would flood the atmosphere with deadly carbon dioxide and ammonia gas. As a consequence, our air would eventually be rendered unbreathable. All life on Earth—plant, animal, marine, *everything*— would go the way of the dinosaur. The planet would literally suffocate.''

Although Remo had heard doomsday predictions before, the types of people who made them always seemed to have some ulterior motives. Harold W. Smith, however, was a man who dealt with cold, harsh reality and was not the type to indulge in acts of wild speculation. If Smith thought this was serious, in all likelihood it was.

"Okay," Remo sighed. "So now I'm a lumberjack and I'm okay. Gimme an ax and tell me where it is."

"The CCS maintains a headquarters in Geneva," Smith said. "But it might not be so simple a thing as merely destroying the existing plants. In fact, it might not be necessary for you to do so at all."

"They're gonna kill us all, but you want me to save them," Remo said flatly.

Smith removed his glasses. "It is a little more complicated than that," he said, rubbing his eyes. "The *C. dioxa* was actually developed for a reason. It offers a way to study the earliest stages of plant formation and evolution on this planet. It is conceivable that the data collected could have future scientific applications."

Remo didn't seem convinced. "Like what?" he asked.

It was Mark Howard who answered. "They might eventually be able to create a plant that can survive in a completely alien atmosphere," the assistant CURE director offered. "If they can do that, we could send seeds to other planets or moons in our own solar system that could eventually create oxygen atmospheres like ours.''

Remo felt a pinch at his thigh. The Master of Sinanju was tugging at his pant leg with slender fingers.

''It is worse that I thought,'' Chiun whispered quietly in Korean. ''The big one has driven the little one mad.''

Remo shot him a quieting glance. ''So what's our involvement, Smitty?'' he asked.

''Go to Geneva and see who or what is behind the murders of the *C. dioxa* scientists,'' the CURE director said. ''If someone has evil designs on the tree, it may become necessary to destroy it. However, it is entirely possible that someone merely wants the research stopped. In either case, until you determine which it is, I want the two of you to protect the remaining scientist on the CCS team.''

''Maybe chop tree, protect CCCP scientist, save world,'' Remo said. ''Got it.''

He stood. Beside him, the Master of Sinanju floated to his feet. Remo was turning to go when a thought occurred to him.

''What's the name of the guy we're supposed to be bodyguarding?'' he asked.

Replacing his glasses, Smith glanced down at his monitor. ''*Her* name,'' he said, ''is Dr. Amanda Lifton.''

4

Dr. Amanda Lifton, of the Massachusetts Liftons, was frightened out of her Brahmin, Ivy League-educated Mensa brain. The utter, stark, unbearable terror had left her almost beyond the point of all reason. It was only due to her oppressively reserved Lifton upbringing that she didn't run screaming into the tidy streets of Geneva.

If she had been back home in the Boston suburb of Wellesley, she would have been able to work out some of her anxiety on one of the servants. Old Nan, the prim Englishwoman who had raised Amanda, had taken more than her share of clouts to the head during those troubled teen years. Nan was long gone now, but there had to be some dusty butler or upstairs maid who could fill in.

Amanda considered calling Daddy to ask him to send over Reginald for a good old-fashioned shoe beating, but she knew that she couldn't. Not after the very public display of temper she had given vent to at her sister Abigail's wedding. Most of it had been directed at Daddy, but for good measure she'd tossed in a fairly hefty helping of invective for the rest of the Lifton clan.

It had happened six years ago.

"I'm an adult!" she had proclaimed loudly and angrily to the ballroom full of Lifton relatives.

She did this for two reasons. First and foremost was that younger sister Abigail had the gall to go out and get married first. Second was Abby's insistence that Amanda wear the same hideous turquoise gown as the other bridesmaids. Amanda waited for the reception for maximum dramatic effect.

In her tirade, she insisted that she wanted to be treated as an adult. She'd had it with the entire Lifton family. She yelled at her startled relatives that she was going to finally make a clean break from them all. She started her new life on the dance floor, stripping off the appalling gown that Abby knew full well made a Lifton derriere look much bigger than it actually was. Amanda left the dress that malice bought on the floor and, in her underwear, marched proudly from the reception.

She was still reveling in her act of emancipation the next day when the phone rang.

It was precisely 9:00 a.m. Amanda knew it was important when it was Daddy on the line and not some servant or secretary telling her to hold for her father.

She was lounging back in bed, the delicate pink phone pressed to her pale, perfect ear.

"That was quite a performance yesterday, Amanda,"

Daddy said. "Bravo." He spoke in the lockjaw manner of old New England money.

"I meant every word, Daddy," Amanda huffed.

"Of course you did, princess. That is why as of five minutes from this moment you will be cut off from the rest of the Lifton family."

"No great loss," Amanda said, her tone snippy. She flopped one of her fuzzy pink slippers against the soft wrinkled skin on the underside of her pumiced foot.

"That includes the money, Amanda."

The slipper went flying as Amanda shot up in bed.

"I was completely out of line, Daddy!" Amanda insisted. Her free hand clutched a panicked knot of pink sheets. "Is Abigail there? No. Honeymoon. She'll be in the islands. I'll fly down, Daddy. I promise. I'll apologize in person. I'll even wear that damnable dress to do it."

"You will do no such thing," Daddy Lifton said. "You were most impressive yesterday. And you have no idea how much it takes to impress your father."

"Let me find another way," she said fearfully.

"Too late. I've decided to take you up on your exciting little challenge. You are going to be our own little lab experiment, Amanda. You are going to be the first Lifton in more than five hundred years to have to actually go out and earn a living. Isn't that just thrilling, princess?"

"Is Mother there?" Amanda asked weakly.

"She's with the man from Tidwell Vintners. Problem with the '91, don't you know. But she sends kisses and a hearty 'job well done.' This will be our last chat for a while, I expect. The phone company will be terminating service after I'm through.''

"Daddy, you can't *do* this," Amanda pleaded. "I can't go out and make a living. I don't know how."

Her father laughed in that constipated, ultrarefined way of his that sent shivers down her spine. Amanda had only heard him laugh two other times in his life. Once when Gran Lifton had been found facedown in the azaleas, and once during the stock-market collapse of 1987.

"You'll show us all the way, Amanda," Daddy said.

And with that, the line went dead. There wasn't even a dial tone.

Amanda stared at the eerily silent phone.

"I don't *want* to show anyone the way," she cried to the pink papered walls of her bedroom. "I'm an *heiress.*"

The walls cared as little for her plight as Daddy and Mother Lifton. A moment later there came a pounding on her apartment door.

Amanda slipped a fluffy pink bathrobe on over her shimmering pink silk pajamas and answered the door. On her doorstep was her landlord, four movers and a pair of highly paid Lifton family lawyers.

Amanda Lifton was on the street six minutes later.

Daddy let her keep her wardrobe. Everything else went back. Credit cards, jewelry, furniture. The works. She never had a savings account. Never needed one.

Her checking account was vacuumed clean by Daddy's shysters.

Penniless, Amanda found herself on the outside of an empty apartment surrounded by suitcases filled with a lifetime's worth of clothes.

Actually, it was worse even than that. The clothes were only a month old. She had thrown the older stuff out when she'd gotten her new spring wardrobe. As she trudged the streets of Boston, she found herself wishing she'd kept a few of those older things. Maybe some rag merchant somewhere gave cash to indigents for old Versace.

Her endless, terrible wandering proved to be the most dreadful eight minutes of her entire life. She had heard an awful rumor that there were people who stayed out here all the time. She had no idea why. Probably a tax dodge. There couldn't be that many spiteful daddies out there.

Half a block from her apartment Amanda spied a familiar sight. The call letters of the local PBS affiliate shone down on her from the front of an office building like a beacon of hope.

For years Amanda had been volunteering at the station answering phones during its annual pledge drive. Like all good blue-blooded Boston liberals, Amanda Lifton was no hypocrite. For one hour one night a year—whether convenient or not—she actually practiced what she preached. It was her way of staying grounded.

She staggered into the foyer of the station under the weight of a dozen Gucci suitcases and demanded a job. And, in the great PBS tradition of wasting money and not caring, the woman with zero qualifications and a stack of luggage that was vomiting Armani and Christian Dior all over the lobby was hired on the spot.

She started as a receptionist. A day later, when the station manager discovered she was a Lifton, she was promoted to producer of a local-affairs talk show. Two days later, when the same man learned that she was indeed one of *those* Liftons, she was promoted to public-relations director, where her duties consisted of looking out the window and long lunches. Sometimes she was trotted out to wine and dine the various celebrities who showed up at the station, usually around pledge time. One such celebrity was the famous and respected astronomer Sage Carlin. Although it had happened six years ago, Amanda remembered it as if it were yesterday.

Carlin arrived in an old corduroy suit jacket with patches on the elbows. He had a comb-over that looked like a helmet of hair, an overbite, no chin and black-rimmed buzzard's eyes.

In spite of his creepy appearance and his vague odor of fish, Amanda knew Dr. Carlin was brilliant. She wanted to prove to him that she was no intellectual slouch herself.

Amanda explained how she had graduated at the top of her class at Yale. She had taken her degree in botany to the Massachusetts University of Technology, where she received doctorates in morphology, cytology and palynology. Dr. Lifton had been actively courted by some of the biggest pharmaceutical and biotechnology companies in the country. But because Liftons frowned on women in the workforce, Amanda had been encouraged to turn her attention to finding a man of adequate social standing and sire a male Lifton child. "To begin this wretched mess all over again," Daddy had said in one of his more honest moments.

Now all that was gone thanks to her silly outburst at Abigail's wedding.

She was happy during her long diatribe on the travails of her life to find that Sage Carlin was a terrific listener. The whole time she spoke, the famous scientist never took his eyes off her. Granted, he was staring at her chest and not her eyes, but you really couldn't blame him. In addition to being brilliant and beautiful, Amanda Lifton knew precisely how to fill out a sweater.

"I'm sorry to go on like this, Dr. Carlin," she apologized. "It's just that my daddy has been very, very mean to me."

"No need to apologize," Sage Carlin said. "Of the billions of people on this overpopulated planet, you're the one I most want to talk to right now. What's morphlology?"

"You mean morphology," she replied with a smile. "It's the branch of biology that concerns the form and structure of plants and animals."

"Plants?" Carlin asked, intrigued.

"That was a particular interest to me. That's why I went on to palynology and cytology. Palynology is the study of mold and spores—cytology is cell structure and function." She suddenly realized whom she was talking to. "But of course you know that already," she said, face flushing red. "I'm humiliating myself, aren't I?"

"Not at all," Sage Carlin said. "I do some work for a group called the Congress of Concerned Scientists. Perhaps you've heard of it? If you're interested, I might have a job for you."

It was, according to Sage Carlin, a one-in-a-billion chance meeting. That very afternoon he hired Amanda as a palynologist for the CCS.

The team in Geneva soon learned how lucky it was. All her life Amanda had been hiding her light under a bushel basket. She was a natural in her field. In her first months in Geneva, her brilliance put her fellow scientists to shame.

She helped lay the groundwork on the *C. dioxa*. It was she, along with Dr. Brice Schumar, who improved and refined the seed design. The last two seed cycles had only gotten better.

But the greatest victory was personal. She had done what she had—albeit inadvertently—set out to do. She had proved to Daddy, Mother, Abigail and all the rest of the Lifton family that she could stand on her own two feet.

But, sadly, her success was marred by tragedy.

Dr. Carlin passed away. While tragic, it was five years old now, and truth be told, he had always given Amanda the willies. A more recent death and one far more disturbing was the unfortunate accident of her team leader, Dr. Schumar. How he had gotten himself locked in the *C. dioxa* greenhouse was a mystery to everyone. He above everyone else at the CCS in Switzerland should have known enough not to go inside the greenhouse with the skylights closed. The police were saying it was suicide. Amanda had reluctantly accepted their conclusion. Until the next body turned up.

This one was a young American botanist she had recruited herself. Fried to a crisp when a carelessly dropped appliance landed in his bathtub. That the appliance was a microwave and the dead scientist had been fully clothed at the time was glossed over by the authorities. Amanda might even have accepted the official verdict on the tragedy if old Dr. Cross hadn't been found the next day.

The English geneticist had been cooked to death behind the steering wheel of his car. No one quite knew how it happened, but apparently he had been burned to black slag. His fillings and most of his car had partially melted.

Dr. Lewandowski went the same way the day after.

When the Geneva police declared both bizarre deaths to be unfortunate skiing accidents, Amanda began to suspect that their hearts weren't in uncovering the truth.

It became epidemic after that. CCS scientists were all dying or disappearing, taking with them to their graves all knowledge of the process by which the *C. dioxa* had been created. The bodies mounted until there was only one left.

The thought that, at any minute, she might join her deceased colleagues gave Amanda Lifton an involuntary shudder as she walked along the chilly abandoned halls of the CCS headquarters.

The complex was like a high-tech ghost town.

The corridors were a tidy white. Color-coded stripes on the floors directed visitors around the buildings: blue was for the administrative offices, red for the labs and green directed one to the greenhouses.

Amanda walked nervously along the green line. At one point the sole of one lab sneaker squeaked on the concrete floor, and the resultant echo nearly caused her to jump out the nearest window.

She had a right to be jumpy. All the deaths couldn't be coincidental.

Amanda had finally worked up the nerve to phone the head of the CCS about her theory. Dr. Hubert St. Clair seemed very interested in what she had to say. He asked her to meet him at the main greenhouse in twenty minutes so they could discuss the matter.

As she walked, Amanda checked her watch.

It was a cheap digital knockoff she'd picked up in the States. Nothing like the expensive watches she'd had for the first thirty years of her life.

She was thinking evil thoughts of Daddy and the dangerous situation his pettiness had put her in as she passed an empty security desk. The monitors were dead screens. A pile of laminated security passes sat in a box next to a pair of silent telephones.

"No need for security in a building full of dead

people,'' she muttered anxiously as she passed the desk.

She followed the green line around a corner. As she rounded to the next hall, the heel of her shoe squeaked shrilly again on the coated concrete floor.

Her heart skipped and she glanced down at her own clumsy feet. It was in this position—head down and with a scowl on her face—that Amanda Lifton walked straight into the man who was heading up the next corridor.

As she stumbled back, shocked, strong hands grabbed her by the biceps.

Looking up with a start, Amanda found herself staring into the deepest, darkest, deadliest eyes she had ever seen. They were a killer's eyes. Confronted by the death she so feared, Amanda Lifton reacted in the only manner she knew how. Throwing back her head, Amanda screamed.

Amanda kept screaming even after the hands released her.

"What's the hell's your problem?" the killer demanded.

"What did you do?" another voice asked.

There was someone else with the killer. He stood behind the first man, a deeply displeased look on his face.

"I didn't do anything."

"Then why is this thing with the balloons on her chest shrieking?"

"Beats me. She must be self-activating. Maybe

they're like air bags with built-in alarms. Big as they are, they've gotta run out of air eventually.''

Amanda finally stopped screaming to catch her breath.

''See?''

''Who are you?'' Amanda panted fearfully. ''What do you want?'' Her face held a look of a frantic, hunted animal.

The killer began to speak, but paused. Frowning, he glanced over his shoulder.

''Chiun, who are we supposed to be today?'' Remo asked.

The Master of Sinanju padded up beside Remo.

''We are doctors,'' the wizened Korean said. ''I am the esteemed Dr. Marcus Welby and you are my assistant, the bumbling Dr. Kiley.''

''Nah, that's not it,'' Remo said. ''Eh,'' he shrugged. ''Close enough for government work.''

Amanda looked from one man to the other. Neither made a move toward her. Still, she remained cautious, ready to bolt at a moment's notice.

''How did you get in here?'' Amanda demanded. ''This is a secure facility.''

''Tell that to the no one who wasn't guarding the unlocked front door,'' Remo said. ''You got Swiss cheese for security around here, kitten.''

Some of the tension drained from her body. In spite of her initial reaction, these two seemed harmless enough. Probably just lost tourists or CCS contributors. And, in truth, she found the company comforting.

"It's no wonder they left," Amanda exhaled. "Everyone here is afraid for their life right about now."

"Oh, yeah," Remo said, nodding. "What with all those scientists getting bumped off. You're Amanda Lifton, right?"

Amanda's panic returned full force.

"No," she insisted quickly, backing away.

"Says so on your name tag," Remo pointed out. "Not a good picture. They left off your two best attributes."

"She would need to lug a billboard to include those monstrosities," Chiun sniffed.

She was thinking she could outrun them. The old one definitely. The younger one possibly. If she could just get to an office, lock the door. A call to the police or Dr. St. Clair, who she knew was somewhere in the CCS complex.

Dr. St. Clair! He was in danger, too. She had to warn him.

"Okay, buster," Amanda said, forcing strength into her cracking voice. "I want to know who you are and what you're doing here, and I want to know right now."

Remo shrugged. "We're the guys who are here keep you alive," he said.

The words were so shocking, delivered in such an offhanded way, that Amanda felt the fear drain from her.

She cast a tired eye up and down the thin man who stood before her. The same for the tiny, kimono-clad

Asian standing placidly next to him. When she was through appraising them, Amanda did something she hadn't done in weeks. Dr. Amanda Lifton threw back her head and laughed out loud.

5

The laughter lasted only until she started sobbing uncontrollably.

"What'd I do now?" Remo complained.

Chiun slipped around Remo, taking Amanda's hands in his own. "There, there, young lady," he said, patting her hands comfortingly. "Do not let the paleness of his skin alarm you. Remo, go stand in that shadow lest your excessive whiteness give this poor child the vapors."

"Vapors, my ass," Remo groused. "We're in Switzerland, for crying out loud. This is where Aryan clouds are born."

Amanda was still blubbering. Now that she'd started there seemed no way to turn off the waterworks.

"Geez, lady, put a cork in it, will you?" Remo said. "It's not like your dog died. Tell you what. We'll stop by the pound and pick you up a brandnew tweedy scientist to play with."

Amanda shrieked as if in pain. She was going into some kind of hysterical fit, bawling and gulping for air.

Seeing there might be no quick end in sight if he just let her go on leaking like that, Remo sighed loudly. Reaching around behind Amanda, he manipulated a cluster of nerves at the base of her spine.

The crying dried up at once.

"Oh," Amanda said, surprised by the sudden cessation of tears. She tried sniffling, but there was nothing to sniff. She looked up, bewildered. "What did you do?"

"Kept the Alps from flooding," Remo said. "Can we talk now?"

Amanda blinked away her drying tears.

"I'm sorry," she apologized. "It's just been, well, terrible around here lately. Are you really here to help?"

"*I* am here to help," Chiun said. "We have yet to figure out his purpose."

Amanda blinked again. Her eyes were dry. The hysterical attack was over. Biting her lip, she nodded to the two strangers.

"Let's go to my office."

They followed the green stripe back to blue. Amanda's office was in a corridor with many others. The rest were dark and silent.

Amanda took her seat behind her desk. Her pretty face was haggard in the unflattering glow of the table lamp.

Remo noted a photograph on the wall. It was of a single blue tree. Large blue clumps of seeds clutched the undersides of some of the branches.

"That the farting tree?" Remo asked.

Amanda nodded. "That's one of the latest specimens. I took that myself two weeks ago."

"Huhn," Remo grunted. "Doesn't look so tough."

"It isn't," Amanda explained. "The earliest ones were felled by blight. We've created a heartier strain since then, but as with all species where there are only a handful of specimens, we have to exercise great care. Now, are you with the CCS?"

Remo shook his head. "Nope. Got all my brain cells."

"However, he has yet to use either of them," Chiun said. He stood at the door, hands tucked deep in the voluminous sleeves of his crimson kimono.

"But you were *hired* by the CCS," she insisted. "As security after the tragic deaths."

"Would you prefer coyness or outright lying?"

"So you weren't hired by the CCS," Amanda said carefully. She no longer feared these two, but she realized she should still exercise some caution.

"Let's just say we were hired by a friend to see that nothing happens to you," Remo said.

It hit Amanda all at once. She didn't know why she hadn't thought of it before.

"Daddy!" Amanda cried. "I *knew* he wouldn't abandon me in my hour of need. *He* sent you, didn't he? He must have been keeping an eye on me all along. Isn't that right?"

Remo glanced at Chiun.

"Don't look at me," the Master of Sinanju said in Korean. "She is part of your demented race, not mine. If it keeps her from squalling, tell her whatever pretty song she wants to hear.''

Remo turned back to Amanda. ''Daddy sends his love,'' he said.

''Really?'' Amanda asked. ''That doesn't sound like Daddy. Must be a bear market.'' She looked Remo and Chiun up and down, this time with a more critical eye. ''Are you two the best he could do? No offense, but you look like *I* could take you. Daddy's probably kept the best bodyguards for his precious Abigail. She's the perfect one, after all. *She's* the one with the husband and the baby. She's the one who doesn't strip at wedding receptions and insult the whole perfect Lifton family. Well, Daddy can just go die and rot in poo for all I care.'' She folded her arms and slumped in her chair.

''I've changed my mind. I liked her better crying,'' said the Master of Sinanju.

''Are you the last one left from that tree project?'' Remo asked, steering her way from the topic of patricide.

''The last one who isn't in hiding, anyway. Everyone else working on the *C. dioxa* at the CCS is dead or vanished.''

''How about those stupid trees of yours?''

''I don't like you calling them stupid,'' Amanda said, bristling. ''They represent a great step for science.''

''So has every dippy dingdong thing you eggheads have ever come up with. While you're in here making all your great steps, the rest of us schlubs wind up having to paddle through H-bombs and ten versions of Windows."

Amanda's brow sank low. "How little is Daddy paying you?" she demanded. "He must have gotten a great bargain for someone so hostile and close-minded."

"I throw that in no charge," Remo said. "Tell me, are all the trees here?"

"What kind of silly question is that? Of course they are."

"No chance anyone's transplanted some to somebody's backyard?"

"What?" Amanda asked, shocked. "Of course not. That would be suicide on a planetary scale. Who would want to do something so insane?"

"Just a guess? Maybe the guy who's killing off all the people who might be able to stop it from happening."

Amanda considered his words.

This hadn't occurred to her. She assumed that someone opposed to the project was behind the sinister goings-on here in Geneva. It had happened in the world of science before. Within the past few years vandals had been destroying genetically altered crops in particular throughout the world. She just figured this was another of those cases, brought to the extreme.

Amanda hesitated for a moment, finally shaking her head. "That's silly. Of course no one would want to do such a thing, Mr.… What's your name?"

"Forgive him the whiteness of it," Chiun interjected.

"It's Remo," Remo said, shooting a glare at Chiun.

"In Korean that translates into 'slackwit' and 'pasty,'" Chiun confided to Amanda.

"No, it doesn't," Remo said.

"It does now," Chiun insisted blandly. "Remind me to show you the Sacred Scrolls I recorded in the first months of your training."

"You're Remo and you're Chiun," Amanda said. "Remo mentioned your name in the hall." She nodded, locking the information away in her well-ordered brain. "I realize, Remo, that people like you sometimes fear scientific progress. Here at the CCS we have a great respect for the impact of science on nature. I actually helped create a new variety of *C. dioxa* that has a breeding capacity a thousand times greater than the original generation of plants."

"And this dispels my concerns how exactly?" Remo asked.

"Don't you see?" Amanda insisted. "It's a love of the environment that drives our research. We're draining the life from this planet. We need to develop alternatives before eco-catastrophe here destroys everything and everyone. The *C. dioxa* and what comes after it could hold the key to our survival. Not in the immediate future, but hundreds of years from now."

Remo was surprised. Most people in the West thought of time in Western terms—days, weeks, months. Amanda Lifton was a ditz, but she was a ditz who thought in terms of centuries.

"So what?" Remo sighed. "We'll all be dead and buried by then."

"Speak for yourself," Chiun said.

"This is how you have to think when you're talking about the environment. Bad science will tell you there are quick fixes to everything. There aren't. I've conditioned my mind to be patient. And believe me, I've had to. You know, originally the *C. dioxa* seeds were as big as your thumb. I was able to refine them to the size of a raisin."

"Big deal," Remo said.

"It will be for future generations," Amanda said. "When terraforming becomes a reality. My small seeds break open after just a few days on the ground, releasing hundreds of tiny seedlets that can be carried on the air. Forestation of an entire planet could take place in a few decades."

"The same true if these things get loose here?" Remo asked.

Amanda frowned. "I don't like your attitude or your insinuations," she said. "Everyone who comes to work for the CCS signs a confidentiality contract. Our work is known only to us, and we are all above reproach. No one in this organization would wish any harm to come to this planet."

"If no one outside here knows about your plant, how come I do?" Remo asked.

Amanda faltered. "Well," she said, "obviously *Daddy* would have his sources."

"For someone passing herself off as a brainiac, you're pretty dense," Remo said.

Amanda sat up straighter in her chair. Her dark Lifton eyes peered condescendingly down her long Lifton nose.

"I don't care where Daddy found you, I will not be spoken to in that manner. I am a Lifton and *you,* sir, are the hired help. What's more, you are a crude, nasty moron." She folded her arms firmly.

"This moron's your best bet at staying alive."

"And you're an imbecile," she snapped.

"Although right now the imbecile and the moron are thinking about heaving you to the wolves and heading back home."

"And you're a mean, mean, mean meanie," Amanda Lifton concluded. "And I don't know why Daddy would hire someone as nasty as you to watch out for me. He must hate me."

Somewhere in the middle, her tirade had stopped being about Remo. The tears were starting to well up in her eyes once more. Before the floodgates could fully open, and to Remo's eternal gratitude, someone chose that moment to knock on Dr. Lifton's office door.

When the man stuck his head in the room, Amanda stopped her latest outburst in midsniffle.

"Dr. St. Clair," Amanda said. "Oh, I'm sorry. I'm late, aren't I?"

Although Remo had never met him before, there was something familiar about the man at the door.

The turtleneck, the jacket with the elbow patches, the bizarre lump of combed-over hair.

"I got worried when you didn't show up at the greenhouse," Hubert St. Clair said. He was eyeing Remo and Chiun. "Hello."

"What's that on your head?" Remo asked.

Amanda shot to her feet. "These are private bodyguards," she explained quickly. "My father hired them to protect me."

"Ah," St. Clair said. His eyes twitched back and forth between the two Sinanju Masters. "This has to do with your theory. It's groundless, I'm sure. We've just had a string of bad luck here at the CCS. Nothing sinister here at all."

"I wish I could be so sure," Amanda said.

"Tell you what," St. Clair said. "I've got something I need to show you in the greenhouse. You can try to convince me something's wrong on the way there. Your friends are welcome to come along."

Remo shot the Master of Sinanju a glance. The old man, too, had detected the anxious undertone in Hubert St. Clair's voice.

"What the hell," Remo said. "I'd like to see the thing that's going to kill us all."

Amanda gave him a silencing glare.

The four of them left the office together. Amanda and St. Clair led the way, she insisting that something nefarious was going on at the CCS. Remo and Chiun followed.

The main CCS complex fed into an ultramodern corridor that looked like an oversize version of the plastic tubes hamsters run through. The clear hallway led to a blockish structure that was attached to the side of the greenhouse.

Hubert St. Clair had wrapped a handkerchief tight around his finger by the time they reached the doors. As he led them through both sets of doors, both Remo and Chiun noticed his agitation-level rising. It seemed to have more to do with their high-tech environment than anything else.

When the second set of doors slid open, revealing the vast interior of the greenhouse, Amanda Lifton let out a shocked gasp.

"The trees!" she cried.

In the center of the huge room were the remains of the only existing *C. dioxas.* The trees had been chain-sawed. The trunks sat in a tangled pile of limbs on the floor. Soft blue leaves revealed pale undersides, drooping in withering clumps. Naked stumps spotted otherwise bare planting beds.

There was still a sharp taste of ammonia in the air.

Amanda ran inside the greenhouse.

"I'm sorry, Amanda," St. Clair said as the rest of them crossed over to the remains of the *C. dioxas.* "I had to have them destroyed. While I don't think there's anything sinister going on, with all the terrible coincidences that have hit your team, there wasn't anyone left to see to it that the proper safeguards were maintained. It was too dangerous to allow them to live."

"*I'm* still here," Amanda insisted.

"Yes, you are," St. Clair said vaguely. "Would

you excuse me for a moment? I have to make an important call.''

With a tight smile plastered unnaturally across his face, he headed for the door.

Chiun's eyes trailed him suspiciously.

Amanda dropped to her knees next to the pile of blue wood. ''Six years of my life, gone,'' she moaned.

With slender fingers she caressed a wilted blue leave.

''Yeah, that's rough,'' Remo said, unconcerned. Hands on his hips, he was looking around the big chamber. ''What kind of greenhouse is this? It isn't even hot in here.''

The skylights were rolled open, revealing a blue patch of clear Swiss sky. Glass pipes affixed with hundreds of nozzles latticed the vaulted ceiling.

''This is a natural climate as much as possible,'' Amanda replied sadly. She didn't look up at him as she spoke. ''We keep it open to the elements when we can.''

''So what's all that junk?'' He waved a finger at the elaborate networks built into the ceiling.

''We can shut off the outside world and create any of dozens of microclimates of our own choosing in here,'' she explained. ''All that is used to simulate the various environments. Mostly we just use it for watering the plants. Or *used* it,'' she corrected bitterly. ''The *C. dioxa* cannot yet extract enough water to survive from the air. That would have come in future generations. Those nozzles provide seeding for the clouds.''

"Get outta town," Remo said. "You grow actual clouds in here?''

Amanda didn't answer him. "I can't believe this is happening," she said to herself.

When Remo looked down he found her still crouching next to the trees. The panicked daddy's girl had fled, replaced for a moment with a coolly professional young woman.

Remo squatted beside her, taking a withered *C. dioxa* leaf between his fingers. It felt warm to the touch.

"It's hot," he said. He rubbed his fingertips together. They tingled.

"A chemical reaction," Amanda said absently. Her mind was somewhere else. "Actually, most people shouldn't be able to feel it. Where's Dr. St. Clair?" she asked, standing abruptly. "Maybe we can still salvage this somehow.''

"That little twitchy guy?" Remo asked. "He just went out there to try to kill us or something. Hey, you ought to try touching one of these leaves, Little Father. It's pretty weird.''

"What do you mean 'kill us'?" Amanda asked.

Chiun was standing imperiously next to them, his eyes directed on the greenhouse control room. "My pale son is correct," the old Korean said. "That one means you harm.''

"Are you two nuts?" Amanda said. "You're talking about Hubert St. Clair, the head of the Congress of Concerned Scientists. Oh, this is it. I'm calling Daddy. He probably got someone else to hire you for him. He has no idea he's throwing away perfectly good, potential trust-fund money on two flimflam—''

She was interrupted by a sudden loud clanking sound. It rattled throughout the greenhouse. When she looked up, she saw that the skylights were rumbling shut.

''What's going on?'' she asked.

''First guess would be your boss trying not to kill you,'' Remo said blandly.

Amanda spun toward the greenhouse doors. Like the skylights, they were sliding shut. They closed, followed by the hiss of the hermetic seal inflating. Through the special plastic panel next to the closed doors, Amanda saw Hubert St. Clair sitting uncomfortably at the control panel. He held an interoffice phone gingerly to his ear.

Feeling the first thrill of worry, she hurried over to the door, Remo and Chiun in her wake.

''Hubert,'' she said into the speaker next to the door, ''could you please open the doors? I'd like to get out now.''

On the other side of the glass, St. Clair hung up the phone. He unwrapped the handkerchief from his hand.

''You've been a big help, Amanda,'' the CCS head said over the speaker. ''The pristine world of the future will thank you for your contribution.''

''Hubert?'' she asked, worry changing to panic.

"Hubert!" she yelled when he got up and walked from the room.

The second set of doors slid shut, sealing the airtight outer chamber.

Eyes wide, Amanda wheeled on Remo and Chiun.

"Told you he wanted to kill us," Remo said.

Amanda couldn't believe what was happening.

"This is insane," she gasped. "Dr. Schumar died in here, but he was asphyxiated by the *C. dioxas*. The trees are all dead. They've stopped producing carbon dioxide or ammonia. What does he think he's doing?"

As if in response, a new mechanical sound echoed throughout the greenhouse. When they looked up, they saw the massive fans that were positioned high up on the walls chugging to life. At the same time, thick mist began pouring from a network of twisted cones.

"Mind telling me what that's all about?" Remo asked.

"I told you. It's for the clouds," Amanda explained. "They're part of the artificial-environment program."

Propelled by the fans, the mist was swirling into the center of the ceiling. The sky beyond the glass faded as the cloud cover thickened.

"Okay, this has gotten too creepy even for me," Remo said. "Little Father?"

The Master of Sinanju nodded agreement. Twirling, he faced the closed door. Bony hands appeared from the folds of his kimono, daggerlike fingernails unfolding like desert blooms. With nail edges sharper than titanium glass cutters, Chiun attacked the plastic pane.

To the old man's shock, the surface gave. The glass refused to cut.

Remo was stunned when his teacher's deadly nails left little more than a scratch on the hard veneer.

"What is this substance?" Chiun demanded.

"It's a special polymer," Amanda explained. "We needed to create a totally incorruptible environment."

"Anyone else here wish we'd run for the doors when we had the chance?" Remo asked.

The Master of Sinanju's wrinkled face had grown concerned. "Remo, help me," he snapped.

Chiun placed his palms flat against the pane.

Remo joined his teacher. The surface of the door felt alien to the touch. Whatever it was made of, it wasn't ordinary plastic. Still, it was on a frame and so should pop free. With a shared nod, the two Masters of Sinanju exerted pressure against the door.

The door met them with as much force as they put out. They pushed harder. Still nothing.

"It does not move," Chiun hissed.

"Reverse pressure," Amanda insisted. "The door frame is built to withstand vastly different interior pressures. It's part of our simulation of different atmospheres."

"It extends to the walls, too," Remo said. "They would have buckled otherwise."

"The ceiling's the same," Amanda offered worriedly.

She was eyeing the ceiling as she spoke. Sparks of electricity crackled within the swelling storm clouds.

"Lightning?" Remo asked, his voice flat.

"I keep telling you, we *had* to have a natural environment," Amanda insisted.

Chiun's face was harsh. "There is nothing natural in this chamber of horrors," he spit. Hazel eyes watched the blackening clouds.

There was an overhang above the door at which they were standing. It would protect them from the rain.

"No biggie," Remo said. "A little rain never hurt anyone. Still, we better get out of here before winter sets in. I left my snow pants back home."

Glancing around, Remo's gaze fell on the pile of *C. dioxas*.

"One battering ram coming up," he said.

Ducking out from under the small overhang, he raced back across the greenhouse to the trees.

The biggest trunk was nearly two feet around. Remo dumped it from the pile. With the flat edge of his hand he sheered off the branches and chopped off the top.

As he worked, he watched the clouds from the corner of his eye. Whites and blues flashed like indoor fireworks. He was flipping the bare, eight-foot-long tree trunk into his arms when the first crackling roar sounded above him.

The short hair on his neck and arms shot to immediate attention. An explosion of electricity lit the room. Before the lightning bolt could eat up the inconsequential space between floor and ceiling, Remo was already reacting.

He flipped the trunk in his hands straight up and flung himself to the floor. The bolt sought the tallest object in the room which, a moment before, had been Remo. It slammed the top of the *C. dioxa* trunk, pounding down into the packed dirt floor. When Remo scrambled to his feet an instant later, the end of the trunk was charred black and smoking.

A squeaky voice called to him from across the greenhouse.

"Remo, stop your tomfoolery!" the Master of Sinanju shouted.

Thunder bellowed too close to be real. The ground beneath Remo shook as if struck by the colossal foot of some gigantic primordial beast.

"I'll tomfool you, you old buzzard," Remo grumbled.

He was grabbing up the log when he noticed something in the dirt near one of the plant beds. With a deeply worried look that had nothing to do with the storm raging above his head, he snatched up the small object and stuffed it in his pocket. He grabbed up the trunk and was heading back for the doors when the first drop of rain fell.

The thick droplet smacked into the blue tree trunk in Remo's bare arms. Unlike normal rain, it hissed.

The raindrop spit and smoked, burning his nostrils as he ran. A hole as big around as a quarter burned the log.

"This ain't water," Remo snapped as he rejoined Amanda and Chiun under the overhang.

Amanda examined the hole burned in the trunk. "I think it's acid," she said, fear tripping her voice.

"Acid rain," Remo muttered. "Gotta admire him for sticking with what he knows."

Amanda shook her head. "This can't be," she said to herself.

"Is," Remo said. "And unless you want all of us to be was, you'll get out of the way."

Numbly, Amanda backed to the wall.

Chiun grabbed the smoking end of the log. The two Masters of Sinanju steered the blunt end into the greenhouse door. It struck with a wall-rattling thump. They brought the log back, slamming it into the plastic once more.

Behind them, the rain was opening up. Heavy droplets splattered the ground, fizzing and popping wherever they struck.

Remo and Chiun steered the log at the space where the two doors met. On the third try, Remo thought he felt movement. They brought the trunk back, pounding again and again. The log began to splinter. Blue slivers of bark sheered away, revealing powder-blue pulp.

"It isn't working!" Amanda insisted. She was watching them work, eyes darting now and then out to the greenhouse.

The storm was worsening. Sloppy acid droplets spattered onto the trunks of the felled trees. The wood steamed as holes ate through the tough bark. Amanda jumped when an acid raindrop struck the floor near her foot.

"This roof won't hold if it gets worse," she said, troubled eyes directed up at the small overhang.

Remo and Chiun brought the log back, slamming it forward one last time. The room shook and Remo heard a tiny hiss.

"That got it, Little Father," he said.

The Master of Sinanju nodded curtly. As Remo held the log in place, Chiun hurried to the door.

The seal had cracked. Chiun attacked the opening. As he pried the space larger, the inner seal inflated to fill it.

"What the crap?" Remo groused. He jammed the end of the log into the space between the doors.

"It is attempting to seal itself," the Master of Sinanju said tightly even as he began assailing the securing lip with his long fingernails.

"That's a special security feature," Amanda explained. "To keep the environment pure."

"You know, lady, I'm getting pretty tired of hearing that," Remo griped. "By the sounds of it, you thought of everything except how to get out of this goldfish bowl."

His words sent a cold shock of memory through her fear-rattled brain. "There's an emergency switch that opens the door!" Amanda announced frantically. "I forgot all about it." She shrank from Remo's glare. "We never needed it in our work," she explained hastily. "I don't think anyone on the team even knew it was there. I only found it when I was studying the greenhouse schematics after Dr. Schumar's death.''

"Where?" Remo snapped. He glanced around the door. All he could see was the speaker.

"There." She pointed across the greenhouse floor to a series of support columns that rose from the floor, stretching to the vaulted ceiling.

"It's on the third or fourth column," she said.

Remo wheeled on the Master of Sinanju. The old man was still trying to pierce the inflated seal between the doors.

"Go," Chiun commanded. "But have a care."

Remo nodded tightly.

The acid was splattering mostly the main floor. If he hugged the walls, he might be okay. A rumble of thunder shook the greenhouse, and a desperate crackle of lightning screamed into the pile of *C. dioxas* as Remo slipped out from under the protective overhang.

As he moved, he felt the telegraphing waves of something familiar zeroing in on him. A video camera.

Somewhere in the dank depths of the CCS building, Hubert St. Clair was watching him.

Remo saluted the camera with his middle finger even as he ducked and dodged the raindrops. He was right. They drizzled out to almost nothing at the edge of the greenhouse. The nozzles were concentrated in the center of the room.

There was an artificial randomness to the rainfall. Remo's body tuned to the mechanical pattern. Twirling and skittering at the storm's edge, he managed to avoid the fat raindrops.

He found the emergency switch on the third column. A padlock and chain secured it in place. Remo snapped the chain and pulled the switch.

When he glanced back, he saw that the switch hadn't worked. Chiun was still crouched before the doors. Standing next to the Master of Sinanju, Amanda Lifton was growing frantic.

"Stupid geniuses," Remo muttered.

From where Remo danced amid the raindrops, he had a clear view of the roof that was protecting Chiun and Amanda. It was held in place by twin bands angled to the wall. Pooling acid was burning away the securing braces. Even from this distance, his keen eyes could see the metal dissolving.

"Damn," he grumbled. "Chiun, that thing's gonna—"

He never finished. Even as he was shouting, a band snapped.

The roof twisted to one side, spilling a wave of acid. A split second after the first band broke, the second followed suit and the entire overhang collapsed.

Remo could only stand and watch, helpless, as the Master of Sinanju was buried beneath a ton of hissing metal.

He took a step forward. But the room seemed to anticipate his move.

All around him the storm seemed to find sudden focus. The spitting nozzles shut down on the far side of the greenhouse. All at once, they opened up above him. And as Remo stood alone and defenseless on the greenhouse floor, a downpour of acid washed down from above like liquid fire.

6

Herr Hahn knew death. He knew it up close. Had kept quiet company with it for years.

The blood, the anguish, the final screams. He knew all the familiar faces of his old companion. He wasn't some dime store philosopher who would have claimed death as a friend. Herr Hahn had no friends.

No, death to him was not a friend, but an ally. It had worked with him, at his side since his youth. In one sense it was a protector, for without the deaths he inflicted on so many others, Herr Hahn would surely have himself died long ago.

To some he was known as an assassin. He rejected the term. These days an assassin conjured up images of maniacs with political or social motives. The trade, as practiced by Herr Hahn, had no such pretenses. Someone could hire him to kill a president or a plumber. Hahn wouldn't care either way. Of course, the money was the same in each case. For this expensive reason he rarely found work killing plumbers.

In such a skilled profession as his, Herr Hahn was unique, for he was content to be called a murderer.

After all, a murder was a pure and honest-sounding thing.

Professional murder had paid the bills a long time now. And as long as his old ally death continued to see to it that others died instead of Herr Hahn, he would be murdering for many more years to come.

Dealing death was on his mind this day.

Herr Hahn was tucked safely away in the security room of the Congress of Concerned Scientists building in Geneva. On closed-circuit TV, Hahn watched as the drama unfolded within the big greenhouse.

Herr Hahn had set up the elaborate greenhouse system for his employers here at the CCS. As he watched the three people in there now, he realized he might have been unintentionally sloppy. Of course, he couldn't be blamed. After all, these visitors deviated from the norm.

When Hubert St. Clair had instructed Herr Hahn to oversee the death of the woman, Hahn didn't anticipate anything interesting. Even with the addition of the two others he didn't expect anything other than the usual. They'd all three cower underneath the overhang for a time. Eventually and inevitably the acid would do its work, and that would be that.

It should have been the same as the rest of the scientists he'd eliminated. Perhaps this was a little more dramatic than some of the others, but the end result would be identical. Boring and inevitable.

Yet as he studied the monitor, he was finding things a little less predictable than he had come to expect.

These three were **lasting** longer than he ever would have thought.

When the young **one** suddenly raced out from beneath the overhang, **Hahn** sat up straight.

This was new. Such behavior went against every survival instinct Hahn had seen in his many other victims. To leave an area of safety—even a temporary one—ran contrary to normal human behavior.

It was panic. Had to be. Sheer, blind panic. That was the only logical explanation.

In such circumstances panic always killed. The young one would soon die in the artificial storm.

When he didn't, Herr Hahn felt the first tickle of some strange alien emotion deep in his round belly.

The young one seemed unharmed by the growing storm. More incredibly, he had cleared one of the trees of limbs, lifting it with seeming ease. Without a sign of strain on his face, he'd raced back to the others.

Hahn had no great control over where the rain fell or lightning struck. The random program that controlled the storm was intended to mimic the real thing so as to give the trees the closest thing to a natural environment as possible.

All Hahn could do was ratchet up the acid output in certain quadrants. He did. As the liquid sprayed from specially designed nozzles through which water ordinarily flowed, the two intriguing men in the greenhouse were already ramming their log against the thick plastic door.

It was incredible to watch.

They were obviously possessed of physical strength far greater than appearance indicated. They had the perfect camouflage, these two men. Nothing about them would indicate anything extraordinary. And yet here they were, battering the door to their final prison.

Their great efforts wouldn't matter. The doors and walls had been designed to withstand pressure greater than any mere mortals could produce. Even men as unique as these two obviously were.

Hahn watched them work, almost grateful that he hadn't met them some other way. Although he was the best at what he did, these two could present—

A light flashed on his monitor. Blinking disbelief, Hahn leaned forward in his chair.

The door to the greenhouse was open. Just a hair so far—and so far the seal was still secure—but these two had somehow managed to do something the engineer of the greenhouse had insisted would be impossible. And Hahn trusted this particular engineer's word, for it was Herr Hahn himself who had designed the room for the CCS.

On the monitor Hahn saw that they'd pried the edge of the trunk between the doors. The old Asian attacked the inflating hermetic seal with his long fingernails.

For the first time in his professional career, Herr Hahn felt his certainty in his inevitable success begin to fade.

This couldn't be. They *had* to die.

As Hahn watched, the Lifton woman suddenly pointed back out across the greenhouse.

She obviously knew where the emergency switch was. Not that it mattered. Yes, he had gone out to get the log, but the young male would never go back out again.

Hahn watched, stunned, as the young American darted back out into the greenhouse. He grew even more shocked when the thin man with the abnormally thick wrists threw an obscene gesture toward Herr Hahn's security camera.

How could he possibly have known he was being watched?

The American made it to the switch. The acid had to have chewed through the lock and chain, because he simply plucked them off and threw them to the floor.

Others in his business thought Herr Hahn cautious in the extreme. Today, Hahn was grateful for his care and planning. He had disabled the emergency switch before his targets had even entered the greenhouse.

He watched on the monitor as the young one yanked down the switch. When the doors remained closed, Hahn allowed a slip of air to pass his thick lips.

Not that he really expected anything to happen. It was just that, given the strangeness of this situation—

A green light suddenly winked on in the security panel.

Hahn's eyes grew wide. His hands sought out control buttons even as he stuffed his feet back inside the open well beneath the desk. He swept the panel with his eyes.

A breach in the doors. But that couldn't be. The emergency switch was dead. He was sure of it.

The old Asian was still attacking the seal. But now plastic shards had begun to fly like string confetti in a homecoming parade.

Impossible! He was using his fingernails to whittle away at the supposedly invulnerable polymer. Somewhere, somehow, a break had been made in the airtight seal.

He glanced at the monitors. This couldn't be happening.

Hahn was watching two screens at once. The young one was across the room while the old one and the girl stood under the door overhang. Through the murky air Hahn thought he saw something that gave him hope. He zoomed in on the roof.

Yes. There it was. The acid was rotting away the securing bracket. No sooner had he focused the camera than the metal twisted and snapped. The roof lurched and collapsed.

Two dead, one left. Hahn reached for the control panel.

The overhang was no longer there. There was no protection, no way out. Hahn could cut off the sprinklers on half of the room, concentrating the downpour where the young one stood.

Hahn flipped the last switch. Gripping tight the

edge of the control panel, he threw his attention back to the monitors. To watch the younger man finally do as he was supposed to. Melt into a pile of steaming flesh and bone.

THE DELUGE that would have turned a common man to sludge failed to kill Remo Williams for one simple reason. Remo Williams was not a common man.

He was off at a sprint even as the acid was falling. It hadn't even touched ground before he was nearly out of range.

The nozzles had been turned off to the right of the greenhouse. That was where Remo ran.

Remo was running full-out even as he felt the first drops of acid kiss the back of his T-shirt.

As he ran, he rolled the skin of his back, flexing and twisting the muscles. His skin became a life-form independent of the rest of his body, rippling in undulating waves. The movement kept his shirt out of complete contact with his skin, preventing the acid that was bleeding into the disintegrating fabric from finding root in soft flesh.

He was at a crouch once he reached the storm line. With a fall and a roll he was out of it. Acid that had pooled on the floor chewed away at the knees of his pants.

The nozzles where he'd been standing clicked off with a drizzling hiss. In another moment he was sure the ones directly above him would switch on.

He was out in the open now. Exposed. There was

no longer any place for him to hide. His eyes strayed to the remnants of the door arch.

Even if Chiun had survived under all that metal, it would only be a matter of time before—

Remo blinked. The twin doors into the control room were no longer closed. The clear panes had been pried apart. A narrow gap opened into the room beyond.

A weathered face appeared in the narrow opening. Chiun's worried expression changed to a look of agitation.

"Remo, act your age," the Master of Sinanju admonished. "It is unseemly for the Transitional Reigning Master of Sinanju to be stomping around in rain puddles."

With that, Chiun disappeared.

Above Remo, the nozzles switched on. It no longer mattered. Remo was already gone.

He took a running leap over the collapsed roof.

"Banzai!" he yelled as he dove over the twisted debris and through the open door. His palms hit the floor in the small control room and he flipped up and over, landing on the soles of his smoking loafers. "Tah-da!" he announced, throwing his arms out wide.

Amanda was standing next to the Master of Sinanju. Rather than be impressed, she wore a frightened expression.

The instant Remo hit the floor, the Master of Sinanju jumped forward, tapered fingernails flashing out like deadly knife blades.

"What are you doing?" Remo asked, twisting away.

"Stay still, imbecile!" Chiun barked.

Like a demented tailor, the old man attacked Remo's steaming T-shirt. The cotton sheered away in long strips. As it fell to the floor, the acid continued to chew at the material.

Once the shirt was gone, Chiun sliced off the growing holes at Remo's knees. He came away with two circles of cloth with widening holes at the center. He threw them to the floor with the steaming T-shirt strips.

When Chiun at last stood back, Remo looked down on his tattered outfit. He was shirtless with two holes in his knees and a pair of smoking loafers. He glanced sheepishly at the Master of Sinanju.

"You think maybe you could skip over this part in the Sinanju Scrolls?" he asked.

"If not for the ever vigilant eyes of my dead ancestors, I would be tempted to throw out the entire chronicle of your apprenticeship and claim the records were lost when you burned down my house," Chiun replied thinly.

"That sounds like a no," Remo sighed. "And I didn't burn down our house."

Scuffing his soles on the concrete floor to remove the excess acid, he turned his attention to Amanda.

She stood panting near the door. Beyond, the storm still raged in the greenhouse.

"I—I can't believe this," Amanda stammered.

"Yeah, my boss has tried to kill me a couple of times, too," Remo commiserated. "If he's thinking of making it a regular thing, I'd ask for a raise and a better parking space. Say, you wouldn't have a spare shirt around here?"

Amanda glanced at him. "Oh," she said. "There might be some clothes in the offices."

She pressed a button on the control panel and the outer doors hissed open. In a daze, she headed into the hallway. Chiun followed her out.

Remo cast a final glance into the greenhouse.

The storm was powering down. The electricity had been cut to the lightning and the fans. Only a little liquid still drizzled from the overhead nozzles. The ground steamed. The acrid air burned Remo's nostrils.

Whoever was operating the environmental controls was admitting failure and shutting off the systems.

Remo left the small control room, his face as dark and doom-filled as the dissipating clouds in the big glass greenhouse.

IN THE SECURITY ROOM on the other side of the CCS complex, Herr Hahn switched off the monitors one by one.

For a long moment he sat alone in the silent room, staring at the dead black screens.

This simple killing was apparently going to be more difficult than he had originally thought.

Without realizing it, a smile slowly spread across his broad face. In the pit of his stomach, a new emotion.

Excitement.

It had been a long time since Herr Hahn had faced a real challenge. These two promised to give him something his professional life was sorely lacking.

Like a man with renewed purpose, Herr Hahn got to his feet and waddled out into the dimly lit corridor.

7

The sunrise was new.

He had been in this place many times now and it was always night. But there it was. Or *nearly* was. Although the sun had not yet actually peeked over the horizon, Mark Howard knew on some instinctive level that it was coming even as he walked along the empty Folcroft corridor.

Through the closed and barred windows he could see the sanitarium grounds bathed in the purple of predawn. The same color streaked the sallow sky.

It was always winter in this place. It remained the same even as the rest of the world enjoyed the change of seasons. Dark shadows painted the land. The tree trunks were arms, their dead branches fingers. Grasping, clawing for the dawn that had been so long coming. Finally, almost here.

Mark was used to the dream by now. It had started the first week he'd come to work at Folcroft. For months it was a nightmare, but he'd had it so frequently now that he had built up a callus in his mind.

When he passed the same window at the end of the hall, the same owl sat in the same branch of the same tree. Its eyes glowed the same color as the sky and the land. He saw for the first time that the swollen moon was gone.

Mark was looking out the window when, with a loud hoot, the owl suddenly flapped its big wings. His heart tripped when the night bird took flight. It vanished in the pale darkness of early morning.

That was new, too. He had gotten used to everything being the same. The changes in the dream this time were bringing back some of the earliest feelings of dread.

He pulled his gaze from the window.

Mark could see now that the hallway was not as misshapen as it usually was. The angles were normal, not twisted. The lines of ceiling and floor led straight to a single door at the far end of the dusty corridor.

It was like any other hospital door at Folcroft. Wires crisscrossed the off-center Plexiglas window.

The Beast lived beyond that door. For a year now Mark had almost glimpsed it in his dreams. It was a thing that lived on fear and in shadow. It played at the fringes of his unconscious mind, never stepping into the light, never taking a form that Mark Howard could fully understand.

He was only happy that the Beast was trapped. The door was a prison that kept it locked away.

As Mark approached the heavy door, he expected to feel the chill that always came at this point in his dream. Along with it, the same inhuman rasping voice he always heard.

They never came.

More changes. A corruption of the familiar that made all of the old terrors seem as fresh as that very first dream all those months ago. His steps growing more cautious, Mark approached the door.

Before he even reached it, he saw that it was ajar. Another first. A small security chain hung slack in the space between door and frame. So fragile. Not enough to hold the monster within.

His heart thudding, Mark reached the door. Hands framing the small window, he leaned in close.

Most of the familiar shadows had fled. He saw now that the room was tidy, like the rooms of all Folcroft patients. A thin sheet draped a plain hospital bed. And on the bed was an emaciated figure with a face as pale as the crisp white linens under which it lay.

Mark blinked. There was no sign of the Beast.

And when the voice spoke, it came not from the figure in the bed but from Mark Howard's own mind.

The time is nearly here....

Something stabbed into Mark's shoulder. He jumped, grabbing for whatever had touched him. His fingers wrapped around something cold and dry.

Nearly here...nearly here...nearly here...

"MARK, WAKE UP."

The voice spoke with crisp irritation. The dream fled and Mark Howard's tired eyes blinked open.

He was sitting in the office of Dr. Harold W. Smith.

The CURE director stood over him, shaking Mark with one arthritic hand. Smith's lemony face was drawn tight with annoyance.

"Dr. Smith," Mark said, embarrassed. He suddenly realized that the thing he had grabbed on to in his dream was Smith's gnarled hand. He released it, his face flushing.

Smith straightened. "We were in the middle of our morning meeting," he said. "I had taken a moment to retrieve something from the mainframes. When I looked up, you were asleep."

"Oh." Mark cleared his throat. "I'm sorry. I've been having a problem with…" His voice trailed off. "I'm sorry, Dr. Smith," he repeated.

A notch formed on Smith's gray brow. "Is there something that you wish to tell me?" he asked.

When Mark looked up, he found Smith peering intently down at him. The look of accusation of a moment before had begun to change to one of concern. There was almost a paternal glint in those cold eyes.

"It's something—" Mark shook his head. "I can't really describe it right now. It's something strange."

"I see," Smith said slowly. "Does it have anything to do with your, er—" he hesitated "—ability?"

Although the CURE director chose not to discuss it much, he was aware that his assistant was possessed of a unique intuitive sense. In the past Howard's gift had given them foresight into some CURE-related matters.

"I don't think so," Mark said. "If it is, it's not in any way I'm familiar with."

Smith nodded. "Very well," he said. He began to turn away when he abruptly paused. "Mark, you've been working nonstop since you started here. Perhaps it might be a good idea for you to take a few days off.''

Howard seemed surprised at the offer. Before he could respond, they were both interrupted by the jangling of one of Smith's desktop telephones. The CURE director noted that it was the blue contact phone.

"That will be all for now, Mark," Smith said.

Howard was grateful to be dismissed. As he hurried from the room, Smith rounded the desk. Howard was shutting the door as Smith settled into his cracked leather chair.

"Smith," the CURE director announced into the phone.

"Hey, Smitty," Remo said. "I'll give you three guesses who just escaped certain death by the skin of his teeth, and the first two don't count."

Smith leaned forward in his chair. "Did something go wrong?" he asked.

"Depends on your perspective," Remo said. "Since I'm not a French fry right now, that Humbert Humbert guy who runs the show around here probably thinks so."

Smith raised an eyebrow. "Remo, are you saying Hubert St. Clair tried to kill you?" he asked.

In the Geneva headquarters of the Congress of Concerned Scientists, Remo leaned back against Amanda Lifton's desk. Chiun and Amanda had left him alone while he placed the call. He looked down at his tattered clothes.

"Technically, kill," Remo said. "Specifically, acid

dip. Six of one, half dozen of the other. I think he was just going after that dingbat lady scientist, and me and Chiun got caught in the cross fire. And speaking of her, the Ivy League must have started passing out diplomas with every bikini wax."

"Dr. Lifton is supposed to be quite gifted," Smith said.

"She's a flaky debutante with boobs till Tuesday," Remo replied. "I doubt she could invent her way out of a bra with both hands." He tipped his head, reconsidering. "Actually, that's probably how she got the job here."

Remo quickly briefed Smith on the events in the CCS greenhouse, including the destruction of all the *C. dioxas.*

"You said St. Clair was on the phone before the attack against you began?" Smith asked once Remo was finished.

"Yeah, but I wasn't listening to what he was saying," Remo said. "Could have been calling his bookie. It sure as hell wasn't his dry cleaner."

As he spoke, he picked up a framed photograph from Amanda's desk. Dr. Lifton was posing with Hubert St. Clair and a half-dozen others. Although he could have picked her chests out of a lineup blindfolded, in this picture it wasn't hard to tell which one was Amanda. The rest of them were all dressed like St. Clair. They all wore bell-bottoms and corduroy jackets. Remo frowned at the picture.

"Must be the office Halloween party," he muttered.

"What?"

"Nothing, Smitty," Remo said, putting the photo down. "I don't know what the what is here right now, but I searched the place and came up empty. That Dilbert guy flew the coop. I need you to track him down."

He heard the sound of Smith typing rapidly at his computer. "There is an executive committee that oversees the CCS," the CURE director explained as he worked. "While the current director is Dr. St. Clair, he is answerable to the rest of the leadership. They could be involved." The typing stopped. "The CCS owns a home for St. Clair's use when he is in Geneva," Smith said. He gave Remo the address.

"Thanks, Smitty." He started to hang up.

"Remo," the CURE director said. "Are you certain all the trees were destroyed?"

Remo snapped his fingers. "Thanks for reminding me," he said. Digging in his pocket, he pulled out a tiny object.

It was as big as a pea. This was what had caught his eye in the greenhouse when the lightning struck.

Remo held up the blue seed for inspection.

"Is something else wrong?" Smith asked after the dead air had gone on between them too long.

"Maybe," Remo said. "Although it could just be the end of the world. I'll get back to you." Slipping the lone *C. dioxa* seed back into his pocket, he hung up the phone.

8

"Where are all the seeds?" Remo announced when he rejoined Amanda and Chiun in one of the CCS labs.

He had brought a framed photograph with him from Amanda's office.

The Master of Sinanju was sitting cross-legged near a big picture window that offered a breathtaking view of the snowcapped Alps. He had removed a handful of his special gold-and-silver envelopes and a stack of writing paper from his kimono folds. The old man was ignoring the scenic view, concentrating on composing another of his mysterious letters.

Amanda was laying out a dress shirt and a pair of pants she'd scavenged from the CCS offices.

"What?" she asked, looking up.

When Amanda saw the picture Remo was carrying, she frowned. It was the photo of the *C. dioxa* that had been hanging on her office wall. The same one Remo had asked about when she first brought them to her office.

"What are you doing with that?" Amanda demanded.

"The seeds," Remo pointed out. He held up the photo in one hand; in the other was the seed he'd found in the greenhouse. "*These* seeds. You said this was a picture of the latest trees. Well, in the picture they've got seeds. The ones that were chopped down in that nutcase greenhouse of yours didn't have any. So where did they go?"

Near the window the Master of Sinanju paused in his writing. When he lifted his head, his hazel eyes caught a good, hard look at the Alps.

"I don't like Switzerland," the old Korean announced.

Scowling, he returned to his writing.

"The seeds must have been there," Amanda said to Remo. "Hubert had the trees destroyed. It wouldn't make sense for him to do that without destroying the seeds, too."

"I don't know if you missed all the fun back there, Chesty LaRue, but Hubert was that weird-looking little troll who just tried to turn you into a silicone puddle."

Amanda's pretty face puckered in annoyance. She tried pushing her shoulders forward to cave in her chest.

"I don't appreciate sarcasm or insults from the help," she said unhappily. "And I've been thinking about all this. Something's wrong here, I know it. But I just can't believe that Hubert St. Clair is behind it."

"Believe what you want," Remo said. "But you need to get those things checked. Your reception's way off."

Remo picked up the dress shirt, shrugging it on. He rotated his shoulders. "This doesn't feel right," he said.

"Well, it was the best I could do," Amanda said, trying to pretend she wasn't watching him dress. "That was Dr. Riviera's. He died a month ago in a snorkling accident in the Bahamas."

"Your boss probably stuffed shark-nip down his skivvies and tapped a cork in his pipe," Remo said. He wasn't used to long sleeves. And the shirt was too tight at the wrists. He'd have to pick up a new T-shirt.

"The Swiss are forever professing their neutrality," the Master of Sinanju proclaimed near the window. "Tell me, Remo, what use is there for an assassin in a land where everyone is afraid to choose sides?"

"No use at all, Little Father."

Chiun nodded. "And their mountains are ugly," he said.

"A blight on the land. We should bulldoze them flat and make the whole damned country a parking lot for Germany."

A thin smile touched the old Korean's wrinkled lips. "Sometimes, Remo, you are almost not a disappointment to me," Chiun said.

"I like you, too, Little Father," Remo said. "Care to tell me what all those letters are for?"

"Still none of your business," Chiun replied ominously. He offered Remo the top of his bald head.

"I have a feeling they are," Remo muttered. He

grabbed up the pants Amanda had found for him and ducked behind the open door of the lab.

"Maybe Hubert—I don't know—bumped the controls with his elbow on his way out the door," Amanda said. "It could happen. He doesn't like to touch buttons or switches. Maybe he doesn't even know what almost happened." Her face grew suddenly concerned. "Oh, or maybe they got to him, too!"

"Fine with me," Remo said, zipping his fly as he came out from behind the door. He tossed his old pants onto a table. "Someone doing my job for me for a change. I'm sick of always doing all the grunt work. We're going, Chiun."

The Master of Sinanju swept up his writing material.

Cradling an elbow in one hand, Amanda was chewing on the back of her thumbnail. "You're absolutely *sure* there weren't any seeds on the trees?" she asked, her voice very even.

"Picked clean," Remo said certainly. "My guess is we'll find Hubert Appleseed wearing a tin pot on his head and spreading doomsday seeds from the back of his electric car. That is, assuming we don't all asphyxiate first."

With that, Remo and Chiun left the lab.

Amanda's face had grown pale. Assuming Remo was right, with the rest of the *C. dioxa* team gone, she alone in all the world knew the truth of his words.

When she pulled the lab door closed a moment later, Dr. Amanda Lifton's hands were shaking.

9

Remo and Chiun had taken a cab from the airport to the Congress of Concerned Scientists complex. Since they were without transportation, Amanda offered to drive to Hubert St. Clair's Geneva retreat.

"This is *your* car?" Remo asked when she led them to her economical Citroën.

Some of the color had returned to her cheeks. She fumbled in her purse for the keys.

"What's wrong with it?" she asked.

"For starters, where's the rest of it?"

"There's nothing wrong with economy," Amanda insisted. "Who needs a big Detroit gas-guzzler with a TV, a bar and a chauffeur anyway?" Her eyes welled at the memory of better days. "Not me. Excuse me, I've got something in my eye."

She turned, blowing her nose on her sleeve before turning back to unlock the car.

Chiun sat in the front next to Amanda. Remo had to cram himself in the back on a pile of stuffed toys and with an umbrella stabbing him in the side.

Amanda Lifton drove like someone who was used to giving orders from behind a martini glass in the back seat. When she had taken one too many corners on two wheels, Remo finally snapped the umbrella in two and threw it out the window.

"What did you do that for?" Amanda demanded.

"I'm not getting paid to be shish kebabbed," he said.

"Umbrellas aren't free, you know," she said. "I'm telling Daddy you owe me a new one."

"Take it out of your stuffed-animal budget," Remo grumbled, knocking around the pile of toys. "What are you, five?"

"He's not very nice at all," Amanda said to Chiun.

"No, he is not," Chiun agreed. "And since he is by nature a not-nice person, it is making it all the more difficult for him to do one nice thing for another person as is required by our traditions."

"*He* has to do a good deed?" Amanda asked. She snorted derisively. "Good luck."

"Thanks," said Remo who, while Amanda and Chiun were talking, had been heaving most of her stuffed toys into the street.

Two miles north of the city they passed the European headquarters of the United Nations. They followed the Rue de Lausanne to where it ran parallel to the shore of Lake Geneva. The snowcapped Alps held up the sky. The Mont Blanc massif cast a looming shadow over the gleaming lake.

"You sure you know where St. Clair's house is?" Remo asked as they headed into the hills.

"Of course," Amanda said. "I practically grew up in Switzerland. Abigail and I used to winter here with

Mother and Daddy. I've been to a bunch of CCS functions at Hubert's house. It used to be Sage Carlin's when he was CCS head.''

It was the name that finally jogged Remo's memory.

"Sage Carlin," he said, snapping his fingers. "I *knew* St. Clair looked like somebody."

"Yes," Amanda said uncomfortably. "Dr. Carlin was a legend at the CCS. Some of the men there sort of adopted his look after he died. I guess they think they're kind of a living memorial to Sage."

"You mean they look like that on purpose?" Remo asked. He shook his head. "Trying to end the world is starting to look like the least crazy thing about that place."

Amanda took a sharp turn onto a winding road. The homes grew more palatial as they climbed. The more opulent they became, the more despondent Amanda grew. By the time they stopped at the gate of Hubert St. Clair's chalet, she was practically in tears once more.

The home beyond the fence was one of rich woods and elaborate peaks. It was perched on an outcropping. Far below, the crescent shape of Lake Geneva sparkled in the cold mountain sun.

Porches encircled both floors of the house, one above the other. Big sheets of plate glass reflected sunlight.

When Remo and Chiun got out, Amanda was still sniffling behind the wheel.

"Look," Remo said, trying to strike a sympathetic

tone, "why don't you wait here while we check this out."

"No," Amanda insisted. "It's just tough. All this money. I used to have this. This used to be me." She straightened her proud Lifton spine. "But I'll be fine."

"Okay, come. Just stay out of the way," Remo advised.

It was as if her tears were wired to a switch. They just stopped. The old Lifton arrogance resurfaced.

"Don't you condescend to me," Amanda ordered. She blinked her eyes clear as she got out of the car. "You work for me, remember?"

"Okay, okay," Remo sighed. He turned to Chiun, pitching his voice low. "Let's keep an eye on the flake, okay, Little Father?"

"What did you say?" Amanda demanded. "Was that about me? I don't appreciate whispering behind my back. Especially when you're doing it right in front of me. If you have something to tell me, you tell me to my face."

Remo rolled his eyes. "*I* should wait in the car," he said. "And you wanna yell a little louder? There's a pastry chef in Munich who can't quite hear you."

"You've got a lot of attitude for a guy who wears just a T-shirt," she accused.

"You should have seen him when *I* found him," Chiun said. "He was a naked foundling, even whiter than he is now. Hard to believe, yes, I know. And even after all my years trying to de-white him, this is still only the best I could do."

"Tell you what. Why don't you two wait in the car and I'll go jump in the lake?" Remo snarled.

With his heel he kicked open the driveway gate. The brittle lock snapped, and he stormed onto the grounds of Hubert St. Clair's estate.

THE FIGURE WAS outlined in green.

From his boat moored out in Genfersee—the name his German forebears had given Lake Geneva—Herr Hahn watched Remo head up the driveway. The other two, which Hahn knew were the woman and the elderly Asian, trailed him up to the house.

The two men didn't walk so much as glide. Their grace had been apparent on the security cameras at the CCS, but it was far more obvious here, where he wasn't actually seeing their features. Here, they were only warm green ghosts moving with inhuman grace across his glowing monitor. A beautiful, perfect symphony of movement.

"What are you?" Herr Hahn asked the ghosts on his screen.

After the events at the greenhouse he was being even more cautious than usual. Hahn had assumed they would come here in search of Hubert St. Clair. He had already been given orders to destroy the house and all its contents. He had lingered a little longer in the hope that his assumption was correct. Now that they were here, he felt a fresh tingle of excitement. So new a sensation he wanted to savor it.

There wouldn't be much time to do so. In a few moments they'd all be dead, and Herr Hahn would have to satisfy himself once more with ordinary targets.

His ample stomach continued its thrilling butterfly dance in concert with the boat's rocking motion as the three green ghosts climbed the porch steps.

THE GRAVEL PATH LED from the driveway around to the back of the chalet where the broad deck looked out over the lake. Remo was first onto the porch. When Amanda followed Chiun up, she managed to make four steps squeak three times and nearly put an eye out on a hanging potted plant.

"Did your father disown you because you were a klutz?" Remo asked.

"No," Amanda snapped back as she stilled the swaying plant with both hands. She suddenly frowned. "Why? Did Daddy tell you that was why?"

"No," Remo said. "And be quiet." He was glancing around the area.

Lake Geneva was a living postcard photo, shimmering in the early-afternoon sunlight. Pleasure boats bobbed gently while *Mouettes Genevoises*—the small motorboats that shuttled between the old and new cities of Geneva—skimmed the silvery surface. A lone cruise ship carted tourists on camera excursions north to Montreux and Chillon. And somewhere down there, Remo sensed the distinct pressure waves of some kind of mechanical equipment directed at them.

"You feel that, Little Father?"

Chiun nodded. "Whatever it is, it is farther away than most detection devices."

"Spying at a distance," Remo sighed. "Welcome to the future."

"Why?" Amanda asked. "What is it?" She was squinting around the back of the house.

A cold wind blew up the steep mountainside. Farther down, a road snaked across the hillside. Here and there, a few rooftops peeked out between frozen rock and winter trees.

"Nothing," Remo answered. "We're just being watched is all."

Amanda gripped his arm. "Where?" she whispered, worried once more about joining the deceased ranks of her fellow CCS scientists.

"Can't tell really," Remo said. "The waves are focused as they come at you, but they break down over distance. My guess would be the lake. It's coming from that direction, and it's got a clear shot up at the house. Mountains are way too far for us to feel anything."

Turning from the lake, he headed for the door.

"You're still going in?" she asked. "Don't you want to get whoever's down there?"

"Too big an area to search. But you wanna go frisk some flounder, hey, be my guest."

A wall of glass panes lined the deck. One was a sliding door, which Remo pushed open.

Amanda noted as Remo and Chiun slipped inside that the two men failed to make a single sound as they walked. She tried to follow their catlike lead but found the hardwood floor creaking underfoot as soon as she followed them inside.

Amanda cringed at the sound. When Remo caught the look on her face, he shook his head.

"Don't sweat it," he said. "Nobody's here."

"Yes," the Master of Sinanju agreed. "However someone has been here recently."

Remo sniffed the air. "Smells like lard and sausages. One of the rooms back at the CCS smelled like that, too."

Chiun nodded agreement. "A German," the old man concluded darkly. "There was a time, Remo, back during the days of that little man with the funny mustache, when all of Europe smelled like this. To this day there are still corners of France that smell like Germany."

"No wonder," Remo said. "They fling open the door and throw up their hands every time some mailman in Düsseldorf hammers a new spike in his helmet. Still, stinking like a German beats stinking like a Frenchman any day of the week."

"Shouldn't you two be quiet?" Amanda whispered. She was glancing nervously around the big living room.

There were a few pictures on the walls. Remo could tell by their weird Sage Carlin–inspired uniforms which men worked for the CCS.

"I told you, no one's here," Remo said as he tore his gaze from the pictures.

He had detected another scent in the house. Nose in the air, he tracked it like a bloodhound to the cellar stairs.

"What is it?" Amanda asked when Remo stopped at the top of the staircase.

"I smell ammonia," Remo replied. "Back home I'd think it was just the laundry room, but since this is Europe, where washing day comes only after a good healthy round of black plague…"

Voice trailing off, Remo headed down the stairs.

HERR HAHN WATCHED the three glowing figures descend.

They managed to amaze him yet again. There was no searching of the rest of the house, as Hahn had expected. No trial and error of any kind. They entered the house, steered a beeline for the cellar door and went down.

Their certainty was unnerving. It was as if all the old rules were gone. All of his understanding of human behavior and ability, honed by years of experience, didn't apply to these two.

Yet as troubling as it was, it was also exhilarating.

To be the best in his field meant so few challenges.

Feeling a melancholy twinge for what he was about to do, Hahn placed his chubby hand on the portable console that sat on the map table in the cabin of his boat.

As he watched the silhouettes of the men and woman creep deeper into the basement, one fat finger lovingly caressed a gleaming silver toggle switch.

"THIS IS WHERE he stored them," Remo said.

Amanda saw nothing but a dirt cellar floor. An

empty floor. But even she could now smell the thin odor of ammonia that lingered in the musty air.

"Judging by the marks in the earth, there were more than thirty sacks stored here," the Master of Sinanju concluded.

"Burlap sacks," Remo said. "Big ones."

"That would probably be enough to hold all the seeds from the greenhouse plants," Amanda said. She shook her head in disbelief. "But he couldn't have. He *wouldn't* have."

"I thought we were past that," Remo said. He was looking at something in the corner. "Did he use that?"

Amanda saw that he was nodding to an antique wooden butter churn. Souring milk was slopped on the tarp on which it sat. Remo noted an old oil lamp hanging next to the churn. Both appeared to have been used recently.

"Hubert has a thing about machines," she explained. "I don't think he's really comfortable with technology. He uses all kinds of excuses just to get other people to turn on his lights or answer his phone for him."

"Not too crazy," Remo muttered.

His eyes strayed to the rear of the main cellar room. He saw something lying in the dirt near an open door. Going over, he picked up the tiny blue seed.

"That shouldn't be out of the CCS complex," Amanda said, coming up beside him. "God help us, he *has* gone insane."

"He churns his own butter, won't turn on a light

and has dressed like that for how long and you're just noticing?'' Remo asked dryly.

The door opened into a separate room off the side of the basement. A few rectangular windows pulled streaks of daylight down to the dirt floor. When the three of them entered the long, dark corridor, Amanda's nose rebelled at the smell. The dirt floors and stone walls had suppressed it in the outer room.

''That's oil,'' she complained. A thought suddenly occurred to her. ''Oil,'' she repeated. ''Oh, my.''

They were passing by another open room. An old furnace hummed away in the dark recesses. A much newer device had been attached to the front of the ancient furnace.

''What's wrong?'' Remo asked.

''Oh,'' Amanda said. ''Maybe nothing. ''It's just that when I first started at the CCS I remember seeing schematics for an underground system of oil tanks in Dr. Carlin's office. I thought it was strange because most of the power around here is hydroelectric. I didn't know why he'd want to store that much oil. The tanks were huge.''

''Your point being?'' Remo asked.

''The tanks were built into the side of a mountain. *This* is the side of a mountain. And this used to be Dr. Carlin's house when he was at the CCS.''

Remo stopped dead.

''Oh,'' Amanda said when she saw the look on his face. ''You think it might be something? I only remember because it was right after that prediction he made during the Gulf War. When he said those oil-well fires would burn for months and change the environment of the entire Gulf region for years to come.'' She grew more worried when she saw Remo's expression grow even darker. ''They didn't,'' she added hopefully.

''We should leave,'' Chiun said evenly.

Remo was thinking of the pressure waves from the surveillance equipment they'd both sensed coming from Lake Geneva. He suddenly felt like a mouse just before the steel bar snapped shut.

''Right behind you, Little Father,'' he said.

Shepherding a suddenly very worried Amanda Lifton before them, the two Masters of Sinanju began to cautiously retrace their steps back out to the main cellar.

REMARKABLE!

Hahn watched the infrared monitor image through excited, unblinking eyes.

They were heading back up the basement hallway. Could it be? Could it *possibly* be that they had guessed what was in store?

The three green blobs were back in front of the open door that led to the furnace. They were coming back out.

Maybe they had seen the modified furnace. Hahn had rigged it for Sage Carlin years ago. Activated it just this afternoon. Could they know?

He wished he could have asked them, but of course that was impossible. It was time for them to die.

The silver antenna was already up on the remote

transmitter. It was aimed across the deck of Hahn's boat at the magnificent chalet nestled among the lower Alps.

A cold wind blew across the lake, swirling through the open cabin door, cutting Herr Hahn to the bone.

Eyes on the chalet, Herr Hahn flicked the toggle switch.

The monitor flashed bright, consumed from corner to corner and top to bottom by a wash of brilliant green.

And in the rocks above Lake Geneva, an orange fireball vomiting up from the very bowels of Hell itself erupted from the smoking crater where Hubert St. Clair's house had been.

10

The click saved their lives.

They heard it as they passed the open door to the furnace room. It was a soft thing that became inaudible in the ensuing roar.

A brilliant orange flash burst from the black mouth of the dark room. A wall of searing flame and heat whooshed forward, erupting into the hall.

When the click sounded, Remo and Chiun went from a walk to a sprint. They tore down the slender passage a heartbeat ahead of the blast.

Chiun had scooped up Amanda. In his arms the world around her seemed to slow, then freeze.

Not enough time to make it out into the main cellar.

Frozen flames, locked in time, rocketing in at impossible speed.

Amanda suddenly airborne. Remo's arms encircling her waist. Chiun, flames licking at the hem of his kimono, launching himself up at one of the dirty basement windows.

The glass shattering. Then flying at Amanda. No way to avoid it. She was a deadly human spear, fired at speeds greater than the explosion or the flames, faster even than conscious thought.

Out! In the cold mountain air, with bony hands grabbing her once more.

Running.

Time tripping back to normal speed.

The house exploded. Windows burst, scattering diamond fragments across the Swiss hillside. The wood splintered apart and spread like burning matchsticks as the ball of orange flame burst from Earth's ruptured molten core.

The intense heat chased them down the driveway and out into the street. Still Chiun ran, Amanda thrown over one shoulder. Even when he stopped, he danced through falling fragments of Hubert St. Clair's chalet.

Chiun set Amanda to the street. She reeled in place as she tried to get her bearings.

It all seemed to have happened in an instant. In a fiery blur she'd gone from standing in the cellar to dodging flaming house chunks out beyond Dr. St. Clair's twisted front gate.

The heat from the oil-fed fire pushed them back. Acrid smoke poured out of the jagged hole where the upper story had been. The roof had been blown off completely.

Amanda fought the fire for oxygen, panting to catch her breath. For a moment, her Lifton pretensions burned away. The money, the cars, the hotels—none of it seemed to matter as much as her life. She looked gratefully at the two men who had saved her.

She saw only Chiun. Worry formed deep in the lines of his weathered face as he watched the fire.

"Where's Remo?" Amanda asked.

She glanced back at the chalet. The bottom-floor walls were starting to collapse into the central crater. Flames of orange crackled and danced.

"He did get out, didn't he?" she asked, her voice growing very small.

Chiun didn't reply. His expression carved in stone, he watched impassively as perdition claimed the sunny Swiss mountainside.

HERR HAHN KEPT his eyes off the thermal-imaging unit from the moment he pressed the toggle switch. With that much heat exploding into light, if he'd seen it he would have been blinking away stars for the rest of the week.

He watched out the boat's cabin window as a thick curl of angry black smoke rose from the hills above the cold waves of Lake Geneva.

Thanks to all that oil buried in the underground tanks, the fire would burn for hours.

An oil-well fire in the Alps.

As the hired killer of the Congress of Concerned Scientists, Hahn had found the notion intriguing. It gave him the opportunity to test his engineering and technical skills. Of course it was an extravagant way to demolish the chalet, but the CCS wasn't lacking for donations. And this method had one side benefit, unknown when the tanks were first installed. The two men who had survived the CCS greenhouse could not possibly have made it out alive.

They along with the pesky girl—who was his true target—were cinders by now.

Savoring the victory over the only interesting targets he had ever encountered, Hahn gathered up his binoculars from the table in his boat cabin. There was a plate of pfeffernuesse next to them. Hahn blew powdered sugar from the lenses before aiming the binoculars at the hillside.

The sound of emergency vehicles already rose in the distance. Sirens howled over the cold wind.

What was left of the wooden house was engulfed in flames. As Hahn watched, the burning walls fell into themselves.

It would be days before fire officials learned about the oil tanks, days before they realized why the fire had taken so long to put out. By the time it was extinguished, there wouldn't be so much as a tooth or scrap of bone left of Herr Hahn's latest victims.

Herr Hahn was about to lower the binoculars when he caught a brief flash of movement near the driveway of St. Clair's chalet.

Fire and police officials wouldn't be there already. Probably gawking neighbors.

Hahn shifted his great bulk in his creaking chair, backtracking with the glasses.

When he found the source of movement, Herr Hahn shot to his feet as if someone had wired his chair. The pfeffernuesse plate tumbled to the floor along with a stein of thick German beer. The plate shattered, and little cookie balls rolled across the cabin floor.

It couldn't be.

The old Asian stood at the mouth of the driveway. Along with him was the Lifton woman. As Hahn watched in shock, the Asian ran back up the driveway.

The old man rounded the ruins of the house. The heat from the fire should have been unbearable. Yet he seemed unmindful as he ran.

Hahn's brain could not reconcile this with the world he knew.

He *couldn't* have gotten out. Hahn had tracked them with the thermal sensors to the last possible instant. They were trapped in the basement. He had detonated the explosive cap attached to the furnace when they were standing in front of the door. In Herr Hahn's world, men did not outrun explosions.

Maybe there were two old men. Another woman who resembled Amanda Lifton. He didn't see the younger man. Maybe he didn't have a twin. Maybe the sole young one had been properly killed in the blast that had obliterated the twins of the old Asian and Amanda Lifton.

This ludicrous speculation flitted through Herr Hahn's brain in a shocked instant. All such conjecture ended the moment Hahn saw a new figure race out from behind the wall of flame.

It looked as if the fire was holding on to him, but Herr Hahn soon realized that the young one's shirt was ablaze. He stopped, did a little pirouette, and the flames winked out. It was as if that simple move had created a vacuum, extinguishing the fire.

The old Asian raced up to the young American. Sharp hands slapped furiously at the back of the young one's shirt.

They appeared to argue for a moment, the young one pushing away the old one's slapping hands. But then the attention of both seemed to be drawn in another direction. Like two heads controlled by a single mind, the two men turned their eyes down the hill.

They didn't search the waters of Lake Geneva. There was no uncertainty. No hesitation at all. It was as if they were possessed with an ability to focus in like laser beams on something that was breaking into their conscious sphere.

They found the boat.

They found the man on the deck of the boat.

Together, they stared down the binoculars of Herr Hahn.

And then they began loping down the hill toward him.

"YOU DIDN'T HAVE to slap me like that," Remo complained as they bounded down the steep hill toward the distant lake.

"True," Chiun replied. He leaped over a boulder, landing at a sprint. "I could have left you to cook like a pig on a spit."

A broad black rock surface appeared suddenly on the hill before them. Remo's legs split like a hurdler's as he soared over an angled crevice in the rock face. Chiun bounded down after him. They continued on.

"I was already out," Remo snarled.

"I thought I saw an ember."

"Ember shmember. You were ticked because you thought I'd got myself blowed up real good. If Amanda had slowed me down a second more, I might have."

"Do not blame the woman," Chiun said, leaping down over a knot of pines that was growing up from a sheer rock face on the mountainside. "And if I am upset with anything, it is your new habit of causing every dwelling we enter to spontaneously combust. Really, Remo, how do you expect me to get home insurance for any future Castle Sinanju if you persist in playing with matches?"

Remo ignored him.

The mountain angled flat. Remo vaulted a hedge, landing in someone's backyard. Chiun floated in after him.

They flew past another chalet set into the hill and exploded out onto a narrow road. The lake was closer than it had been, but it was still too far away. More rooftops peeked from pine trees below. Beyond, the boat still sat in the cold waters of Lake Geneva. The man with the binoculars was no longer on the deck. Both boat and lake vanished as they raced into another grove of trees.

"That wasn't St. Clair," Remo said. "If he's the one at the greenhouse, too, I can't wait to get my hands on him."

"We may not get the chance," the Master of Sinanju pointed out.

In spite of an area of over two hundred square miles, Remo's keen ears isolated the same, lone sound Chiun had detected over all the other lake noise.

It was the sound of a boat engine misfiring.

Remo's face grew grim. Feet flying over treacherous rock, the two men continued racing down the steep slope.

"START, DAMN YOU, start!" Herr Hahn snapped.

As a rule, he rarely spoke. But with no one around to hear him, it didn't matter. And right now, maintaining his habitual silence was the least of his troubles.

A choking splutter sounded at the rear of the boat.

He stabbed the ignition switch. Nothing. No time to check the engine. The last he had seen, they were halfway down the hill. The two men were still three-quarters of a mile up on rough terrain, darting in and out of tree cover and between tidy Swiss homes. But the speed at which they were descending was inhuman.

In the boat cabin, Hahn's round face glistened with sweat. His armpits were moons of freezing perspiration.

"Start, start, start…"

The boat engine coughed and spluttered but wouldn't turn over. Herr Hahn didn't believe in prayer, but at that moment he said a silent entreaty to every thief, pirate and murderer who had come before him to deliver him from the two men who were running at him with death in their eyes.

Holding his breath, Hahn struck the button again. The engine coughed once and roared to life.

Hands shaking, he grabbed frantically at the steering column and the throttle stick. Shoving the throttle to the max, he sent the boat bobbing and zooming across the frothy waves of Lake Geneva.

BY THE TIME Remo and Chiun crossed the last lawn and broke through the tree cover at the shore, the boat was already halfway across the section of lake that separated the new and old cities of Geneva.

Remo was heading for the water, but Chiun touched his arm.

"He is too far gone," the Master of Sinanju said.

Remo stopped, squeezing his hands in impotent frustration at the rocky shore. The boat weaved through shuttle traffic and sped toward the big white shape of the cruise liner.

"Damn," Remo said. "Judging by the whiff in the air, that's definitely the guy who was in St. Clair's house. If he'd used binoculars instead of some electronic whatsit in the first place, we could have had him."

Chiun nodded tight agreement. He watched the distant boat through narrowed eyes before finally turning away.

"Come, Remo," the old man said. A long nail flicked at the holes burned in the back of Remo's shirt. "Even the Swiss must have laws against exhibitionism."

Remo looked up the near-vertical hill they'd just descended. A cloud of black smoke belched high into the clear blue sky. He sighed bitterly.

Together, the two Masters of Sinanju began the long climb back up to the burning chalet.

11

Young Chim'bor feared the Sky Forest.

It wasn't the same as the other fears he had lived with all his life. Those were old and familiar.

As a member of the Rsual tribe, which lived in small encampments in the dense jungles where the Jamunda River met the mighty Amazon, Chim'bor had spent much of his adolescence identifying fears— both real and imagined.

Where Chim'bor grew up, there were fish so small that they could swim up a man while he bathed in the waters of the Amazon and kill him from the inside. There were mosquitoes that carried diseases that poisoned the mind and snakes with darting fangs and a taste for flesh.

These were real fears.

There were also fears of a supernatural nature. Animals that inhaled the life's breath from tribesmen, gods that punished with torrential rain or blistering sun, shadowed ghosts armed with spears that stalked those who were alone.

These fears were imagined.

Some fears were a combination of both. The pulp

of certain trees was stuffed with larvae that were a feast for the tribe. Others caused death the instant they touched the tongue. Legend had it that the succulent larvae had been mixed with the poisonous by tricky gods to test the Rsual men. It was a life test to see who could choose wisely.

Another fear in a world of fears. All known.

Everything—from the great white rapids in the north to the mossy valley in the south—was known to the Rsual. It was only a span of a few miles, but it was the entire Rsual world. Everything to fear within that small area had been identified and classified by tribal elders generations ago.

To know one's fears made one master of them. That was what made this new fear so terrifying to Chim'bor.

The Sky Forest.

To the Rsual, it was alien. Like one day discovering a river or rock that had not been there the day before.

It had been brought to the land of the Rsual by whites.

Chim'bor was fourteen when the invaders first arrived five years ago. A man by the standards of his tribe. He would never forget that first frightening day.

Chim'bor and his brother Sor'acha had been searching for *gualla* near the valley far from the main village. This juicy fruit was difficult to harvest. Since it grew so far up the trunks of the trees, it took two natives to collect it.

They were using the network of vines they'd installed when they were children. Chim'bor climbed while Sor'acha waited on the ground to catch the dropped fruit. When Chim'bor grew weary later in the day, the two brothers would switch places.

Early in the morning Sor'acha was watching as Chim'bor stretched from tree to tree far above. Taking hold of one of the upper branches in his small hand, Chim'bor shook it violently. Green fronds rattled an angry protest, and three of the fat yellow fruit plopped to the ground.

When Chim'bor looked down, he found that Sor'acha wasn't there to catch them. His brother no longer stood amid the great gnarled roots at the base of the tree.

He found Sor'acha standing a few yards away, an ear cocked to the jungle. Strange noises rumbled from the thick undergrowth of the valley.

On callused hands and feet, Chim'bor scampered down the tree trunk. He hurried over to his brother.

"What is wrong?" Chim'bor asked.

Sor'acha silenced him with a raised hand. "The ghost faces have returned," he whispered. He was peering intently through a gap in the brush.

Bright sunlight flooded the region beyond. Strange for a land where sun rarely reached past the thick treetops.

The vast valley beyond had been largely cleared over the previous season. There had been many days of toil for the whites and their earthmoving machines. The jungle canopy had been hacked down for miles within the valley. What had been dense jungle was transformed to desert.

"You should not look there," Chim'bor warned. Like most of the Rsual, he avoided the valley since the arrival of the whites.

"I am the older brother," Sor'acha replied. "You do not command me. Besides, do you not wish to know why they are here?"

Although Chim'bor didn't, Sor'acha was determined.

At nightfall, they crept out of the jungle and entered the barren valley. The moon hung bright and big in the sky as they slipped across the barren ground. A man-made hill rose in the center of the valley, its top flat.

The whites were gone. What they'd left behind intrigued Sor'acha and troubled Chim'bor.

A small forest of trees had been planted atop the wide flattened hill. The plants were of an unnatural blue. It was as if the color had bled from the sky to stain the trees.

The small trees were all roughly the same height— twice as tall as Chim'bor and his brother. In the bright moonlight the forest stretched off as far as the night eye could see.

Sor'acha laughed. "Only whites would cut down trees to plant trees," he said. He took hold of one of the saplings. It was warm to the touch.

"This is a place of evil," Chim'bor warned. "The whites have stolen the sky for their trees."

Sor'acha lingered at the edge of the new forest for

a time, but there was nothing more to see. Eventually, Chim'bor convinced his brother to leave.

They returned for the harvest six months later.

Again, Sor'acha let his curiosity get the better of him. Although Chim'bor was reluctant to visit the Sky Forest of the whites, his brother insisted. The two traveled back through the jungle to the valley and the hilltop forest.

They crossed the wide stretch of parched land that separated jungle from hill. The earth was hard-packed as they scampered up the side of the valley's central hill. When they reached the top, Chim'bor couldn't believe his fearful eyes.

The trees were now as tall as the ones in the jungle far behind them. A dense forest of blue stretched across the flat hill at the valley's center.

"White sorcery!" Chim'bor hissed.

Sor'acha wasn't listening. From where they hid at the edge of the hill, he spied what looked like blue fruit clinging sparsely to the undersides of some of the branches.

Although the whites were nowhere to be seen, there was still activity at the forest's edge.

Dozens of squirrel monkeys jumped and screeched at the periphery of the blue forest. They had come out of the jungle to venture across the clear-cut plain and climb the hill. Pounding the ground and hissing at air, the monkeys looked possessed by demons. None dared enter the field.

All he saw filled Chim'bor with dread.

"Please, Sor'acha," Chim'bor implored. "Let us leave this place."

But his brother wouldn't budge. "For all the work they have done, the fruit of these trees must be even more sweet than the *gualla*," Sor'acha insisted.

He thought they should pick some of the fruit, but Chim'bor would not be persuaded. The younger native stayed back while his older brother crept over the hill's edge to the forest of blue trees.

Shrieking, the monkeys scampered away from his feet, clearing a path to the woods. They flooded back in behind him. To Chim'bor, it looked almost as if the monkeys were trapping his brother in the white man's forest.

Sor'acha made it to the trees.

As Chim'bor watched, his brother took the bark in his strong hands and began climbing. He cupped his feet to the rough surface, pushing off. With quick, even strokes, Sor'acha scampered quickly up.

He was halfway to the top when Chim'bor realized something was wrong.

Sor'acha was moving too slowly. As though he was having a hard time climbing. It looked as if he was forcing himself to go higher and higher. As he went on, the struggle to climb became more obvious. It was with great difficulty that he finally made it to the top of the tree. One hand snaked out to a piece of blue fruit.

As his brother climbed, Chim'bor had slowly climbed up over the edge of the hill.

Something was very wrong.

Before he even knew it, Chim'bor was running. He was halfway to the Sky Forest when Sor'acha looked his way.

His brother was still stretching determinedly for the blue fruit. But on his dark brown face was a look of deep confusion. His cheeks bulged as if he was holding his breath.

When Sor'acha finally plucked a single piece of fruit from the rest of the cluster, he held it in triumph for only a second. The breath exploded from his lungs, and he let go of the trunk.

He dropped twenty feet from the treetop, hitting the hard-packed ground below with a bone-crushing thud.

Chim'bor ran through the pack of screeching monkeys. The animals parted in fear, scattering as he kicked at them with his bare feet. When he slid to his knees next to his brother's lifeless body, a lone monkey was plucking the blue fruit—which Chim'bor now saw was a small cluster of several seeds—from Sor'acha's dead hand.

The other monkeys immediately attacked the one with the seeds, clawing and biting at it. Shrieking, the monkey raced down the hill and across the plain. The other animals chased it back into the jungle.

Chim'bor didn't care about the monkeys.

Sor'acha lay flat on his back, his dead eyes staring glassily up at the cluster of blue seeds in the tree high above. He had taunted the demons of the Sky Forest, and they had exacted the ultimate price.

Had he only listened to Chim'bor. Had he only left the blue seeds to the demons of the Sky Forest.

As the tears burned hot in his eyes, Chim'bor looked up. The instant he did, his anguish turned to terror. For, as he knelt over the body of his dead brother, a demon appeared in the Sky Forest.

The screeching monkeys might have drawn it out. More likely it was Sor'acha's theft. Either way, he saw a white shape slowly coming toward him.

It vanished amid the blue tree trunks. Frozen in fear, Chim'bor heard a ragged, heavy breathing coming from among the trees.

The demon reappeared. Closer now.

Chim'bor's heart pounded. He couldn't breathe, couldn't move.

The demon emerged into the light.

It was taller than a Rsual native. It had the limbs and body of a man but no face. The demon was wrapped from head to toe in a strange white garment.

The faceless demon loomed above Chim'bor. It struggled to breathe through an invisible mouth. When it spoke, the demon's language sound almost like that of the whites, who had summoned it to Rsual land.

"Sweet Georgia Brown," the demon rasped, "what do you termite eaters think you're doing here?"

With the words, Chim'bor finally found his feet.

More demons were coming out from the depths of the Sky Forest. Some had faces. Tanks were strapped to their backs, clear plastic covering their mouths.

It no longer mattered. Sor'acha's body was nothing. The whites and their demons could have the jungle. As more of the creatures emerged from the Sky Forest, Chim'bor ran screaming from them. When the Amazon jungle swallowed him and the Sky Forest and the faceless demons were long behind him, he still ran. He ran all the way back to his village.

After that day, he couldn't stay in the land of the Rsual. Chim'bor left his tribe. He fled the forest to the white man's city, hoping distance would extinguish the flame of constant fear.

He stayed there for five years, working at a boat-rental shop at the mouth of the Amazon. Sometimes he would pilot a charter boat himself.

Every now and then he would hear stories out of the jungle. How the Sky Forest had claimed a few other Rsual lives. How the valley became choked with smoke for a full year, so that no one could see for miles around. And how it had been decreed that the entire region was to be avoided by all future generations of Rsual for the dark magic that had been performed there.

Chim'bor heard it all. And stayed away.

For a long time he and his fears lived a life of self-imposed exile. Then one day the Sky Forest came to him.

A group of whites arrived at the docks in Macapa. They brought with them many provisions stored in bags and crates.

He assumed they were tourists, since these were the only ones still fascinated by the Amazon jungle. If they were tourists, they were part of some strange white adventurers' club, for all the men wore the same strange outfit. They perspired heavily in their corduroy jackets.

Brazilian natives struggled to load their cargo into three rented boats. The last items aboard were three dozen large burlap sacks.

Chim'bor was carrying the last of the sacks to the final boat when it slipped off his shoulder and dropped to the rotted wharf. When it hit, one stitch in a corner seam popped open and a single small object launched free. It rolled across the dock, tapping against the side of a big crate.

The skipper of one of the Amazon tour ships had a small squirrel monkey as a pet. Before Chim'bor had even seen what came out of the sack, the monkey had scooped it up. After devouring it, the animal scurried up to the bag Chim'bor had dropped.

Chim'bor was hefting the bag back into the air when the monkey reached out and clawed at the corner seam of the sack. The bag split open, and dozens of seeds spilled onto the warped dock.

Blue seeds.

When he saw them, Chim'bor dropped the sack in shock. The seam split wider. Hundreds of small seeds scattered across the ancient dock.

"What are you doing!" one of the whites yelled.

The monkey threw itself into the pile of seeds. As Chim'bor backed away, the animal was shoveling them into its mouth. It took the boot of a sailor to get the animal to stop.

"Sweet Georgia Brown, what's wrong with you?" the leader of the whites demanded.

He and the others began desperately shoving the seeds back into the torn burlap sack.

That voice. Chim'bor knew that voice. Although he hadn't been able to see a face at the time, the man on the Macapa dock had the same voice as the demon from the Sky Forest.

"I know we're supposed to embrace the simplicity of the native, but I just don't see it," the demon said to his companions as they picked up every last seed. "Give them half a chance, and they'd be just like everyone else on this planet. With air conditioners and chlorofluorocarbon fridges in their mud huts. They're not fooling anyone. You're not fooling anyone," he repeated to Chim'bor.

Chim'bor just stood there as the demons—who now resembled ordinary men—finished gathering up the seeds into the torn sack. Pinching the corner, they pulled it carefully off the dock. They put it in the last boat, balancing it on some of the other sacks.

Through it all, Chim'bor said nothing.

The boats were all loaded. The head demon put the others dressed like him onto the boats. He then returned to a waiting car and drove off into the city.

The monkey had been in hiding until now. It joined Chim'bor on the dock, jumping and screeching as the three boats pulled away into the river.

As they chugged out into the current to begin the journey that would take them into the dark heart of the rain forest, Chim'bor looked numbly at all the provisions lashed to their decks. Tools and supplies. Food, medicine. Enough for a long, long time.

And in the rear of each boat, burlap sacks filled with enough blue seeds to remove breath from the land of the Rsual forever. Perhaps even all of Brazil.

Despite the oppressive heat, as he stood on the Macapa dock, alone save the company of a single shrieking monkey, Chim'bor of the Rsual could not stop himself from shivering.

12

In the privacy of his office, Dr. Harold Smith was reading the latest news reports out of Geneva. A mug of chicken broth from the Folcroft cafeteria sat on a tray at his elbow, along with a plastic-wrapped packet of four small crackers. Smith was frowning at his monitor when the contact phone rang.

He quickly put down the spoon with which he'd been stirring the hot broth and scooped up the phone.

"Report," he ordered.

"St. Clair flew the coop," Remo announced. "And if you thought his last method of attempted murder was kinky, you'll love what he had for an encore."

"I have just seen a report about some kind of explosion that leveled his home," Smith said cautiously. "Authorities are saying it's some sort of gas line, although there are none in the region."

"Not gas—oil," Remo said. "By the sounds of it, this gaggle of mad scientists buried tanks in the mountain to force-feed the fire. I'd say it was crazy, but everything about this cracker factory is nuts. Did you know the guys here are all running around dressed up like Sage Carlin?"

Smith's face grew disturbed. "I had uncovered that in my research of the CCS," he said seriously. "Apparently, since his death a cult of personality has developed around Dr. Carlin."

"I'd say that's a twist," Remo muttered, "seeing as how Carlin didn't have one of his own."

"Hmm," Smith mused. "This could be instructive, Remo. The two methods of attack they have used thus far are suggestive of dire ecological predictions made by Carlin and the CCS through the years. It could be a pattern."

"Maybe," Remo said. "But I don't know if you can read too much into it, Smitty. It could be that they were gonna do this cockamamy stuff anyway and we were just tossed on the barbecue at the last minute. I think they were in the market to trash St. Clair's house. And they burned up those trees of theirs with the acid. They might just be covering their tracks. And speaking of the trees, it looks like St. Clair picked them clean of seeds before he took off."

A thin intake of air passed Smith's bloodless lips. "You are saying Hubert St. Clair is in possession of the *C. dioxa* seeds?" the CURE director croaked.

"Looks that way, Smitty," Remo said.

Smith's gnarled hand clenched tighter around the receiver. For a silent moment he tried to comprehend the consequences of St. Clair's actions. His silence spoke volumes about his gravest fear.

He forced calm into his voice. "Do you have any idea where he has gone?" Smith asked finally.

"Nope. That's what I'm calling you for," Remo

said. "My guess would be a tree farm in some psycho version of Hooterville where he can plant his little seeds in the ground and watch them shoosht up to the sun and the sky."

Smith jammed the phone between shoulder and ear. Dropping his hands to the edge of his desk, he began typing rapidly at his hidden capacitor keyboard. Trails of light followed in the wake of his drumming fingertips.

When he was through, Smith frowned. "I don't have a record of St. Clair leaving Geneva on any commercial flights," he said. "One moment, please, Remo."

After another quick search, his gray face grew more animated.

"Here it is," Smith resumed. "The CCS jet left Cointrin International Airport a few hours ago. It is en route to Brazil."

"I guess he's going for something bigger than just some dinky little tree farm," Remo said, concerned. "How are we supposed to find him if he heads into the jungle?"

"With luck you can head him off before then," Smith said. He continued to type quickly away at his keyboard. "According to the records I have accessed, the CCS keeps a few suites year-round in a Macapa hotel. They are reserved for members of the organization when on trips to the rain forest. The hotel staff has been alerted to the arrival of St. Clair and his CCS group."

"Okay, get us there fast and we can maybe pull the plug on Mr. Greenjeans before he gets started."

"My thinking exactly," Smith said. "There is an Air Brazil flight to Rio de Janeiro leaving from Heathrow this evening." He issued a few commands from his computer. "I have arranged for the three of you to catch a connecting flight to London from Geneva in one hour."

"There's only two of us, Smitty," Remo said slowly.

"I want you to take Dr. Lifton with you," Smith said.

"Aw, c'mon," Remo complained. "Do I have to?"

"We can't afford to risk her life. Once you leave, whoever has twice attempted to kill her could return at any time. Presumably, they are working on the order of Dr. St. Clair. We cannot allow them to succeed. She has full knowledge of the *C. dioxa* and is apparently the only one left from the CCS who wishes to stop it from being introduced into the wild. You and Chiun will be the best bet for her survival. And she, perhaps, of ours."

In the Geneva apartment of Amanda Lifton, Remo cast a hooded glance around the living room.

The place was all fuzzy pinks and fluffy whites. Most of it looked like the FAO Schwarz version of the elephants' graveyard. Heaps of stuffed toys were arranged in corners, lined on tables and parading snout to tail across shelves.

They'd stopped at a store on their way there to get

him a change of clothes. Since he hadn't yet changed, Amanda had spread newspapers on the sofa for him to sit on before she went in to take a shower. It was fifteen minutes later, and the water was still running.

As soon as she was out of the room, he'd wadded up the papers and threw them on the floor. The white sofa was smeared black where he was sitting. The back of the couch was lined with stuffed animals. Amanda apparently had great affection for them. Remo saw that each one had a pretty little pink bow with a tiny silver name tag.

"If civilization has to rely on her, we'd all better start practicing holding our breath," Remo grumbled. "And speaking of the guy who made the chalet go poof, we almost caught him but he got away. I don't know how deep he is in this, but maybe he could help us track St. Clair if it becomes necessary."

"Do you have a description of the assassin?"

The Master of Sinanju was sitting on the floor near Remo, a blank sheet of parchment spread out before him. He clucked his tongue disapprovingly.

"He was not an assassin, Emperor Smith," Chiun called in annoyance. "An assassin is an individual skilled in the art of precision location and removal services, not some boom-flinging Hun. And most important, an assassin is only an assassin who succeeds in eliminating his target." Shaking his head, he dropped his voice. "I can tell him until I am blue in the face, but no matter how long we work for the lunatic he will never get it right."

He returned to his blank parchment.

"Did Chiun say that this man was German?" Smith asked.

"Yeah," Remo said. "He stunk German, anyway. Fat and fortyish. Got away on a boat."

"Nothing more to go on?" Smith asked.

"Sorry," Remo said. "We were pretty far away, not to mention doing the vertical plummet at the time."

"I will check the marinas on Lake Geneva," Smith said. "Perhaps the employee records of the CCS will prove helpful. In any event, your tickets will be waiting at Cointrin when you arrive. Stay in touch."

Smith broke the connection.

With a sigh, Remo hung up the phone. "We just got saddled indefinitely with the nutty heiress," he said.

Chiun didn't look up. "Consider yourself fortunate if that is your greatest worry this week, Remo Williams," the old man intoned. He seemed to be trying to burn words into the parchment with the act of thought alone.

It was the same parchment the tiny Asian had been staring at for the past week. Sitting on the floor of Amanda's apartment, he was still struggling with how exactly to enter his confession about Remo's whiteness into the Sinanju Scrolls without making it sound like a confession.

Even though Remo knew that he was the one being blamed for something that he obviously had no control over, this particular distraction of Chiun's was better than those maddeningly secretive letters the old man had been writing. At least here Remo knew what he was in for.

"I don't know why you think it's such a crime for a Master to train a white pupil," Remo grumbled. "You know as well as me that I'm not the only one to learn Sinanju."

Chiun knew to whom Remo was referring. One of the greatest foes they had ever faced was a white trained in Sinanju. Jeremiah Purcell was now in a perpetually medicated state in the security wing of Folcroft, a threat to no one.

"It is not the same," Chiun said. "He was the disciple of my wicked nephew. I am responsible for you, not him."

As Chiun continued to not write, Remo cast a depressed eye around Amanda Lifton's apartment.

"Maybe the nice thing I'm supposed to do is set fire to this place," he said suddenly. "Probably not. I guess her neighbors could choke from inhaling all this saccharin."

He knocked most of the stuffed toys off the couch as he spread his grimy arms across the back.

"Are you gonna be through in there sometime this week?" he yelled into the bathroom.

"Almost finished!" Amanda called out over the spray of the shower. "Be careful of my petsy-wetsies!"

"You betsy-wetsie," Remo called back as he used a stuffed kitty to wipe the oily soot off his shoes.

When he was done, he threw cat and shoes into the rubbish and pulled a brand-new pair of eight-hundred-dollar loafers from a plastic bag.

13

The big, sprawling plantation was a throwback to the long gone days of bright and shining British colonialism.

The clapboard house and its wraparound porch were painted a clean and tidy white. Although the African sun burned down hot all year, the boards never warped, were not allowed to get too dry.

Mosquito screens enclosed the neat little gazebo that sat to one side of the front yard. When the days stretched long into twilight and night drew in like a lazy fog, the orange glow from a lone pipe bowl could often be seen through those screens. Swinging lazily with the back-and-forth motion of the old porch swing.

The sun had set on the British Empire, but some small vestige of it lived on in that big old house.

Odd that the neighboring farmers would think that, since the sole occupant of the house was not English, but American. But he had that cool confidence, the superior mannerly attitude of the velvet-gloved conquerors their ancestors had come to know, then fear and, finally, to hate.

A few years before, attackers had targeted the whites who lived in Zimbabwe. Gentleman farmers who had inherited the land they lived on from their fathers, who in turn had inherited it from their fathers before them, were being slaughtered in their homes. No one lifted a hand to stop the bloodshed. In fact, it was encouraged. But even when the president had given his approval to the murder of whites and the seizing of their land, the gangs of killers who roamed the wilderness cut a wide swath around that clean little house with the neatly trimmed rosebushes and the American owner who liked to sit out in the gazebo on warm summer nights to smoke his pipe and watch the stars.

They left the man and his house alone for one simple reason. Fear. The occupant of the house had a reputation in this part of Africa. Yes, he was quiet and genteel. And, when properly provoked, he was more deadly than any workaday mob that might assault his little bit of paradise.

Fear kept them away and kept the little farmhouse safe.

As he spread manure and mulch around his rosebushes, Benson Dilkes didn't look like a figure to provoke fear. He was flicking an aphid off a leaf and tsking in annoyance when he heard the telephone ring in the house.

Brushing the dirt from his hands, he climbed to his feet.

Dilkes was a handsome man, with a tan, rugged face and laugh lines that crimped the corners of his eyes. Although his dark hair was peppered gray and the calendar of his life had recently slipped past his sixtieth year, he still retained the vigor of youth.

He mounted the porch, grabbing a sweating glass from a metal table before going inside.

The phone was old and clunky. A good solid number from the days when a phone could be used to club a man to death or strangle him with the cord. With the new phones these days, the best a person could do was call a target a thousand times and hope he got head cancer.

Thankful once more for uncomplicated retirement, Dilkes scooped up the phone. "Hello." He took a sip of his drink.

"I think I might have a problem, Benson."

The voice surprised Dilkes. The man on the other end of the line rarely spoke and never, ever called.

"Is that you, Olivier?" Dilkes asked slowly. The answer caused him to put his drink down. Carefully.

"Yes." Even that one word was difficult to get out. "Benson, I just left an *event*. There were two targets of interest that were not acquired as I had hoped."

"*You* failed?" Dilkes asked. At this point he doubted he could mask his surprise even if he tried. He sat on the edge of a chair, concern etched in his deep tan lines.

"These men are special, Benson. Different than what I am used to. I was hoping you could offer some insight. Perhaps you know something about them."

Could it be? Was that actual fear in that accented voice? The younger man had always had ice for blood.

"I'll help if I can, Olivier," Dilkes said. "What information do you have on them?"

"Very little, I am afraid. One is an elderly Asian. Perhaps Korean or Japanese. I was too far to see clearly. The other was just an ordinary Caucasian."

Benson Dilkes felt the floor go out from underneath his feet. For an awful moment, the room swirled.

"My God, it's them," Dilkes croaked.

The voice on the phone grew excited. "You know them? Who are they?"

Dilkes picked up his drink, draining it in one gulp.

"I know *of* them. Run, Olivier," he insisted. "Get far away from those two. My God—you're lucky to be alive. Run as far as you can and don't look back."

"Why? What are they?"

Dilkes closed his eyes wearily, sinking back in his chair. "You never listened, Olivier," he said, shaking his head. "You were an exceptional student, but you were always only interested in your gadgets and toys. You loved those Rube Goldberg contraptions of yours, but you never bothered to learn the history of what we are."

"I am listening now. Tell me who they are."

Dilkes sighed, opening his eyes. "Sinanju, Olivier. Those men were Sinanju."

A pause on the line. "I thought they were mythical."

"They are absolutely real," Dilkes insisted. "The old one was the reason I left America twenty-five years ago. He is the Master. I've since learned that he's taken a pupil. An American, if the stories I've heard are accurate."

"The younger one acted like an American." There was a growling contempt in the voice.

"It was them. It's amazing you met them and got out alive," Dilkes said. "Olivier, do you have any idea how rare a thing that is? In all of recorded history, there are only a handful of men who've done what you have."

It was the wrong thing to say. The fear that had been there at the start of the conversation was slowly overcome by arrogance.

"I almost had them, Benson."

Dilkes sat up rigid in his chair. "No," he insisted. "No, you didn't. And don't even think about going back after them. You live in isolation, Olivier. You've never appreciated that there are forces out there that you and I will never understand. You've achieved a well-deserved reputation, but it's only the reputation of an individual. Sinanju is the reputation of our entire career."

"Thank you, Benson. I will try to come down for a visit in the spring."

"You're a dead man if you try to engage them," Dilkes said in final warning.

The phone buzzed loud in his ear. With a hot exhale of air, he dropped the receiver back in its cradle.

So few men in his line of work lived to enjoy retirement. He had just spoken to another that would not.

Getting up from his comfortable living-room chair, Benson Dilkes went back out to his yard and his prize roses.

14

He sent back the ice because it wasn't cold enough.

His lunch was too hot. Then it was too cold. Then it wasn't lunch at all anymore because he'd thrown it on the waiter's tidy uniform.

The bulbs in the overhead lights were too bright. Someone was sent for replacements.

While he waited, some marauder with mallets for hands improperly fluffed his pillow. Since everyone knew a pillow once improperly fluffed could never be fluffed properly again, both pillow and fluffer would be thrown off the plane the minute they landed in Brazil.

In the back of the jet, people searched for a persistent rattle that only he could hear. Agents and record company executives, promoters and accountants, the flight crew and various personal staff scurried around the cabin, chasing after a sound that wasn't there. They'd been looking, straining their ears, since the jet took off from London.

"I want it found by the time we touch down or there'll be sackings all around," Albert Snowden snapped over his shoulder. He was chewing on an ice cube as he talked. "Still not cold enough," he snarled, spitting the too-warm ice into the forehead of the lentil-covered waiter.

As the terrified man scurried around the floor of the plane in search of the wayward chunk of ice, Albert settled angrily back in his seat.

He was always angry. Even an entire private planeload of people—*his* people, *his* employees—bending over backward to service his every whim couldn't soothe the perpetual state of agitation that was, for Albert Snowden, the very stamp of miserable life itself.

He had always been peevish. Even back when he was a nobody working a starvation-wages job as an English teacher at a boys' school in Saint Albans, twenty miles outside of London.

Albert Snowden. He hadn't gone by that name in years.

The last time he'd used it was that long ago winter when he'd taken a sabbatical from teaching. He went to London to indulge in his avocation. Rock and roll music.

Everyone thought Albert was insane for even thinking he might have a career in music. Crazier still for thinking he could front a band.

"You're tone-deaf, Albert," his voice coach had told him. "When you sing, it sounds as if your genitals are being pressed between two very large flat rocks. That is not a pleasing sound to hear, Albert. I would demonstrate to you on an animal, but the RSPCA would stop me for inflicting pain on that animal. Which they will do to you if you subject an audience to that voice of yours. Go back to teaching. Go back now. If not for me, man, do it for queen and country.''

But in spite of such negative encouragement, he had persisted in his dream.

A few days after firing his voice coach—who had taken to wadding cotton in his ears during their sessions—Albert was at an open-mike night at a London club. As luck would have it, he met up with a young American who was looking for a lead singer for his band. Called Fuzz Patrol, the band would consist of only three main members. In those heady days of joyful masochism, Albert and his voice just happened to be in the right place at the right time. He quit teaching altogether and joined the band on the spot.

They started out in small venues, eventually graduating to bigger clubs.

From the moment he began with Fuzz Patrol, Albert was on the lookout for a suitable stage name.

As fate would have it, he happened to be pricked by a bee before a small gig in Los Angeles one night. After he threw a forty-five-minute temper tantrum backstage, someone suggested he call himself Prick. They claimed they'd come up with it from the bee. A lot of people who had known Albert thought otherwise.

That night for the first time, Albert introduced himself to an audience as Prick. The name just felt right. From that moment on, Albert Snowden was dead. It was Prick who stepped off that stage and into a new life.

The name change seemed to work like a lucky talisman. It was during that small L.A. booking that Fuzz Patrol was spotted by a scout from a major record label. That very night they were signed to a multirecord deal.

After that, the sky was the limit. Fuzz Patrol got national exposure on the late-night talk shows. Hit song followed hit song as their albums all went multiplatinum. They became a powerhouse in rock, both in the U.S. and internationally.

Success should have brought great happiness. But like so many people who finally achieved precisely what they set out to, Prick was unsatisfied.

It came as a shock to the rock world when Prick announced he would be leaving Fuzz Patrol. After much soul searching, he had decided that going solo was the only way he could do the sort of music he wanted to. The truth of the matter was, in the few short years they'd been together, Prick had *become* Fuzz Patrol. Few people outside the music industry even knew the names of the other band members.

"Why split the money three ways when I only have to split it once?" he reasoned privately to his wife at their rural English estate.

"You're so right, luv," his wife had replied. "By the way, have you met my new boyfriend? You've had his wife up for a few weekends here and there."

As Prick's wife led the handsome stranger over to

their very liberated bed, Prick merely sat and watched. He had important business on his mind.

Some had their doubts about a solo Prick. After all, he was neither the brains of nor the talent behind Fuzz Patrol. In truth, he was just a shrieking English teacher whose incredible luck had already defied all odds.

Once more the former Albert Snowden proved his critics wrong. Prick went on to establish a solo career every bit as successful as his time with Fuzz Patrol. For fifteen years he reigned supreme at the top of the adult contemporary charts.

But satisfaction still proved elusive.

He had all the money in the world and the coveted life of a rock star. He had limos, jets, drugs and mansions.

But in a strange way, Prick missed his old life. He missed his days as a schoolmaster, standing in front of a classroom full of eager little dullards hanging on his every word. Like most small men, Prick longed to tell people what to do. That was where his political activism came in. His love of wagging his finger at people as if they were nuisance children thrust him to the front of every cause célèbre.

He screamed along with the glitterati of rock on "We Are the World," the theory being that really bad music ends hunger.

He helped Famine Relief send bundles of grain to rot on Ethiopian docks.

He held hands with William Hurt and some smelly stranger with sweaty palms in Hands across America, for what reason he had no idea. He thought it had something to do with homeless red Indians or helping the endangered something-or-other.

In the arena of celebrity do-goodism, Prick was king. He could always be counted on to toe the Russian, Castro or just plain Commie line on all the right issues, provided his stance didn't negatively impact his own personal bankbook.

And above all other causes, Prick loved the rain forest.

The jungle had a primal pull on him. It was distant, huge, tropical and as alien as hell. He could say all kinds of outrageous things about it, and reporters who'd only ever seen pictures would ooh and aah with serious faces. One had to wear a serious face when discussing globally serious issues.

Prick claimed an area of rain forest the size of Alaska was stripped bare every minute of every day. Even though this would have cleared the entire continent of all vegetation in just over eleven minutes, no one challenged him. He insisted the pharmaceutical companies were in league with the lumber companies to systematically obliterate the plant that cured cancer. He decried the forced extinction of species in numbers that had never existed in the entire history of the planet. He carted natives around with him like sideshow freaks, turning their genuine plight into a sanctimonious exercise in self-promotion.

The rallying cry to save the rain forest had been adopted as his mission in life. The rain forest was therefore considered by Prick to be like his Sussex estate. His own personal property.

Like a supreme overlord returned from battle, Prick watched his vast jungle property from the window as his private jet roared up the snaking Amazon toward Macapa, Brazil.

This was a necessary homecoming.

His recent benefit concert for the Primeval Society in New York had been a disaster. The big moment that was supposed to come with But Me No Butz and Glory Whole had turned into a sissy-girl slapfest. The audience had left before Prick's closing number. Even his wife, who so loved the sound of her own voice as emcee that she sometimes continued to drone on while the acts performed, had fled the scene. At the moment she was shacked up in their Manhattan penthouse with a pile of Kleenex and the least fey member of Glory Whole.

It had been such a bad time back there that Prick was looking forward to this special time in his jungle. He was slated to perform at the Pan Brazil Eco-Fest, a concert organized to raise awareness of rain forest devastation. With no wife and no acts bigger than himself, this was the perfect chance to recharge his precious bruised ego.

Men scurried all around him, searching under seats and in cupboards for the nonexistent rattle Prick insisted he could hear. A flight attendant was taping down bottles and glasses in the bar to keep them from shaking.

The only men not engaged in the vain search were sitting across from Prick.

The two barefoot men carried spears. They were nude except for matching red loincloths and beads of bone around their necks. Their black eyes were flat, their faces impassive as they stared blankly ahead.

Prick had found the natives on one of his many trips to South America.

Rich white men plucking natives from the jungle for their own purposes was by and large frowned upon in the modern age. In fact, America had fought a civil war over this very practice. But it was apparently still okay to do so just as long as the motives of those doing the plucking were judged pure.

Prick had even cut a record with his natives. It was mostly him screeching while they beat on hollow logs. For some reason, it didn't catch on with the listening public.

Prick didn't look at his natives. He was still staring out the window. The lush green jungle spread out like rumpled carpet as far as the eye could see.

Prick's frazzled manager hurried up the aisle, stopping next to his client.

"We're landing in ten minutes," he said.

Prick didn't even raise his eyes to the man. "Did those idiots send the helicopter like they said they would?"

"It's ready and waiting," his manager said.

"It bloody well better be," Prick growled. "I've had enough disasters for the rest of my life. Another screwup like New York, and you're all in the dole queue. You're just lucky I don't have you speared through the head for that.''

He waved a thin pale hand at his two natives.

"Yes, Prick. Thank you, Prick," said his manager, eyeing the two natives uncomfortably.

The men made the manager nervous. They'd been even creepier ever since their single lost the bullet and their album tanked. A record company exec had vanished at around the same time. No one was speculating out loud what had happened to him, but after the disappearance the manager had seen one of the natives wearing the man's very expensive Rolex as an ankle bracelet. And he swore the natives looked a little fatter.

"What the hell are you staring at?" Prick snapped.

The manager jumped. "Nothing," he said.

"I'm not paying you to do nothing. Leave me the hell alone."

The grateful manager almost tripped over his own feet in his haste to leave.

"And about that rattle," Prick called after him. "It's more like a hum. I want it found and I want it dehummed before we land."

"Yes, Prick," his manager said with a sharp nod.

As Prick continued to stare out the window at his jungle, the cabin exploded in a flurry of fresh activity. The crew began searching frantically for a hum that didn't exist.

15

Remo called Smith from the airport in Rio de Janeiro. The CURE director had already arranged for a flight on a turboprop to Macapa.

"Who were you talking to?" Amanda demanded once Remo hung up the phone and they were heading across the tarmac to the smaller plane. The air was hot and sticky. She was directing the skycaps who were hauling her luggage. The dainty pink bags were showing signs of wear.

"I've got an idea for a game we can play," Remo said. "It's called none of your business."

"Heh-heh-heh," said the Master of Sinanju as he padded along beside them. "None of your business."

Amanda shot the old man an evil look. "I'm starting to think you're not so nice, either," she accused. To Remo she said, "It was Daddy, wasn't it?"

"Wasn't who?"

"On the phone. You were just talking to Daddy. He wanted to check up on you, make sure I was okay. Only, it's just he won't give me the unlisted numbers. They changed them after I was—" the words were hard to get out "—cut off. Mother has a card sent to

me on Christmas. Although not last year. Or this year.
Yet. I thought I was gone for good. This is so unlike
him to take the time to look after me like this.''

Remo could see the flood waters rising in her eyes
again. They were at the air stairs. He stopped.

"He's a regular Robert Young,'' Remo agreed.
"Now can we change the subject from Daddy War-
bucks? Speaking for the orphans of the world, if I
have to hear one more story about your childhood of
ponies on the patio and hot and cold running wet
nurses, I'm gonna heave all over this Mary Kay luggage of yours.''

Her tears dried up. "Don't you dare,'' she snapped.
She shooed the men with her luggage off to the cargo
hold. "You made a big enough mess back in my
apartment. And don't think I'm not keeping a running
total of what you owe me. By the time we're through,
Daddy will be writing a check to me, not you.''

Pushing past him, she mounted the stairs.

The plane was nearly empty. Chiun sat alone on
the left side of the aisle while Remo and Amanda sat
in the two seats across from him.

Once they were back in the air and Amanda got
her first good glimpse of jungle, her expression soft-
ened.

"It's amazing, isn't it?'' she said quietly as she
looked out the window.

Remo leaned over her, peering out at the sea of
green. Clouds of burned-off mist rose into the early-
morning sky.

"Glad I don't have to mow it," he shrugged, flopping back in his seat.

"It's not only jungle down here," Amanda insisted. "A lot of Brazil is covered by savanna. It's like Africa in a lot of ways. Have you ever been to equatorial Africa?"

Remo was doing his best to ignore her. Chiun wouldn't let him.

"She is talking to you," the old man said blandly. He was staring out at the left wing.

"I know. But can't we pretend she isn't?" Remo asked. "I've had to put up with it the last six thousand miles."

"No," Chiun replied. "Because then she might try talking to me."

"Now, now," Amanda admonished, wagging a finger at the Master of Sinanju. "I know you're not the grumpy Gus you pretend to be."

There was a flash of silk, so fast Amanda didn't see it. Remo barely managed to snatch her hand out of the way of Chiun's razor-sharp fingernails.

"Oh," Amanda said softly. "Oh, my."

Remo's hands as they held hers were strong, but not coarse. They were the hands of a real man and not those of the perfumed sons of privilege she had dated all her life. She felt a shudder of electricity shoot through her as Remo held tight for a few lingering moments. For an instant in her tripping heart she wondered if he felt it, too.

"Hey, headlights, if you don't want a stump where

your rings used to go, you'll refrain from cheesing off the pissy old Korean guy.'' He let her go.

Amanda wasn't sure what to think. She'd definitely felt something. And while this Remo was a barbarian and, worse, an employee, there was something raw and primal about him.

''I thought we were getting a little better acquainted,'' she ventured hesitantly.

''Nope,'' Remo said. ''Just didn't want your blood squishing up my new shoes.''

She pouted her perfect lips. ''Afraid of commitment, I see,'' she complained.

Remo gave her a baleful look. ''Is this you coming on to me? 'Cause if it is, I wish you'd go back to yelling.''

Across the aisle, the Master of Sinanju huffed angrily. ''And I wish this craft would crash and spare me from having to listen to either of you,'' he groused, getting to his feet.

Amanda was sending a hectoring finger back his way when Remo intercepted it. With a disapproving harrumph, Chiun glided up the aisle and sank into an empty seat.

''Can't keep your hands to yourself, can you?'' Amanda said, doe-eyed optimism returning.

''Put it back in your pants, Amanda,'' Remo said as he let go of her hand. ''Besides, I'm just the help, remember?''

He got up and moved across the aisle to the seat Chiun had vacated. Amanda followed him.

''I've dated the help before,'' Amanda confided.

"The pool boy, some gardeners. About a dozen drivers."

"Beats a cash bonus, I guess," Remo said. "Assuming you keep your yap shut during. Which I doubt."

He got up and sat in his original seat. Getting up once more to follow, Amanda settled back into hers.

"Why are you running away, Remo?" she asked. "What are you men so afraid of?"

"The usual stuff. Commitment leading to long-term relationship leading to me not being able to watch *The Three Stooges* in peace because you're harping at me to trim the hedges and take the cat to the vet. You want a window into a guy's mind? That's it."

Amanda's face darkened and she folded her arms. "It wasn't like I was proposing or anything," she grumbled.

"You certainly were not," a squeaky voice chimed in from farther up the cabin. "I am having a difficult enough time explaining you, Remo. When you finally do wed, it will be to a Korean maiden, not some melon-dugged ghost face. Besides, this one is damaged goods."

Amanda was embarrassed enough already. When Remo responded she felt like melting into her seat.

"How you figure that, Little Father?" he called.

"She was left at the altar," Chiun called back. "Do you not listen? She keeps going on about it."

Amanda's face grew horrified. "I was not," she

insisted to the nearest person, a passing Brazilian stewardess who had no idea what was being said.

"He was probably marrying her for those millions she keeps going on about," Remo said to Chiun.

"I was not left at the altar," Amanda hissed. "There was some...*unpleasantness* at my sister Abigail's wedding. That's all I said. You two are the ones who don't listen."

"I listen perfectly," Chiun said. "You talk wrong."

Remo shrugged. "Sue me for only listening to every fourth word," he said. "I'm taking a nap." Reclining his seat, he closed his eyes.

Amanda couldn't believe his nerve. The way both of these men acted it was as if she was their servant and not the other way around. She hoped that by hiring them to protect her, Daddy was signaling a thawing in his attitude toward her. The quality of help he was employing had obviously taken a dramatic downturn since she'd been frozen out of family affairs. She wanted to give him an earful before the inheritance she was counting on was completely frittered away.

Casting a last, longing look at Remo's slumbering form, she turned her eyes back to the window and the lush majesty of the Brazilian rain forest.

THEIR PLANE TOUCHED down in Macapa early in the afternoon. Remo and Chiun waited until the few other passengers on board had deplaned before gliding down the retractable stairs and out into the eighty-degree heat.

The air in Macapa was like a hot shower in July. The humidity was already soaking Amanda's blouse by the time she stepped off the plane.

"There's no one here to carry my bags," she said.

"Yeah, how 'bout that," Remo said.

Frowning at Remo, she looked to Chiun.

"The Master of Sinanju does not lift," he sniffed.

"I can vouch for him on that one. No luggage, no bodies, no nothing. But don't worry. We'll wait."

Scowling, Amanda collected her suitcases alongside the other passengers.

"A gentleman would help me carry these," she growled as she struggled under the pile of pink Gucci.

"I think I saw one over there," Remo said. "Lemme see if we can catch him."

He and Chiun struck off for the small terminal. Amanda puffed to catch up.

"If you're my bodyguards, you should stay with me," she complained. She adjusted a suitcase strap that was biting into her shoulder. "I've got half a mind to— Hey."

Remo heard the sound of luggage thudding to pavement. When he turned, Amanda was standing stock-still up to her ankles in suitcases. She pointed to the private hangars beyond the terminal.

"That's the CCS jet," she said. She blew a clump of damp stringy brown hair from her face.

Remo looked back to where a sleek white jet peeked out from a shadowed hangar door.

"You sure?" he asked. One jet looked like the rest to him.

Even standing on a South American airport runway

in sweat-stained, off-the-rack clothes and amid a pile
of ragged seven-year-old luggage, the girl who had
grown up on jets still managed a look of supreme
Lifton condescension.

"Okay, so you're sure," Remo said. "Stay put."

"I'm standing out in the open in broad daylight,
you idiot," Amanda snapped.

"So what do you want from me? Weave a little.
Come on, Little Father."

Amanda was hauling her luggage straps back up
over her shoulders and cursing under her breath as
the two Masters of Sinanju headed over to the long,
flat building.

The big hangar door was rolled open wide. When
they paused near the corrugated steel wall, they
sensed no one inside.

"I smell oil," Remo said. "Not more than normal,
though."

Chiun was peering in at the shadowed ceiling of
the hangar. "There are none of those devices for
spraying acid," he observed. His hands sought refuge
in the voluminous sleeves of his kimono.

Remo glanced across the tarmac. Amanda was halfway toward them, lugging her heavy bags.

"Let's hope it just doesn't mean there's a whole
new surprise inside," Remo muttered.

Without another word, the two men slipped around
the wall of the hangar and disappeared inside.

FROM THE MACAPA airport security shed, Herr Hahn
watched the two Masters of Sinanju duck inside the
hangar.

He was sweating and panting as he sat in his chair. It wasn't fear, but exertion. He almost hadn't gotten here before them. Even now his own private jet was cooling down on the other side of the airport.

He was himself again. Back in full control.

Oh, there was a moment or two back in Geneva when he had allowed fear to take control from reason. But even that had been exciting in a bizarre way.

Other men in his profession had walked that uncertain path before—between success and failure, life and death. Possibly even Benson Dilkes himself, although Herr Hahn had his doubts about that. Since Hahn had known only success, his failure back in Switzerland had given him a certain twisted thrill. But that was gone now.

These two celebrated assassins had become the challenge of a lifetime. Herr Hahn would meet that challenge with greater caution than he had ever exercised before. And in the end, the victory would be savored as none other.

Hahn wasn't sure what they were able to sense. He knew to his marrow that they'd felt his binoculars trained on them back in Geneva. Did whatever sense they possessed extend to electronic surveillance equipment?

He had no way of knowing if they'd noticed the heat-sensing equipment at Hubert St. Clair's chalet and had simply chosen to ignore it. If so, with luck, they might do the same thing here.

There were only a few cameras at the small airport. Two at the main terminal, the rest positioned around the private hangars. Herr Hahn chose not to focus all cameras on the two men. Rather, he let the devices pan back and forth in their normal automated cycles.

He saw them deplane, then missed them for a full minute as the woman got her luggage. The cameras rotated, and he caught just a glimpse of them on their way into the hangar.

The woman was alone. She was heading in the direction of the Masters of Sinanju, but right at this one moment she was completely vulnerable.

How easy it would be to slip out of the security shed unseen. A single bullet would put an end to her. Just as it had to the dead security officer who lay on his back on the floor near Herr Hahn's briefcase.

But a gunshot would bring the two men running.

This wasn't about the simple way out. This was all about tactics and victory. And maybe—just maybe— one last single moment of delicious fear before Herr Hahn achieved the greatest triumph in his professional career.

DENSE JUNGLE FOLIAGE around the back and sides cooled the hangar by ten degrees. Alert now to the unexpected, Remo and Chiun made their cautious way around the CCS jet.

The door behind the cockpit was down, the attached stairs almost welcoming them inside.

"If it's a trap, I'm not getting anything from it," Remo said cautiously.

The Master of Sinanju's face was impassive. "I sense no danger, either," he admitted.

"Good," Remo said. "If it starts shaking us like a paint mixer or launches us into space, we can both take equal blame."

"Very well," Chiun agreed. "But if something goes wrong, the Sacred Scrolls will show your equal blame to be greater than mine." He nudged Remo up the stairs at the point of a long nail.

The recycled air inside the jet had grown foul the instant it was exposed to Macapa air. Remo noted another smell lingering along with the stale air. It was the same odor they'd picked up back in Switzerland.

"I smell German," Remo said. "Think it's our guy?"

The Master of Sinanju nodded. "It is too weak for whoever it is to have flown here on board this craft. The German who boarded this plane did so long after it landed."

Remo nodded. "Thought so," he said. "He must have gotten here ahead of us."

They stepped more cautiously as they continued deeper into the plane.

There was a conference area halfway down the jet. A big map of the Amazon had been left unfolded on a low table. Remo saw that a large circle had been made in blue ink around an area of jungle miles inland.

"Well, they don't think very highly of us," Remo complained. "Why didn't they draw a bunch of arrows and write 'This is not a trap' at the bottom?"

Disgusted, he tried folding the map. It was like those from the gas station. He could never fold them back up right, either.

"Chiun?" he asked after his third try.

Frowning with his entire face, the old Korean snatched the map from Remo's hands. It folded quickly before vanishing up a wide kimono sleeve. He twirled away in a flurry of robes.

There was nothing else for them inside. When they went back into the hangar, Remo popped the door to the cargo hold. A vague whiff of ammonia told them where the seeds had been stored. The hold was empty.

"We know for sure where he brought them now," Remo said. "They just better be at that hotel, because I don't feel like schlepping off into the jungle."

He was interrupted by Amanda Lifton, who chose that moment to stick her head in through the main hangar door.

"Remo, Chiun, come quick!" she cried. *"Hurry!"*

Fearing the worst as she ducked back outside, the two Sinanju Masters flew for the door. When they emerged into the sunlight, they found Amanda standing a few yards from the hangar, surrounded by her pastel pink luggage. She was staring across the tarmac, a look of near rapturous bliss on her sweating face.

A new private jet had landed and taxied to a stop. People milled around the plane.

"You're not going to believe it," Amanda said. "I just saw him." She was craning her neck for a better look.

"Who?" Remo asked. "St. Clair?" He looked hopefully at the small crowd.

He didn't see the head of the CCS. All attention seemed to be focused around the thin, balding man in sunglasses who had just stepped into view.

When she saw the man reappear, Amanda grabbed Remo by the arm. Her digging nails pressed white finger marks in his skin.

"Geez, lady, lay off," Remo snarled.

A single tap on the back of her wrist and her hand sprang back open. Amanda hardly noticed.

"Don't you recognize Prick?" she asked.

Remo turned to the Master of Sinanju. "Did she just insult me again?" he said, assuming this was some new slang phrase he'd missed.

"Do not look at me," the old Korean said. "English when practiced by the modern British is confusing enough. I have long given up trying to keep track of whatever it is you Americans do to vulgarize it."

"Prick is a world-famous singer," Amanda explained. "You *must* have heard of him."

Remo looked back over at the new arrival, eyes narrowing. The man in the sunglasses wore an open-necked shirt and a pair of torn jeans. Remo realized that he had indeed seen him before.

"Oh, yeah," he said, nodding. "He's the one and only loudmouth in the music business who's always spouting off about something or other like he's the world's freaking nanny. Good thing there's not more like him or no one would ever take music stars seriously.''

A pair of loincloth-wearing natives stepped down from the plane. They carried spears, blowguns and copies of *Rolling Stone* with their pictures on the cover. Remo recognized them from the Primeval Society benefit concert in New York.

Amanda watched Prick eagerly as he and the tribesmen stepped over to a waiting limo. The flush to her cheeks was no longer due solely to the Brazilian heat.

''He's done a great job focusing attention on the plight of the rain forest,'' Amanda breathed.

''Beats working for a living,'' Remo said. ''You think he has to use that name because of truth-in-advertising laws?'' To the Master of Sinanju, he said, ''Chiun, can I see that map for a minute?''

The old Korean produced the map they'd found on the CCS plane from the folds of his kimono, handing it to Remo.

''He's here for the big Pan Brazil Eco-Fest,'' Amanda said as she watched photographers swarm the limo. Something big and papery crinkled in front of her face, blocking her view of Prick. ''What's that?'' she asked. Leaning back, she saw it was a map.

''Your buddy St. Clair and his hired killer left it for us to find,'' Remo said. ''Any idea what's there?'' He pointed to the circled section.

Amanda shook her head. ''No,'' she said worriedly. ''The CCS does a lot of work down here. It could be a project I don't know about. Did you say the killer was here?''

Remo nodded. "He must have got here just before us."

Suddenly, Prick was forgotten. "And you let me out here to fend for myself alone?" she said, aghast. "He could be anywhere, and you *abandoned* me? You—you *incompetents!*"

Frantically, she grabbed up only one of her bags. Using it as a pink shield, she covered her head and went running for the terminal.

Remo handed the map back to Chiun. "I'm glad we don't really work for her," he groused. "That servant-bashing is starting to get on my nerves." He cast a raised eyebrow at Amanda's abandoned luggage. "Should I?" he sighed.

"Why?" the Master of Sinanju replied blandly. "There must be something in them the street urchins of this squalid land could use."

Turning, he padded off toward the terminal.

Remo nodded. "Consider it the first shot in the battle for servants' rights," he said to himself.

With a mental image of dozens of Brazilian beggars dressed in Amanda Lifton's pink nighties, he struck off after Chiun.

HERR HAHN WATCHED them go.

First the girl, then the men.

Hahn had seen everything he wanted to see on the security monitors. They had taken the bait. The Masters of Sinanju had the map.

It was still possible he could get one or two of them

before they left Macapa but, if not, true success would inevitably come up the dark depths of the Amazon.

Hubert St. Clair wouldn't approve of his actions. But this was no longer about his employer.

Leaving the body of the murdered security officer to rot in the heat of the small shed, Herr Hahn hurried out into the stifling Brazilian afternoon.

16

The grand old-world style of the four-star Macapa hotel belonged to the Portuguese colonizers who had left Brazil one hundred years before. Remo and Chiun stepped easily through the revolving door. Amanda struggled to haul her last surviving bag inside.

A huge chandelier hung over the central staircase. Red carpets stretched across polished marble floors. A fountain gurgled in the middle of the lobby.

When she took one look around the ornate lobby, Amanda almost burst into tears.

"Isn't it magnificent?" she said with a melancholy sniffle. "I used to live in places like this. I practically grew up on room service."

For years Remo had lived the life of a hotel vagabond. His home of a decade had put an end to that nomadic existence. Now his house was gone. Smith had been tolerant of Remo and Chiun living at Folcroft, but that wouldn't last forever. Remo knew as he looked across that fancy hotel lobby that he was looking into his own inevitable future.

"It's not all it's cracked up to be," Remo muttered.

"I wasn't talking to you," Amanda snapped. "You

think a lunatic might be on the loose down here, and you left me out to fend for myself. Plus you left my bags to get stolen. Believe me, mister, Daddy's going to get an earful about you. I was talking to Chiun.''

She pointedly offered Remo her back. ''Isn't it magnificent, Chiun?''

The old man's hazel eyes were flat as he examined the lobby. ''I will be waiting outside,'' he announced abruptly.

Turning on his heel, he headed out the front doors.

''What did I say?'' Amanda asked.

''Don't mind him,'' Remo said. ''It's just a thing we both have about hotels.''

As they headed for the front desk, Remo heard a commotion at his back. When he glanced over his shoulder he saw a familiar figure step through the revolving door.

Prick surveyed the lobby like a visiting king. His entourage—including his two rain forest natives—hurriedly filed in around him.

''We better hurry up,'' Remo grumbled to Amanda. ''It's crowded enough in here without his ego.''

Amanda was looking longingly back at Prick as Remo dragged her over to the desk.

The clerk ignored them. He was staring excitedly past them, dark eyes directed at the singer at the door.

Remo rang the bell.

The desk clerk continued to ignore him.

Remo took the desk clerk by the bow tie and

stuffed his head into one of the mail slots behind the desk.

"You're violent," Amanda accused.

"You're just noticing?" Remo asked blandly.

As the desk clerk flailed frantically, another clerk and the hotel manager breezed in to help Remo.

"Would you like a room, *señor?*" the manager asked, a nervous eye trained on his employee with the wedged head.

"No," Remo said. "What room is Hubert St. Clair's?"

"Ah," the manager said, casting a glance over the register. "He is on the tenth floor. Room 1008. Shall I tell him he has a visitor?"

"No," Remo said. He held up a warning finger. "And don't you go telling him we're on our way up after we're gone, or I'll mail your head to Caracas."

The manager assured the very dangerous visitor that he wouldn't dream of alerting Dr. St. Clair, thus depriving Dr. St. Clair of the unexpected joy of his surprise guest's wonderful visit.

"No cops, either," Remo warned. "Your head to Caracas and your ass to Pittsburgh if I see one cop down here."

The manager had no idea why he should even consider summoning the police. He was sending his assistant to the kitchen to get some cooking grease in order to unstick the head of the desk clerk as Remo and Amanda left the desk.

By now Prick's entourage was fully assembled. He had just finished a quick photo session with the organizers of the concert he was to perform at and was sweeping across the lobby toward the desk.

Amanda gasped. "He's coming this way," she hissed. "Pretend we're not together."

"Isn't he married?" Remo asked.

"Right, like *that* means anything," she mocked. "He's got more money than God. Not as much as Daddy, but I'm sick of being poor. You wouldn't understand."

"I'm rich in other ways," Remo said.

"Spoken like a pauper," Amanda replied from the corner of her mouth. "How's my hair?"

Unseen by Amanda, as they walked across the carpet Remo slid his feet back and forth in a few blindingly fast sweeps. He touched his finger to her head, and the resulting static electricity sent every strand of hair sticking up wildly in every direction.

"Perfect," Remo said.

"Good," Amanda whispered. "Now stay back and look servile."

She was smiling at Prick as he walked by. She wondered why, instead of smiling back, his handlers hurried him away as if she were some kind of lunatic. She wondered about this only until she caught her reflection in a decorative lobby mirror and saw every hair on her head standing up on end.

Like a shrieking tumbleweed, Amanda dove onto the elevator.

Feeling good about doing two nice things for himself in the same week, Remo followed her on board.

HE WATCHED them step onto the elevator.

There were only the two of them—the apprentice Sinanju Master and the Lifton woman. The Reigning Master of Sinanju had gone outside.

Herr Hahn didn't know much about the Korean assassins. Probably their reputation was mostly just legends and tricks. The young Sinanju Master was certainly fast. He had seen that now firsthand.

Hahn switched his attention to the front desk. Hotel employees were still trying to extricate the desk clerk's head from the mail slot. Someone had a foot braced against the wall as others tugged at the man's ankles. Another man was dumping a frying pan filled with grease over the back of the desk clerk's neck.

The American Master of Sinanju had speed and finesse. But he was, in the end, just a man. No matter what Herr Hahn's mentor might think. He refocused his attention to Remo and Amanda.

They were standing at the back of the old-fashioned elevator car behind the elderly lift operator. While the Lifton woman tried to push down her suddenly wild hair, the young Master of Sinanju just stared.

His eyes were cold and dead. Herr Hahn had seen hints of such coldness in eyes before. In his own, in those of Benson Dilkes, in the eyes of a hundred other contract killers. But this was cold to a degree that even Hahn had not seen. To look in those eyes was to peer into the very act of sudden, violent death itself.

"Just a man," Hahn assured himself.

He shifted his gaze from Remo's dead eyes, turning attention to the tenth-floor monitor.

The room he was in was cramped, the air fetid. A battered air conditioner labored loudly in the grimy window. It did nothing to cool the room or clean away the smell. For all the times he had delivered it, Herr Hahn never much cared for the stink of death.

The body of a hotel security guard ripened on the floor behind him. The wide slit across his throat smiled red at the dirty ceiling tiles.

The elevator car finally rose into view on the tenth floor behind a closed metal grate. The elevator operator pulled the gate open and ushered Remo and Amanda off the car. The elevator was descending as they made their way up the hall.

As he watched them go, Herr Hahn leaned forward eagerly, suddenly unmindful of the stink and the worthless, spluttering air conditioner. He was finally going to see close up the vaunted Sinanju assassin. And with any luck, the next minute would give the hotel staff two more bodies to dispose of.

"YOU DID THIS somehow," Amanda accused. As they walked along the hallway, she was still trying to flatten her frizzed-out hair.

"I thought you were going for a look," Remo said. "Here."

He took hold of a wall-mounted light fixture with one hand and touched a finger of the other to Amanda's shoulder. The sharp jolt of static electricity made her jump. Her hair wilted before her face.

She pushed her bangs from her eyes. "I don't know how you did that, but I'm telling Daddy."

Remo stopped dead. He turned very slowly.

"You know, Amanda, in case you didn't notice, you're a whole big grown-up person. I don't know what kind of sicko relationship you think you've got going on with this father of yours, but it sounds like he doesn't give a fat flying fig about you. You've got a whole life and a career without him, so maybe you should just go live it and tell him to go diddle Colonel Mustard in the conservatory. And for the record, it's as creepy as a spider down your shorts to hear a grown woman call her father 'Daddy.'"

Spinning, he resumed walking. After a moment's hesitation, Amanda trotted to keep up.

"You really think I've got a life of my own?" she asked uncertainly.

"Yeah? Why not? I mean, you built that tree that's gonna kill us all. Not many debutantes can say that, can they?"

She tried to put on her pouty little girl's face. For the first time in her life, it somehow didn't feel right.

"I'm still angry at you," she said.

"That's the biz," Remo shrugged.

They followed the hallway to the end. Remo stopped outside of room 1008. He had a choice between being either subtle or unsubtle. After events of the past few days, he opted for the latter.

Remo slapped his palm against the flat face of the door just below the room numbers. The door ripped from its frame as if struck by a runaway Brinks truck. The numbers popped free, spinning in place.

Even as the door rocketed into the room, Remo knew something was wrong. He heard the telltale electronic click the moment the bolt cracked the frame. It was followed by a sharp hum.

Fearing yet another unorthodox attack, Remo shoved Amanda out of the way. The wind whooshed from her shocked lungs, and she and her suitcase went flying.

As Amanda fell one way, Remo dove to the other. They landed on opposite sides of Hubert St. Clair's open hotel room door.

Remo whirled, prepared for the predictable flame or acid booby trap. Neither materialized. He heard the door hit the floor inside the room, then nothing.

The only sound was the persistent soft electronic hum coming from the interior of the room. Remo was about to assume this latest trap was a dud when he noticed something strange emanating from the room.

A faint purplish light spilled from the open doorway and into the hall. And as Remo watched, the hallway's rich red carpeting began to visibly fade. The shiny bronze room numbers that had fallen to it were growing dark.

On the other side of the door, Amanda climbed to her feet. Leaning against the floral wallpaper, she cast a worried eye at the faint purple glow.

"What's wrong now?"

Remo shook his head. "Don't know," he said. "But I wouldn't move if I were you."

Two doors down, a hotel guest had left out a pair of shoes to be polished. Remo went over and took one, returning to the edge of the purplish light. He tossed the shoe into the area of the rug where the light splayed out of the room.

It immediately started to crackle and spit. As Amanda watched in growing shock, the shoe began to shrivel.

It was as if they were witnessing a lifetime's worth of aging in an instant. Even Remo's eyes had a hard time following the rapid process.

The shoe went from light brown to shrunken black in a matter of seconds. With a puff of surrender, it collapsed in on itself, deflating into a smear of black dust.

To Amanda it was like witnessing in person some trick from a Hollywood horror movie. The shock that she had just been standing in the very spot where the purple light was cascading from the room had just begun to register.

"What is it?" Amanda whispered. She was plastered hard against the wall, sick eyes focused on the weird light.

"Beats me," Remo said with a frown.

Spinning, he went back down the hallway. There was an empty room-service tray covered by a silver dome before another door. Casting aside the lid, Remo grabbed the tray and hurried back to the end of the hall.

He stopped a few feet from the open door. Lifting

the tray chest-high, Remo let it fly. It whistled down the hall like an airborne saw blade.

For an instant, Amanda thought it was zooming at her. But as the tray entered the purple haze, it cut sharply left. In the blink of an eye, it was gone.

Amanda wasn't sure exactly where the tray had gone until she heard a loud crash from inside the open room. It was like flicking a switch. The light abruptly winked out.

Remo tossed one of his new loafers in front of the open door. Nothing happened. He waved his hand around the corner. Still nothing. Sticking his foot back in his shoe, he ducked inside the room.

Amanda peeked around the door. "Is it safe?"

"Since I don't have an all-over tan, I guess so," Remo said.

Amanda stepped gingerly onto the warm hallway rug. As she walked into the room, Remo pointed back to a long insulated cord on the floor.

"Trip wire," he said. "It was hooked up to the door."

Amanda looked over at the remains of the door. It had broken into two large chunks. A snapped piece of wire hung from the dented doorknob. The longer section of wire ran across the rug and up into the center of the living room.

Amanda frowned when she saw where the wire ended.

Remo's silver room-service tray had slammed into a squat metal box. The box had a digital input face on one side. Extension cords ran to wall sockets.

A broad white object that looked like a satellite dish had been knocked off by the hurled tray. It sat on the floor next to a beige sofa.

"What the hell's this supposed to be?" Remo asked, crouching next to the device.

Amanda hurried in behind him, leaning down to examine the strange contraption.

"It looks like an excimer laser," Amanda explained. "They use them for glass etching, sterilizing wines, that sort of thing. I've never seen one jury-rigged like this."

"So what was that purple light?"

"The excimer is an ultraviolet-emitting laser," she explained. She snaked a hand to the broad silver dish. "It looks like someone has tampered with this one to work on a wider beam. Anything that stepped in front of it would get cooked."

"I hate your friends," Remo muttered. He kicked over the box. Something deep inside it continued to hum.

"This is very odd," Amanda said. "Trying to kill someone with ultraviolet light. Why not just shoot us?"

"Smith thinks they might be copying some environmental doomsday scenarios."

"Who's Smith?" Amanda asked.

Remo suddenly realized he'd misspoken. He glanced over at Amanda. "Our boss at the bodyguard agency," he ventured. "He's like Charlie. Chiun and I are the Angels. Except there's only two of us and no knockers. Well, that is until you showed up with those. Thank you."

"When you made those calls, you said you were talking to Daddy," Amanda said suspiciously.

"You were in the shower for forty-five minutes back at your apartment, Amanda," Remo said. "By the time you got out, I could have called ten pizza parlors and half the people in the greater Geneva phonebook."

She seemed unsure of him for a moment. The cloud of doubt passed away.

"Well, your boss might be on to something," she said. "You've heard what the results might be if the Arctic hole in the ozone layer enlarges?"

"Heard *and* seen," Remo said dryly.

There seemed some special meaning to the last words, but Remo didn't elaborate.

"This would be one of the results," Amanda said. "We've just been attacked by ultraviolet rays. Another dire prediction by the CCS."

"As world-destroying crazy men go, you've at least got to give St. Clair marks for ingenuity," Remo said.

Amanda shook her head. "Hubert didn't do this," she insisted. "He'd have to *tell* someone to do it. I told you, Hubert's afraid to screw in a light bulb."

"I smell a tubby German," Remo muttered.

"Whoever did this was very clever," Amanda said, nodding to the excimer laser. "What he did here is amazing."

"A laser's just a gun is just a spear is just a rock,"

Remo intoned. "So said Master Thuk. Well, I added the laser part."

He started to go from room to room in the suite, checking closets and under beds for the missing seed bags. As he searched, a thought occurred to him.

"Hey, Amanda, if this German guy is so bright, maybe he worked at the CCS. Any fat German scientists there?"

"Several, actually," Amanda admitted. "The two that were on the *C. dioxa* project are dead. The rest disappeared like everyone else when the bodies started piling up." She considered. "There was Mr. Hahn. He has a German surname. And he insisted people call him 'Herr.' He got very angry if they didn't."

Remo was shutting a closet door. "Was he a scientist?"

"No," Amanda said. "Actually, no one ever seemed to quite know what he did for the CCS. He was with Hubert in Geneva a lot these past few months."

"He's probably the guy."

"No," she said, shaking her head. "He was Swiss. He didn't talk much, but he definitely had a French accent."

"Wouldn't that make him French?" Remo asked.

"There is no Swiss language, Remo," she explained. "The people there speak mostly German, then French and Italian."

"No kidding?" Remo said. "No wonder they're neutral. They can't decide whether they should in-

vade, surrender or make bets on which one it'll be."
They were back out in the living room. "Okay, St.
Clair and the seeds definitely aren't here. I guess I
better collect Chiun and that map." He turned to her.
"You know, Amanda, maybe it would be safer for
you to get a room and hunker down here until we get
back."

Her face darkened. "What kind of bodyguard are
you?" she asked. "You were hired to protect me, not
go traipsing off up the Amazon after Hubert."

"I'm a bodyguard who's gotten fond of breathing.
I'm thinking the rest of the world is with me on that
one. Now, which is it, stay or go?"

Amanda took a long, deep breath. There was a hint
of something singed in the air of the Macapa hotel
room—the result of the laser. But it was still air. Life-
giving, nurturing, breathable air. Her face steeled. The
world needed someone of Lifton character to save it.

"I'm going with you," she insisted.

Remo didn't seem to appreciate the great Lifton
resolve that had just gone into her decision.

"Your funeral," he shrugged as he left the room.

17

"He was Swiss."

Although the Lifton woman's voice was muted through the speaker, it was clear enough to his ears.

Herr Hahn had buried the microphone inside the metal chassis of the excimer laser. It was an example of the meticulous attention to detail for which he was professionally known. The kind that many of his peers—like Benson Dilkes—thought to be redundant. The kind that had kept Herr Hahn alive for years.

Of course he hoped the laser would kill them. But if it didn't, he'd at least be able to hear them.

Hahn couldn't see either of them. He'd lost sight of them from the hallway security camera after they ducked into the room. But he could hear every word. And the words spoken by the wretched Lifton woman were worse than the fact that they hadn't been killed by his laser.

He was Swiss.

The rage with which those three small words filled him!

He regretted now not killing that spoiled rich American whore when he had the chance. A bullet in her wretched head. Splattering brain all over the Macapa runway. Who cared if he was caught? *Let* them catch him.

Swiss. How dare she? How dare that little *thing*... that inconsequential little *bug* call him that?

Hahn's ears rang. Blood pounding.

They were still talking. Their words were like buzzing static over the microphone. Barely registering over the fury that raged through Herr Hahn's non-Swiss brain.

When the young Master of Sinanju suggested that they go retrieve the map from the old one, Herr Hahn blinked the anger way. So enthralled was he in the activity in the hall and the hateful statement of Amanda Lifton, he had neglected to keep track of the Korean Sinanju Master.

All sudden temper fled. Herr Hahn quickly turned his attention to the outside cameras.

There were several active cameras around the hotel. One at each of the entrances, one at the main parking lot, one at the tennis courts and two near the swimming pool. As he scanned the monitors, Hahn felt his flaccid stomach tense.

The Master of Sinanju was nowhere to be seen.

He had last seen the old Korean near the swimming pool, sitting on the patio, a piece of parchment rolled open at his bony knees and an unmoving quill clutched in his long fingers. But when Hahn looked at the pool monitors, he found that the wizened figure was no longer there.

It was the woman's fault. Hahn had allowed himself to become distracted by the Lifton woman and her words of hate. He never allowed for error in his work. Now, thanks to her he had lost one of his targets.

Feeling a tiny thread unraveling from the obsessive order he meticulously maintained, Herr Hahn began scouring the grounds.

When he first went outside, the old man had come around the east side of the building. If he was still outside, he might be backtracking to the main entrance. Hahn scanned the monitors in turn. Front portico, to side lawns, to swimming pool, to tennis courts, to parking area.

The camera that looked out over the hotel's private parking lot was far to the left, tracking slowly rightward. An overlap with the tennis court camera gave him a brief glimpse of the last two courts and a few table umbrellas near the bar. The tennis courts disappeared, and the monitor screen slowly filled with dozens of cars. The camera warped the parking lot under its broad lens.

On another monitor, Remo and Amanda were getting back on the elevator. Hahn's eyes flicked over to them for an instant. And in that moment of skipping between monitors, Herr Hahn caught a flash of shimmering green.

Hahn's eyes jumped back to the parking lot.

The Master of Sinanju was padding around a parked car. Yellow peacocks fanned multicolored feathers on the back of his green silk kimono. His button nose sniffed the air.

Hahn felt the world begin to spin. It couldn't be.

Herr Hahn recognized the car that had drawn the Master of Sinanju's attention.

He had seen it at the rental shop. He had sat behind the steering wheel. He had driven it to the hotel.

The car Chiun was examining belonged to Herr Hahn.

As he watched in sick fascination, the old man wiggled a long fingernail in the space beside the lock. The door popped open silently. Herr Hahn realized that the Master of Sinanju had somehow disabled the car's security system when the alarm on his pocket key chain failed to activate.

As the tiny Asian climbed in the car, Herr Hahn canceled the sweeping motion of the parking-lot camera. He locked the lens squarely on Chiun.

Hahn squinted as he watched the wizened figure spring the glove box. Chiun pulled something out, tucking it inside his kimono.

Hahn knew what he'd found. He had kept a few of the blue seeds that he'd scavenged from the CCS greenhouse. Souvenirs for all the work he'd done eliminating all the *C. dioxa* scientists.

The Master of Sinanju had been smelling around the car like a bloodhound. Was it possible? Could it be that these men from Sinanju were like sharks, able to smell a drop of blood in a churning sea?

Stunned, Hahn just sat there as the Master of Sinanju closed the door of the car. There was something else in his hand. Herr Hahn couldn't quite see what it was.

He was like a delicate bird. So small, so fragile. Standing in the parking lot, Chiun tipped his head to one side. It was almost as if he sensed something different in his environment. Something that had changed since he had entered the car.

Alone in the security room, Hahn's blood froze to ice.

The security camera.

Hahn lunged for the control board.

Too late.

Chiun's head snapped up, focusing squarely on the stationary parking-lot camera.

He raised his hand. Herr Hahn saw now what he had been holding when he left the car. It was one of the big Bavarian pretzels Hahn had brought with him from Europe.

Chiun let the pretzel fall silently to the parking lot. Sleeves flapping like a crazed windmill, the Master of Sinanju began racing toward the hotel.

REMO AND AMANDA were walking back into the lobby from the elevator when the Master of Sinanju came bounding up to them from the main entrance.

"He is here," Chiun hissed.

"St. Clair's flown the coop, Little Father," Remo said.

The old man shook his head. Thunderclouds of yellowing white hair whipped the air angrily.

"His Hun lackey," Chiun insisted. He whirled on a passing bellman. "You," he demanded. "Where are hidden your spying devices?"

"He means security stuff," Remo explained when he saw the man's blank face.

The young man hesitated, but by now Remo's return to the lobby had caught the manager's eye. He was still behind the desk. A custodian was dismantling the mailbox unit in order to unplug the desk clerk's still stuck head.

"Whatever *señor* wants, see to it he gets it, with the compliments of the management," the manager called loudly.

The bellman nodded. At Chiun's urging he quickly led the three of them to a door between the front desk and the gift shop. The long corridor beyond was lined with doors.

He stopped at an unmarked room halfway down.

Remo sensed nothing living inside as Chiun advanced on the door.

"Careful, Chiun," he warned.

He didn't have a chance to get farther before the Master of Sinanju was airborne.

"Aiieee!" the old man cried.

The metal-reinforced door exploded beneath the soles of Chiun's sandals. The metal crunched and caved at the center, tearing from the frame. It flew into the room, Chiun along with it. The Master of Sinanju disappeared into the room, a raging storm of green silk.

"Like I said," Remo muttered. "Let's throw caution to the wind."

As the shocked bellman ran off to report to the

manager, Remo and Amanda trailed Chiun into the security room.

At the sight of the security guard's body, Amanda covered her mouth.

"Oh, my," she said. "Is he dead?"

"That ain't ketchup," Remo replied. "And don't be so shocked, Amanda. If your work's a success, we'll all be wishing we checked out this easy."

The security man's suit jacket was draped over the back of a chair. Remo tossed it over the guard's face.

Other than the body, the room was empty. Chiun whirled, planting hands to hips.

"He has fled," Chiun complained.

The monitor on which Hahn had watched Chiun was still trained on the parking lot. The car was gone.

Chiun's wrinkled face was puckered into an angry fist. But when he saw the vacant parking space, some of the harshness drained away.

"He had presence of mind enough to flee in his own vehicle," the old man said. "He knew to go where I had been and not to run in the opposite direction, as would be the instinct for most men."

"Yeah, you've got to hand it to those Germans," Remo said, annoyed at missing out on catching the killer. "Sure, they try to take over the world every few decades, but they're cool as ice under pressure."

"No, they are not," Chiun said, brow furrowed. He was looking thoughtfully at the security monitor.

"So I guess we've hit another dead end," Remo sighed.

The old man was shaken from his reverie. "Speak for yourself, round eyes," he said.

From the sleeve of his kimono he produced a small sheet of yellow carbon paper.

"After being lured to the vehicle by the stench of pretzeled bread, I discovered this."

He handed over the paper. Remo saw that it was a receipt from a car-rental agency.

"Olivier Hahn," Remo read. "Hahn? Isn't that the name you just mentioned upstairs?" he asked Amanda.

"Hmm?" Amanda asked. She had been staring at the partially covered body on the floor. "Oh, yes. Yes. But I told you, he's Swiss not German."

"Maybe our noses are on the fritz," Remo said. "I'll have Smith check into it." Paper in hand, he looked around for a phone.

"I also found these," Chiun intoned gravely. Once more he reached into his kimono. When his bony hand reappeared, it opened delicately, fingers unfurling like flower petals. In his wrinkled palm were a half-dozen small blue seeds.

Amanda snapped alert.

"*C. dioxa* seeds," she gasped.

Chiun let the seeds drop to the floor one by one. He crushed them under the heel of his sandal. They made a lumpy blue smear on the worn carpet.

"You have created a thing of evil," the Master of Sinanju accused, hazel eyes dark. "All that happens from this point forward rests on your foolish head."

His gaze penetrated deep into her troubled soul.

"I—I didn't mean to." She stopped, unable to go on.

Tears welled in her eyes. Her proud jaw quivered. These weren't the self-pitying tears she was used to.

Daddy, Mother, Abigail, the whole Lifton dynasty—all the power, all the millions—no one and nothing seemed to be as important as it had been just the day before.

She looked down at the body on the floor.

So very, very still. Like they would all soon be. Even her estranged family. In spite of all their Lifton money.

Remo had found a phone. He had already dialed. To Amanda, his voice echoed like distant thunder.

Chiun turned his back on her.

The tears came. Not wild and emotional. They stung hot as they rolled down her pretty face.

She had been comforting herself her past few years in exile by repeating over and over that everything would be okay. She knew now she was wrong on a scale far greater than she'd ever imagined.

Everything was not going to be okay.

She looked at the body on the floor.

Only the first of many.

The world was doomed.

And it was all her fault.

18

Hubert St. Clair wasn't worried so much about who would take the blame for destroying all life on Earth. He was more concerned about who might try to take the credit.

The problem of just exactly where the accolades would fall had been weighing heavily on his mind for months. It bothered him slightly less today. This was largely due to the distraction of the infernal mechanical whine and the constant rattling that made him feel as if his teeth would fly out of his head.

The head of the Congress of Concerned Scientists was sitting in the copilot's seat of an old West German antitank helicopter. The jungle canopy below the belly of the craft was thick and green as the chopper raced over the treetops that crowded the upper Amazon.

Most people would have found the view breathtaking. In a few short years, when these same forests were blue and the sky was adjusted back to preprimordial, those who thought the rain forest breathtaking would be literally correct.

St. Clair didn't much think of the scenery, either

present or future. He was too busy gripping his seat, trying to swallow the terror that had massed in his throat.

It wasn't the helicopter's fault. St. Clair would have been just as afraid in a car or truck or, Lord help him, a bus. He had taken heavy sedatives just to get on the plane from Geneva. The truth was Hubert St. Clair had a deep and abiding hatred of all things technological.

Hubert St. Clair was a Luddite before he even knew what the word meant. Technology had always been something to view with suspicion and dread. Even as a child, he had never felt truly comfortable with everyday appliances. At home he was deathly afraid of getting his hand caught in the toaster or blender or of getting locked in the refrigerator. The sound of the electric can opener sent him running from the room. Outside it was elevators and automobiles. Once he had passed out just from walking by an amusement park. The lights and the screams and the tilt-a-whirl had just been too much.

While many environmentally conscious individuals applauded the use of public transport, Hubert St. Clair couldn't be counted among them. Trains were terrifying metal death tubes that propelled human beings at speeds God had never intended. Buses were just plain evil.

It was odd that a man with his particular phobia had chosen a career in science. He mostly had his father to thank for the path he had taken in life.

"What is the matter with you, Hubert?" was his

father's favorite phrase in summer. "It's only a lawn mower."

"What is the matter with you, Hubert?" his father would often say in winter. "It's just a snowblower."

"It's perfectly safe to get in the car, Hubert," the elder St. Clair had said more times than he cared to all year round. "It's just a car and cars can't hurt you. Now, get out of the goddamn bathroom before I break the door in."

Hubert's problem with technology was evident early on. It didn't get better over time.

His father knew that if Hubert followed the course he was laying out for himself, he was certain to wind up as an underachieving agrarian farmer or forest ranger. Worse, if he could get over his fear of hammers and mistrust of buggies, he might even turn Amish. His father couldn't allow it. Rather than let his only offspring choose his own path in life, the elder St. Clair had chosen for Hubert.

It took years of browbeating and threats. Money held back, money as reward. Handholding through college and graduate school. His father taught Hubert many important things. Not the kinds of things that a father would ordinarily teach his male child, but important things nonetheless. Like that if you hit a light switch really fast and don't look at the bulb, you can pretend lamp light is really sunlight. Or how car trips could be endured if you closed your eyes and blocked your ears and pretended you were sitting on a wobbly bench.

The advice his father gave was probably not the

best he might have gotten. With such a deep-rooted, irrational phobia, some sort of psychiatric help was probably called for. But psychiatrists were for crazy people, and there was nothing really terribly wrong with young Hubert when you came right down to it. And, no, cameras don't really steal part of your soul and extension cords don't slither into bed and strangle you in your sleep.

The elder St. Clair was a physics professor at a prestigious New England university. Once Hubert was finished with school, he made sure his son got a job teaching.

Surprisingly, the academic life seemed to suit Hubert. At least, he didn't seem to complain.

He lived within walking distance of the campus, so he didn't have to drive to work. He turned lights in his office and classrooms on and off without apparent concern. His father was delighted when he visited his son's office and found an automatic coffeemaker in the corner.

By all outward appearances it looked as if Hubert St. Clair had conquered his childhood demons.

When Hubert was offered a job as technical adviser to a public-television show in the 1970s, his father was no longer surprised. Why couldn't Hubert go into a television studio like anyone else? There was no reason that he should be afraid of all the cameras and lights and sound equipment. His son was normal, and normal people did things like that all the time.

A week after Hubert got his new job, Professor St. Clair suffered a massive stroke. In his mind, he died a happy man. But he also died never knowing the truth.

For although Hubert had been able to put up a good front for years, those childhood technology fears had not only stayed with him, they had grown to nearly uncontrollable proportions.

Fortunately, the program he had been chosen to work on was hosted by none other than Sage Carlin, perhaps the most famous opponent of the technological revolution on the face of the planet. That job had changed Hubert's life.

When his PBS program ended its run, Sage Carlin had welcomed Hubert St. Clair onto the board of directors of the Congress of Concerned Scientists. It was there that Hubert finally found men like himself.

The men of the CCS hated technology. They didn't quite fear it in the way Hubert did. But they were convinced that every machine invented was intrinsically evil.

Hubert delighted in the various reports the CCS would periodically issue. He was standing right there as the Congress railed against oil tankers and fast-food sandwich containers. Microwaves and missiles. He signed every worrywart petition by every flighty scientist on every dubiously argued subject that appeared in the *New York Times*.

At the CCS, Hubert St. Clair finally began to get his revenge against the science he hated so much.

Largely due to his passion, he climbed the ranks quickly, until eventually he was second only to Sage Carlin himself. At this point Carlin was at the end of his life and looking for a legacy that would give his existence the meaning he craved.

Sage Carlin wasn't quite the same as Hubert. Whereas St. Clair wouldn't have minded if the whole world was forced to go back to living in moss-lined caves, Carlin had always favored deindustrialization for everyone but himself. But in the end, with his own bright light winking out, Sage Carlin seemed to come over to Hubert St. Clair's way of thinking.

The *C. dioxa* project had been in its infancy when Sage Carlin passed away. Since it would no longer affect him where he was going, his plan was to make the changes to the world he knew were necessary. Afterward, when Hubert St. Clair ascended to the top spot at the CCS, he pressed the project even harder than had his predecessor.

The greatest moment in all his life came that day when he realized the *C. dioxa* team had actually succeeded. Hubert St. Clair had dared to dream big, and now that amazing, wonderful dream was going to come true.

His vision was of a new world.

It was good timing, because he had gotten to a point in his life where he simply could not bear the old one any longer. This brave new world wouldn't be afflicted with the Bronze, Industrial or Technological ages. All of the terrors that had been thrust down around his frightened technophobic ears would become things of the distant past.

Not that he wanted the planet to end. Far from it. There was a future for Earth. Even on a planet where *C. dioxas* thrived and cloud-clogged skies rained ammonia fire, the building blocks of the new age would still be there.

Eventually, the planet would evolve to support other life. It had done so before. Inevitable climactic shifts would force the extinction of the *C. dioxa.* Those plants that mutated would evolve whole new species. The trees had been engineered using genetic material that existed on this current version of Earth. In them would be carried the key to all future life. Life that would emerge once the clouds receded and the sun returned.

Yes, it would be a few billion years from now, but science was nothing if not patient.

When the new Earth dawned, there might very well be a new dominant animal life-form that would succeed man. And with any luck those creatures that eventually climbed up from a future cold pool of primordial sludge would choose farming as a way of life and have sense enough to steer clear of blenders, fax machines and automatic supermarket doors.

As Hubert's helicopter whipped over an endless sea of green leaves, he wondered briefly if he shouldn't leave some kind of message for the future stewards of creation. After all, there was no way he wanted Sage Carlin to get credit.

The other potential glory hogs were gone. Out of necessity to protect his plan, he had thinned the herd of CCS scientists as soon as they'd completed work on the *C. dioxa.* None of them could try to take credit.

Well, actually there might still be one.

The only holdout was that irritating Amanda Lifton. The head of the project, Dr. Brice Schumar, had insisted she was brilliant. St. Clair couldn't see it. All he ever saw—beyond those truly eye-popping knobs—was an emotional train wreck of a woman who had spent large chunks of her day sitting in her office blubbering. She would have been eliminated already if that millionaire father she was always whining about hadn't gone out and hired some outside protection for her.

This was the real baffler. There were only two of them. And one of them looked like he was a million years old.

When he was looking to permanently terminate the *C. dioxa* team, Hubert St. Clair had done some quiet checking around. The consensus in the Swiss underworld was that a man by the name of Olivier Hahn was the best at handling these kinds of delicate jobs. He was a little too fond of technology and had an odd quirk of not wanting people to use his first name, but he had certainly lived up to his hype. Until now.

The last Hubert had heard from Hahn, Amanda Lifton and her two bodyguards had escaped the fiery destruction of his Swiss chalet.

It should have been impossible. When it was his home, Sage Carlin had kept some of the early *C. dioxa* information there. Before he died he had rigged the place so that, if it became necessary, he could obliterate all the data and half the hillside at just the touch of a button. Apparently he had done all this—

Hubert St. Clair later learned—with the help of Herr Hahn.

The explosion that destroyed the chalet was huge. St. Clair had even seen mention of it in Brazil that morning in one of the local English-language papers. Yet, maddeningly, Amanda Lifton had gotten through it in one piece.

"You better not try to steal my thunder," Hubert St. Clair muttered under his breath.

For a moment as he thought about her, St. Clair forgot about the terrifying flying death machine he was sitting in.

The helicopter had been converted to civilian use after being donated to the Congress of Concerned Scientists by the Netherlands. There were no longer missiles hooked to the lateral outriggers. Instead, the riggers had been outfitted with a series of simple metal tubes. An extra-large fuel tank had been installed at the back of the craft, allowing for greatly extended flight time.

The area that was intended to be used for the transport of military personnel had been remodeled. A large stainless-steel hopper filled the back of the helicopter. It tapered to a narrow funnel at the base. The end of the funnel extended through a hole in the floor.

As they flew along, St. Clair felt a sudden vibration in his pocket. Reaching in, he gingerly removed his cell phone.

He hated carting the thing around with him. He was absolutely convinced that the reports were right and the wretched little things caused brain, ear and eye cancer. But circumstances required that he participate in this part of the technology insanity. At least for the time being.

As the helicopter continued to whip over green trees, St. Clair tucked the cell phone under his headset. He tried his best to keep it from directly touching his ear.

"Hello?"

The voice on the other end of the line offered no salutation.

"They are still alive."

Herr Hahn was always short on the phone. St. Clair knew his hired assassin was talking about Amanda Lifton and her bodyguards. The CCS director clicked his tongue unhappily.

Somehow that pesky woman continued to cheat death. But soon it wouldn't matter. No matter how slippery she and her bodyguards were, they'd soon be left gasping for air along with the rest of the miserable planet.

"Again?" St. Clair said, shaking his head. "You know something, maybe we should just call this whole thing off with them. Just let them go."

"That might not be wise," Herr Hahn said. "They seem intent on following you."

"Let them try," St. Clair dismissed. "They've got no idea where I even am."

Hahn's reply caused St. Clair to tighten his grip on the slender phone.

"They traced you as far as Macapa," the killer

said. "I attempted to use the excimer laser on them. It failed."

"That ultraviolet thing of yours?" St. Clair asked weakly. "I thought that barbecued the others like chickens."

"It did. However, this time it did not. Right now they are about to hire a boat to head up the Amazon."

For an instant the threat of head cancer was forgotten. St. Clair pressed the phone tight against his ear.

"They're on the river?"

"Nearly," Herr Hahn said.

This was something Hubert St. Clair had learned early on his dealings with the Swiss assassin. Whenever possible, Olivier Hahn kept his answers short. The better, he thought, to hide his accent. It didn't work. Even with one syllable Herr Hahn was obviously as French as a dirty armpit.

"What does she think she's doing?" he wondered aloud.

"The men she is with are not ordinary bodyguards," Herr Hahn explained. "They are assassins. According to reputation, they are possibly the best in the world. It is likely that they are not even interested in the Lifton woman. Except, perhaps, as a path to you."

"Me?" St. Clair asked, shocked. "They're assassins and they're coming after *me*? You've got to stop them."

"I will," Herr Hahn said. "I said they are possibly

the best in the world. Before this is over we will find out if theirs is a reputation earned.''

St. Clair noted the proud determination in the Swiss assassin's voice. He sounded like every French waiter St. Clair had ever detested.

''I don't want to get caught in the middle of some professional pissing contest you've got going on with those two,'' the CCS head insisted. ''Just kill them. You like that exotic stuff too much. You should use a damned gun. Sneak up behind them and pop.''

''I choose my own methods, and I do not fail.''

''You're right about the first part,'' St. Clair muttered.

Hubert St. Clair had tried to discourage Hahn from the more flamboyant means he'd used against the *C. dioxa* team, but Herr Hahn had become intrigued with the dire environmental predictions made by the CCS over the years. By incorporating them into his execution methods, he brought his art to a whole new level. It became easier to just accept it and let him do his job as he pleased.

''So where exactly are they now?'' St. Clair asked.

''They are on their way to the Macapa waterfront. I strongly suspect they will rent a boat to follow you,'' Herr Hahn said. ''I estimate they are ten hours behind you.''

''You have to stop them,'' St. Clair ordered.

''The defenses I arranged for you at your special site are more than adequate to the task. I am en route there myself. I will rendezvous with you shortly.''

Without so much as a goodbye, Hahn broke the connection.

The Swiss assassin was like that. Arrogant, rude and condescending. No matter how much he tried to be German, the French in him always seemed to come through loud and clear.

St. Clair slipped the phone into his pocket. With worried eyes he watched the tops of the trees speed by.

The CCS head knew the defenses Hahn was talking about.

A sudden split in the jungle canopy and the Amazon became an explosion of blue among the green. In that brilliant blue, Hubert St. Clair saw the future.

The helicopter swooped over a trio of lonely boats. It was the three he had rented to transport the seeds from Macapa to the *C. dioxa* valley. The boats were on course and on time. He could see the heavy burlap sacks baking on the decks.

He could not fail. Not now.

The sweating men aboard the boats had removed their corduroy jackets. They waved them like triumphant flags over their heads as the helicopter soared overhead.

Another boat like these a mere ten hours behind.

St. Clair made a sudden decision.

"Screw you, Frenchie," he grumbled to himself. "You and the twenty-first century had your chance. It's high time we had some pre-Industrial Age killing around here."

Digging back in his pocket, he pulled out his cell phone once more.

19

The botanist from the Smithsonian Institution had been brought in at the last minute as a consultant by an assistant director at the CIA. Although he was a little overwhelmed at first by the Pentagon's War Room, the scientist quickly returned his attention to the matter at hand. Namely, the end of the world. These were the dire words he spoke to those assembled when describing the almost certain damage the genetically engineered trees would cause.

The President, vice president, joint chiefs and a few cabinet members, as well as the heads of the CIA, FBI and NSC, looked on. Some seemed concerned. A few looked skeptical.

"I hope you can do better than that," the White House chief of staff said. His Massachusetts accent was as thick as a bowl of Boston baked beans. "Scientists have been claiming the planet is doomed for thirty years."

The Smithsonian scientist shook his head seriously.

"This isn't doomsaying for political purposes," he insisted. "This is the real thing. Sir?"

Taking the cue, the CIA director pointed to an Army officer at a control console.

A series of panel maps hung high across one big wall. The panels were backlit in bright shades of blue, green and yellow. The colors represented ocean, land and deserts around the globe. The poles were white.

The officer typed in a command at a keyboard. On the wall one portion of the map changed color.

"This is an early projection of species dominance," the Smithsonian botanist explained.

"Why is South America underwater?" the President of the United States asked. His nasal Texas twang was tart.

The scientist shook his head. "That isn't water, Mr. President," he explained. "That is the first five years of *C. dioxa* breeding."

"They'll take over South America in five years?" the President asked doubtfully. "Can a plant do that?"

The scientist nodded. "Alien species introduced into an ecosystem not designed for them are capable of wreaking havoc on an enormous scale. Insects, reptiles, even other trees have all caused ecological problems in parts of the United States in the past century alone. But those were either due to accidents or ignorance. This is far worse. This is a deliberate attempt to alter the environment by introducing a genetically altered species into the wild."

The scientist desperately wanted to impress on these men the seriousness of the threat. In his very marrow he knew the world was heading for a showdown that might be unwinnable. He recognized the danger the moment he had been given the *C. dioxa* information by the CIA. It was made all the more real when he saw the classified satellite photographs of an incongruous patch of land in the Amazonian rain forest. Land the CIA said was owned by Hubert St. Clair's Congress of Concerned Scientists.

"Five years is a long time," the President said. "Maybe we can find something to stop it by then. Some sort of weed killer."

"Five years is nothing," the scientist insisted. "This is the projected course the *C. dioxa* will take. Slow projection, please," he said to the soldier at the keyboard.

As the President and the others watched the big overhead maps, the blue blob slid up from South America into Central America like a spreading ink stain. In a matter of seconds, it had engulfed the narrow strip of land from Panama to Guatemala, along with much of Mexico.

"This is eight years from now," the scientist intoned gravely.

Eyes wide, the President sat forward in his chair. "My God, man, that's practically in *Texas*," he gasped.

He almost jumped out of his seat when the blue blob oozed across the Texas-Mexico border.

"Twelve years away," the scientist continued.

By now blue dots had appeared in Africa and Australia. They began spreading like cancer across those continents. A pair of blue blips popped up in Portugal and France. The original stain had seeped up across the plains states. California was nearly awash in blue.

"Wyoming is gone," the vice president said, his voice soft and even. The blue of the map reflected in his glasses. His jaw clenched as he watched the *C. dioxa* tree line advance on Canada.

"This is only sixteen years from now, gentlemen," the Smithsonian botanist said. "As you can see, the contiguous United States is gone."

The trees had swept up like a tidal wave, rolling through southern Canada. The only part of the U.S. not covered was the high northeast. In a matter of seconds Maine, Vermont and New Hampshire had been gobbled up.

"All that is left of the United States by this point is Alaska and Hawaii. Not that it will matter. The atmosphere will be well on its way to being completely poisoned by the time we get this far. The dominant species will die out first. Of course, in the primary affected areas they'll already be gone. In the rest of the world, it will be a slower process, but inevitable. The higher vertebrates—man included—will go first. But it will race down the food chain until nothing, not even a single microbe, is left."

"This *can't* be," the President said, more to himself than to the others in the room.

"I'm afraid, sir, it is," the botanist said. "If the information I have been given is accurate, the *C. dioxas* grow quickly and spread rapidly. They do not have single seeds, but hundreds of seedlets in a single shell. They break open and are spread on the wind."

Africa, Australia and nearly all of Europe and Asia were gone, awash in the same sky blue. The assembled men watched as the last of Russia was swallowed up.

"The entire land surface of the world will be consumed by this plant within the next twenty-five years. Outside projection." The botanist turned away from the maps. Behind him it was as if the oceans had risen and flooded every continent.

"Antarctica is still white," the chief of staff pointed out.

"Not for long," the botanist said. "The greenhouse gases released by the *C. dioxa* will trap radiant heat. The polar ice caps will melt, flooding landmasses. Eventually, Antarctica will be like everywhere else. Covered with these trees. However, none of us will be alive to see it."

"Can't we fight them somehow?" the secretary of defense asked. "The President's herbicide idea could work. We could blanket our southern border with spray."

The Smithsonian botanist smiled sadly. "Did you ever try obliterating every last dandelion in your yard, Mr. Secretary?"

"Poison miles of land, then. Make it a dead zone where nothing grows or can take root."

"It simply can't be done," the botanist said. "These things are rapid growing. Nature itself will work against us. Once loose, the *C. dioxa* will spread like a disease. Even with our best efforts, the seeds will find purchase in isolated areas. Forests, taiga, mountainous regions. Even overgrown backyards and vacant lots. What I've shown you is the slow projection. I'm already assuming we'll do everything we can to stop them. If we don't try, the process will be even faster. Eventually, mankind will come to see what I already have. In the end we simply will be helpless to do anything to stop them.''

''There must be *something* we can do,'' the President said. ''We can't just let those things overrun Texas like that.''

Lips pursed, he was looking up at the map. He didn't even notice that the Smithsonian botanist was being escorted quietly from the room. The door clicked shut.

''Map, please,'' the CIA director said.

The Army officer at the keyboard obliged. The blue receded from the world. It drained down from North America through Central America until it was once more an inconsequential dot. The upper section of South America was enlarged. The blue dot grew proportionate to the enlargement. It was in the jungles of Brazil, halfway down the Amazon.

''There is a possibility, Mr. President,'' the CIA director said seriously. ''We can destroy the existing forest of *C. dioxas*.''

''How?'' the President asked.

The CIA head and the Chairman of the Joint Chiefs of Staff exchanged a tight glance.

''Bomb Brazil,'' the general said.

The President's head snapped up.

"I can't authorize a military strike against Brazil," the chief executive said.

The vice president was still looking at the map. "We should consider it, sir," he said somberly.

The President exhaled, sinking back in his chair. "How is this even possible?" he muttered to himself. He looked up at the other men in the room. "What kind of strikes are you talking about?"

He hoped for a limited number. He had no strong desire to pummel the Brazilian jungle as his predecessor had Yugoslavia, or his father—who had been President ten years before—had punished Iraq during the Gulf War.

The Chairman of the Joint Chiefs of Staff cleared his throat. "Actually, according to the information I have been given, there is only one type of bomb that would be certain to destroy all the plants. Assuming this is their only location."

All eyes turned slowly to him.

There was a sick look on the old soldier's face. He had never imagined in his entire military career that there would ever come a time when he would advocate such a thing. But if the civilians were right, to not do so would mean the end of the world.

"You want me to drop a nuclear bomb on Brazil?" the President asked. Shock swallowed up his Southern twang.

"We discussed our options before your arrival, sir," the CIA head said. "We would tell you to do this only as a last resort but, Mr. President, this *is* our last resort." He pointed up at the tiny blue dot on the map. "If those plants are not obliterated completely, the entire planet is doomed. Anything smaller than an atomic strike at the heart of that forest runs the risk of scattering those seeds, something we cannot afford to do. This can't be overstated. It's either that dot, or the world."

The room fell silent as the President looked up at the map.

Just a harmless little blue dot. It looked like nothing at all. But he had been partially briefed on the seriousness of the crisis that morning. He had seen all of the intelligence reports. The threat was real.

His options were severely limited. He could either leave the trees alone and let them swallow up the entire planet, or he could become the first President since Harry Truman to drop a nuclear bomb on another country.

Those were the options as outlined by his advisers. But maybe there was a third way.

The President stood.

All eyes were on him as he stared up at the map. He finally turned away.

"I have to make a phone call," the President said.

Waving away protests, he left the War Room, hurrying out to his waiting limousine. The presidential motorcade sped back to the White House.

The President's generally cordial attitude wasn't visible as he hurried through the mansion. Those who greeted him were brushed aside without so much as a glance.

He raced to the family quarters, then hustled to his

private bedroom. He closed the door tightly behind him.

From the bottom drawer of his nightstand he pulled out a red phone.

In the first month of his new administration, he had used that special phone for two separate emergencies. But in nearly a year since those trying times, he had done his best to put the phone and what it represented from his mind. He had hoped that he could survive the rest of his time in the White House without ever having to use it again.

Taking a deep, steadying breath, the President of the United States brought the phone to his ear. As he did, he said a silent prayer that the men on the other end of that line would be able to put an end to this lunatic scheme. Not just for the sake of his beloved Texas, but for the entire world.

THANKS TO THE CAR-RENTAL information Remo had supplied, Harold Smith completed his search for Remo and Chiun's mysterious stalker. He was reading an Interpol report on Olivier Hahn when he heard the muted ring of the special White House line.

Smith collected the red phone from the bottom right drawer of his desk, picking it up before it had a chance to ring a second time.

"Yes, Mr. President," he said crisply.

"We have a problem, Smith," the President said. "I'm not inclined to believe the Henny-Pennies out there, but it sounds like civilization is actually in danger."

Smith blinked away surprise. "Are you by any chance referring to the work of the CCS?" he asked.

The President exhaled relief. "Then you're already on it? Thank goodness. What's the situation?"

"My men are in South America right now," Smith said. "They are on the trail of Dr. St. Clair and his seeds."

"Seeds?" the President asked. "What seeds?"

Smith adjusted his spotless glasses. "The *C. dioxa* seeds that were taken from the CCS greenhouse in Geneva. Isn't that what you are referring to?"

"There are more seeds?" the President said. The words came out in a pained groan.

"I assumed that was what you were calling about," Smith said. "Hubert St. Clair, the director of the CCS, apparently is planning to distribute *C. dioxa* seeds harvested from his European greenhouse somewhere in Brazil."

"He's past the planning stage, Smith. According to the CIA, there's already a whole bunch of those trees growing in an isolated part of the rain forest somewhere."

Smith's chair creaked as he leaned forward. "Are you certain of that, sir?" he asked, his voice steady.

"I saw the satellite photos myself. I'm surprised you haven't. I thought you people were always on top of things like this."

Smith was already at his keyboard. Dumping the Olivier Hahn information into a separate file, he hurried to access the pertinent Central Intelligence Agency files.

He found the report that the CIA head had delivered to the President that morning, along with the pictures of the rain forest taken from orbit. The data wasn't there the last time he checked. Smith's heart skipped a hurried beat when he saw the patch of blue.

"My God," Smith croaked.

"I gather you've seen it now," the President said.

Smith's mind was reeling as he scanned the satellite images. "I have access to the CIA systems, unknown to that agency. There was no indication that they had any special knowledge of the CCS or its plans for the *C. dioxa*."

"By the sounds of it, some special group within the CIA had been looking into the Congress of Concerned Scientists for some time. They just brought it to the CIA director's attention within the past twenty-four hours."

Smith knew of no such group within the CIA that would be beyond his computer access. He made a mental note to check into the activities of the Central Intelligence Agency at the earliest convenient moment. Right now the crisis in South America had just grown far worse.

"My people are on St. Clair's trail, but they don't know what they are heading into," the CURE director said. He pressed his glasses farther back on his patrician nose as he examined the image on his computer. "Did they indicate to you what this strange region is around the trees?"

The blue *C. dioxa* trees were on a plateau in the middle of a valley. They were encircled by a region that looked like some sort of desert. Yet it seemed too light for sand.

"I wondered that, too," the President said. "They said they weren't sure. The shadows cast by the surrounding mountains made it impossible for them to tell."

Alone in his office, Smith shook his head. "This is far worse than I imagined," he said quietly.

"That's what the experts are telling me," the President agreed. "They've recommended a course of action for me to take, Smith. One that I never would have imagined in my worst nightmares. But if there are more seeds—"

"There definitely are," Smith interjected. "And can I assume that the recommendation of a limited nuclear strike against Brazil has been suggested?"

He spoke the words with utter dispassion. Yet a look of quiet nausea had settled across his sharp, lemony features.

"I can't even conceive it, Smith," the President said. "A nuclear strike against a nation in our own hemisphere? An *innocent* nation. I can't imagine that they even know anything about what's going on down there."

"It's likely that they do not," Smith said. "And, Mr. President, as difficult as it is for me to agree with the advice you've been given, it may become necessary. I have seen the report, as have you. You know the danger these plants represent. Given the size of those trees, it would be a miracle if they have not already spread beyond that area. You know what is at stake. If my people are unable to stop St. Clair, you may be forced to make the ultimate decision in order to save the rest of the planet.''

There was a pause on the line during which all Smith could hear was the rhythmic breathing of the President of the United States. The CURE director assumed the President was contemplating the enormity of what was being proposed. When he finally spoke, there was an undercurrent of steely resolve in the voice of the nation's chief executive.

''How soon will you know if they've succeeded?''

''There is a problem with that,'' Smith said. ''I cannot reach them from here when they are in the field. It is they who ordinarily contact me. Unfortunately, as I've said, they don't fully know what is going on. Given the fact that I'm unable to contact them to inform them that the situation has changed, they can't fully appreciate what is at stake. Time is not with us in this situation, Mr. President. According to my people, St. Clair likely has the seeds in his possession and is in the vicinity of the *C. dioxa* valley now. That is the one positive for us in all this, because it works well for containment. But St. Clair cannot be allowed to take them from that area.''

''So what do you propose, Smith?'' the President asked. ''I can't believe I'm even contemplating this, but if I'm going to do it by your own argument I should do it while all the eggs are in one basket.''

''Yes, sir,'' Smith agreed. ''We will need someone on the ground in Brazil. Someone who can inform my people of the new developments and who can relay information back.''

He thought of Mark Howard. Smith had sent the assistant CURE director home for a few day's rest.

Smith placed a flat palm to his desk. His course of action was clear.

''If you call this line within the next few days, don't be surprised when my assistant, Mr. Howard, answers.''

''Why? Where will you be?''

Smith's expression never wavered. ''South America,'' the CURE director said flatly as he hung up the dedicated phone.

20

Mark Howard was sound asleep, stretched out on the sofa in the living room of his Rye apartment.

Except for Sundays he hadn't had a full day off in almost a year. Still, at first he'd resisted the notion that he needed to take a few days away from Folcroft. But Dr. Smith had insisted, and Mark had finally relented.

While work at CURE was certainly a strain, he was equal to the task. The problem wasn't his duties as assistant CURE director, but the dreams that had crept insidiously into his workday. Those unintentional catnaps at work brought him sleep without the rejuvenating effect. When he awoke after falling asleep at Folcroft, he seemed to be sapped of energy.

It wasn't the same here at home. When he slept here, the recurring dream didn't come.

The television was on, but he'd hit the mute button during a commercial. Now, three hours later, the TV played in silence as Mark snored softly on the couch.

In the world of his mind, Mark was standing in a place he'd never been before. Two pillars of rock towered over an ocean. Mark stood at the rocky shore looking up.

High up, a figure stood between the rocks. A flowing mane of yellow hair whirled soft in the wind.

The ocean breeze blew salt mist on Mark's bare skin. When he looked down, he saw that his hands were flecked red. Looking out, he saw that the ocean—more a bay than a sea—had turned to blood. He was gazing in dread wonder at the bay when he felt something grab hold of his ankle.

When Mark looked down, his heart stopped.

A dead man lay in the water at Mark's feet. His cold, lifeless hand was latched around Mark's ankle.

The corpse had Asian features. A flat, pockmarked face was a feast for skittering crabs. Its sightless hazel eyes seemed somehow familiar to Mark. They stared up at the wall of rock that loomed above the blood bay.

Mark tried to pull away, but the dead man held fast. He continued to stare beyond Mark, to the pillars of stone that shadowed the dreary landscape.

There was a hint of something in the distance. A voice. A faraway call on the cold wind. Mark followed the sound, up to the distant figure who watched the sea from far above.

The figure on the rocks spoke not to Mark but to the dead man in the water.

"The time is at hand. At last it is at hand... Father."

Mark blinked surprise. There was a television

across from him now. An afternoon talk show played soundlessly.

His apartment. There were CDs and videos on a shelf across the room. The plant he'd bought, killed and had yet to throw out in the trash sat on his stereo speaker.

At first he was certain he was still asleep. But after a moment, he realized that he was back home. Yet his hands were still cold. When he looked at them, he thought he could vaguely see the specks of fading blood.

But that was impossible. He couldn't have carried them over from his dream. And besides, they were gone now.

He pulled himself wearily to a sitting position. "What is happening?" he pleaded with his empty apartment.

He was clicking the TV off when the phone rang. Grateful for the distraction, he tossed the remote control to the couch and grabbed up the phone from the end table.

TWENTY MINUTES LATER he was standing before the desk of Dr. Harold W. Smith. The CURE director had rapidly briefed him on the crisis developing in Brazil.

"You shouldn't be the one to go, Dr. Smith," Howard insisted firmly.

"There is no one else," the CURE director replied.

"I'm your assistant. Send me."

Smith's hard features relaxed just a bit. "Under other circumstances I might consider sending you.

However, I sent you home for a reason. I wouldn't have called you back in now if the situation didn't require it. I will need you here at Folcroft in order to monitor the situation. I can remain in touch with the President through the scrambled phone in my briefcase, but I will not be able to keep track of all developments on my laptop. You can inform me if there are any changes I need to be made aware of.''

He picked up his battered leather briefcase from where it sat next to his desk.

Mark trailed him to the office door. ''Do you have any idea where Remo and Chiun are exactly?''

''Exactly? No,'' Smith admitted as he shrugged on his overcoat. ''The last time Remo checked in, he was looking for information on the man who has been stalking him. The relevant facts are with the *C. dioxa* data. If he calls back and for some reason I am unable to answer on my cell phone, please relay the information to him.''

''Why wouldn't you be able to answer?'' Howard asked.

The tight look on the CURE director's tart face gave him the answer.

''Oh,'' Mark said, his voice small.

''There is something else, Mark,'' Smith said seriously. ''I cannot rule out the possibility that the worst could happen while I am gone. If the President's hand is forced, Remo, Chiun and I might not be returning. In that event, if the President so chooses, you will assume stewardship of CURE.''

It was as if he were giving the afternoon weather

forecast. Before Howard could say a word, the CURE director had pulled open his office door.

A matronly woman was typing at a tidy desk in the outer office.

"Mrs. Mikulka," Smith announced to his secretary, "Mr. Howard will be in charge of Folcroft while I am away. I am giving him use of my office. Please extend him any assistance he might require."

"Of course, Dr. Smith," Eileen Mikulka said.

Smith turned. "That should be everything. Good luck, Mark. I'll be in touch."

With that the old man walked briskly from the room.

Mrs. Mikulka offered Howard a confused smile before returning to her work.

He looked at the open hallway door for a long moment. Everything had happened so fast. Remo and Chiun gone. Dr. Smith now leaving on a mission from which, by the sounds of it, he didn't expect to return. Mark was certain there were things he should have asked, advice he should have sought.

Mark turned around woodenly. The CURE director's office door closed with a muted click.

21

"Begone!" the Master of Sinanju commanded. He stomped his sandaled foot on the hard-packed road.

The four monkeys that had been following him scurried off into the underbrush, chattering angrily. No sooner had they vanished than their heads emerged from the foliage. Once Chiun, Remo and Amanda passed by, they came cautiously back out of hiding, trailing the old Korean once more as he walked down the narrow road.

"Why are these creatures following you?" Chiun demanded. He stomped again, sending the monkeys scattering. They screeched at him from the bushes.

"Me?" Remo asked. "You're the one they're following."

"Nonsense," Chiun sniffed. "What would they want with me? They are your relatives."

"Actually, they do seem kind of interested in just you, Chiun," Amanda pointed out. She had changed into a pair of khaki shorts and matching blouse. Her last remaining suitcase was slung over her shoulder.

"Do not be ridiculous," Chiun said. "Obviously,

they think Remo to be a long-lost brother and they wish to compare banana recipes with him.''

With the toe of a sandal he launched a pebble from the road. It struck the nearest monkey in the rump, and the animal went shrieking for the underbrush.

The remaining three monkeys were examining the last stomping imprint Chiun had made in the dried mud. After sniffing around it for a moment, they seemed to lose interest in the old Korean. The animals scurried back into the thick jungle brush.

''That's odd,'' Amanda said as the last monkey disappeared into the bushes.

''They must have realized Remo is too big to be one of them,'' Chiun concluded. ''He is more closely related to the orangutan or gorilla.''

''I'm more closely related to you than you want to admit half the time,'' Remo growled. ''So can we can the 'Remo is a monkey' wisecracks?''

As he walked, Chiun stroked his thread of beard. ''Yes, it is true there is some good blood on your father's side. This, at least, has mitigated my difficulty in explaining you in the Sacred Scrolls. But my larger dilemma remains.''

''Sorry,'' Remo said sarcastically, ''but I just can't seem to work up any sympathy for your big dilemma. But you wanna keep harping on this monkey stuff, go ahead. Just remember, I'm the one getting a crack at those scrolls after you. Here's a word future generations of Masters better get used to. White, white, white, white, white.''

Chiun's face darkened. ''You are a wicked son to

put your elderly father in this predicament, Remo Williams.''

"And I'm white. White, white, white, white, white, white, white, white, white.''

"It would kill you to be nice to me just once, wouldn't it?'' Chiun accused.

Remo considered for a moment. "White, white, white,'' he said.

The Master of Sinanju threw up his hands and let forth a stream of angry Korean.

Amanda stayed behind them while they walked. It was in this way—with Chiun complaining loudly in Korean and Remo repeating "white" over and over in English—that they made their to the Macapa waterfront. By the time they reached the shore, the Master of Sinanju had fallen into a sullen silence.

Remo asked around, finally finding the dock where Hubert St. Clair's party had departed that morning. According to the man who had rented them three boats, the group was carting dozens of burlap sacks along with a great many other supplies.

"So what do you think?'' Remo asked, turning to the others. "You want to try flying ahead? There might be an airport around that valley somewhere.''

"I doubt it,'' Amanda said. "There's pretty thick jungle in that region. And we're not sure exactly if that's where Hubert's going. I think our best bet would be to rent a boat and follow him. It sounds like his boats are loaded down, so we should be able to overtake him.''

"What do you think, Little Father?'' Remo asked.

"She is correct," the old Korean said glumly. "And I am not talking to you."

The man who had rented boats to St. Clair had one vessel left. Remo paid for it with his Remo Barkman MasterCard, and within twenty minutes they were chugging up the Amazon.

Exploring the Amazon wasn't the lonely experience it had been a hundred years before. Fishermen and tourists clogged the river in numbers greater than Remo expected. Their young pilot, who they were told was named Chim'bor, steered expertly through the heavy river traffic.

The youth was small and wiry, with gnarled hair and a long dirty T-shirt that nearly covered his threadbare shorts. He seemed preoccupied as the boat putted along. He muttered to himself as he stood behind the wheel in the cabin.

"What's wrong with you?" Remo asked the kid.

The boy responded in a language Remo didn't understand.

"Chiun?" Remo asked.

The old man let out an impatient hiss. "He fears something he calls the sky forest," Chiun replied. "Although his Portuguese is atrocious."

Amanda felt her stomach knot. "Sky forest?" she asked. She shook her head almost as soon as the thought formed. "No," she said firmly. "No, it couldn't be. We were too careful. Hubert couldn't have."

"Couldn't, wouldn't, shouldn't," Remo said.

"None of those seem to apply to this guy. Wake me if there's a fire."

He settled back to the deck in the shade of the cabin, tucking his hands behind his head.

Amanda glanced from Remo's slumbering form to the shore.

A group of children played and laughed at the water's edge. Above them towered trees of green. For a moment she pictured the trees in blue. In her mind's eye, the children became bleached skeletons on a dead, polluted shore.

The future she had helped create. With a shudder she sat on the deck near Remo. Although exhausted from the events of the past few days, she doubted she could relax enough to ever fall asleep again.

FATIGUE EVENTUALLY overtook Amanda. When she slept, she dreamed of children gasping for breath, old women wheezing on beds of blue leaves and of fire raining down from a sunless sky.

In her dream a hand was pressed over her mouth, blocking her breath. Only when she opened her eyes and saw Remo's face close to hers did she realize she wasn't dreaming.

Night had fallen on the Amazon.

"Shh," Remo whispered as he took his hand away. "Stay down. We've got company."

She saw Chiun standing at the port side of the boat. In the midnight darkness, Remo slid over to join him, kicking off his shoes as he went. Without a sound the two men slipped over the side.

Taking care to stay low, Amanda crawled to the railing. Sneaking a peek, she saw lights from two very near boats.

An instant after her head rose into view, she heard the loud clap of single gunshot. The window in the cabin behind her shattered. Chim'bor had apparently been asleep inside. From his angry yelling, Amanda assumed he wasn't hit.

When the gun fired she had dropped to her belly, plastering herself to the deck.

This wasn't like it had been the other times she had been attacked these past few days. There was fear now, to be sure, but not terror. Her worries were larger than herself.

Lying on that dirty deck on a rented Brazilian scow, Amanda Lifton prayed that Remo and Chiun would be safe. Not for her sake, but for the sake of the entire world.

DR. MYRON PHELPS TRIED to adjust the night scope of the sniper rifle, but his pinkie was stuck.

"Ow, ow, ow. Blood blister, blood blister," Myron said as he wrenched the digit free.

Whatever he'd done to the gun loosened the scope. It was wobbling on the stock as he brought it back to his eye. He tried balancing the gun and its wobbly scope while simultaneously sticking his wounded finger in his mouth.

"Did you get them?" Dr. Archie Lancer whispered.

Archie and seven other men hunched behind Myron on one of the boats rented by the Congress of Concerned Scientists. Dressed in their familiar Sage Carlin uniforms, they were all peering into the night at the nearby boat.

"No," Myron snarled as he sucked his injured pinkie. "They moved."

"Are you sure?" one of the seven scientists hovering alongside Archie asked. "Maybe you're not using it right."

"It's a gun, not a particle accelerator," Myron snarled. "You point and pull the trigger."

He demonstrated. This time he was pretty sure he missed the boat altogether. He also managed to get his index finger stuck in that little hole dealie the trigger went in.

"Ouch it all to heck," Dr. Myron Phelps complained.

He didn't know why they had to do this anyway. Hubert was supposed to have a man for this sort of thing. This wasn't the proper job of the CCS board. But Dr. Lifton and her bodyguards were apparently proving difficult to remove, even for Hubert's supposedly perfect assassin.

Myron could almost see why. A minute ago he had had the two men dead to rights as they stood on the deck of the boat. He had even taken a bead on the old one's chest. But then the two of them had vanished.

It wasn't possible that they'd gone in the water. Only a fool would do that, what with all the piranhas in the area. No, they were still on the boat somewhere. Hiding.

He'd worry about them later. Right now he was tracking Amanda Lifton.

He had seen her briefly, peeking out over the railing. Outlined in ghostly green, thanks to his special night scope.

Getting her would be sweet revenge. Not only was she out to stop the CCS from bringing about the death and rebirth of the current Earth, but the stuck-up little socialite bitch had refused to go out with him last Valentine's Day.

He tracked her from her last known location, carefully scouring the deckline at the base of the solid railing.

He found her. A bright green glow shining out through a gap at the rail's base.

Myron pulled his pinkie from his mouth. He aimed the gun very carefully at the warm green glow.

"Washing your hair, my foot," Myron muttered as his finger squeezed the trigger.

Instead of the satisfying crack of the rifle followed by the even more satisfying pop of Amanda Lifton's snooty head, Dr. Myron Phelps saw a sudden flash of movement very close by. And in the instant before his finger completed its violent act, something appeared before him.

Of course that was impossible. Being a man of science, Myron knew that matter didn't just appear from nothingness. But there it was, as big as life. In the shape of a man. More specifically, in the shape of the old Asian man Myron had failed to shoot not one minute ago.

And then the man who shouldn't have appeared in the first place because it defied the laws of physics for him to do so was pulling the gun out of Myron's hands and planting the barrel deep into Myron's disbelieving brain.

Myron Phelps fell to the deck, the barrel of his rifle sticking out of his head like a unicorn's horn.

Behind his falling body, the rest of the CCS group was blinking in unison. The men didn't seem to know which was more shocking, the suddenly dead scientist lying on the deck or the two terrifying men who had appeared impossibly before them as if they'd just beamed down from a Borg cube.

As Remo and Chiun approached, the men cowered together in a corner of the deck.

Remo passed his finger over the terrified group. "Eenie, meenie, miney...you." He pointed at Archie Lancer. "Okay, Poindexter, where are the seeds?"

Archie looked down at Myron. Swallowing, he puffed out his chest bravely.

"I—I won't tell," he said, gulping.

"Fine," Remo said.

Grabbing Archie by a bell-bottomed ankle, Remo upended him and brought him to the edge of the deck.

"Feed the fishies," he said, dunking Archie into the water as far as his chest.

The water stirred from below the surface.

When the piranhas closed in, there was a great churning and frothing. The half-submerged CCS member waved his arms frantically. Then not so frantically. And then not at all. When Archie's arms flopped into the water, Remo dumped the rest of the body into the river.

"Okay, who's in favor of talking now?" Remo asked.

Seven hands shot in the air. The men looked like corduroy-clad Nazis.

"Hubert took them," one scientist offered.

"They're not on board these tubs?" Remo asked.

A second boat was anchored behind the first. It bobbed on the waves. Remo sensed only two heartbeats on board. He assumed they belonged to the Brazilian pilots.

"We started out with three boats. Hubert had us load all the seeds onto one a few hours ago. It continued on without us while we waited here to stop you."

"Swell," Remo groused.

"If the vessel is loaded down, it will not be able to travel fast," the Master of Sinanju pointed out. "If we hasten, we should be able to overtake it."

"I suppose that's some kind of good news," Remo grumbled. He turned his attention back to the CCS scientists. "You've got a lot of stuff here," he said, waving to the piles of provisions stacked all around the overloaded boat. "I'm guessing you've got a plan that doesn't involve suffocating along with the rest of us."

The men glanced at one another.

"We have made, um, arrangements," one volunteered. "It will be necessary for those who understand what's going on to record the planetary ecological changes for whatever agrarian civilizations the new Earth gives rise to. That way they won't make the same environmental mistakes we did." His face grew hopeful. "You're welcome to join us. You could keep us safe if the hordes of dying humans figure out where we are."

"No, thanks," Remo said. "Don't like the dress code. Is St. Clair planting the seeds in that valley?"

"No," a scientist said. "The valley is where we're going to record the last days of the first Earth."

"So where's he planning on planting them?"

"Around," the man said with a timid shrug. "Here. Anywhere. They've been engineered to take root everywhere."

Remo could tell the man was telling the truth. To make matters worse, he was talking about planetary mass extinction without a hint of remorse.

Remo was turning to the Master of Sinanju when he sensed movement in the water. Glancing over, he saw something big and black sliding along the side of the boat.

The animal was so large, the craft rolled to one side as it passed. Remo saw a pair of bright yellow eyes peering over the surface of the water as the creature slipped by.

"What the hell's that?" Remo asked.

The nervous scientists leaned forward. The boat's wan deck lights gave some illumination to the water.

"I think it's a caiman," one scientist said with a

gulp. "They're related to the alligator. They're nearly extinct. It's unusual to find one this far north."

"No kidding?" Remo asked coldly. "Big trip like that, it must be hungry."

Grabbing two clumps of corduroy, he tossed a pair of scientists out in front of the gliding black shape. There was a scream as a pair of jaws yawned wide then snapped shut. A great black tail lashed the air, splashing water across the deck of the rocking boat.

Even as the caiman was turning its attention on the second scientist, Remo was using a hand slash to sever the line between the two boats. The men from the boat-rental agency weren't to blame for the sins of the CCS.

"Let's go, Little Father," he said.

Once they'd slipped over the side, he sent a hard heel into the hull of the boat. The wood and fiberglass cracked, and the boat began to take on water.

By the time they reached their own boat, the lights of the CCS boat were disappearing below the dark water. Screams pierced the night.

When she saw them climbing back aboard, Amanda Lifton's face collapsed in great relief.

"You're both safe," she exhaled, climbing to her feet.

To Remo it almost seemed as if she were legitimately concerned for their well-being. He chalked it up to shock, assuming it would pass the minute she found the fresh bullet hole in the side of her last pink suitcase.

"St. Clair's moved the seeds to one boat," Remo

said. "If we pick up the pace, we should be able to catch up."

Leaving Amanda on the deck, he and the Master of Sinanju headed into the cabin to consult with Chim'bor.

Alone, Amanda gripped the railing. She looked up at the sky, tears of fear and relief in her eyes.

"Thank God," she muttered to the heavens. "Thank God."

22

Remo felt the eyes watching him from out of the darkness. This time he was determined to ignore it. Folding his arms tight, he rolled over onto his side. The eyes watched his back as he lay on the boat's deck.

The Master of Sinanju was sound asleep in the front of the boat. Every once in a while, the godawful honk of the old man's snoring would slice the humid night air.

The distant jungle on either side of the river teemed with life. Animals screeched and howled at the crescent moon. Here and there were lights from small villages. Chim'bor was at the helm. Half-dozing, the native was unmindful of anything beyond wheel and current.

The eyes stared at Remo for nearly twenty minutes. Finally, a figure of shadow crawled across the deck on all fours. When the hand reached out for Remo's shoulder, he rolled flat on his back.

"What?" he demanded of Amanda Lifton.

Amanda seemed startled. "Oh, you're awake."

"Why wouldn't I be? You're the loudest starer I've

ever met. What, do you need me fluff the deck or something?''

She didn't respond as he'd come to expect. As she knelt on the deck, she wore a different expression than he'd seen on her before. As if she'd made some important decision.

Amanda studied the blackness of the night.

''Remo, I don't matter,'' she announced.

''Oh, brother,'' Remo said, his head clunking back to the deck. ''Is this some sort of life crisis because someone ripped the arms off that stuffed panda of yours back home?''

''No,'' she insisted.

''Good, because I didn't do it. And besides, it was an accident.''

She grew angry. But not in the spoiled, pouty, verge-of-tears way that was normal for her.

''None of that nonsense matters,'' Amanda insisted seriously. ''It doesn't and *I* don't. Remo, you've got to promise me something. If it comes to a point where you have a choice between saving me or stopping Dr. St. Clair, please forget about me.''

Remo frowned. ''What's with the attitude transplant?''

''Simple,'' she said. ''I've finally come to realize that there's something bigger than me out there.''

''You're kind of old to be just figuring that out now, aren't you?'' Remo asked.

''Listen to me,'' she insisted harshly. ''Daddy sent you to protect me, right? Well, you're through. I'm firing you. I don't want your protection anymore.''

"Maybe you should have thought of that back when I told you to stay at the hotel."

"No," she insisted. "I had to come. If I can offer any help, I will. I'm responsible for all this. But you've been putting yourself in danger to protect me. No more. You're through doing that. That's an order."

"I don't get it," Remo said. "I thought you got off on bossing people around."

"I do. I mean I did. I mean—"

She stopped to collect her thoughts. When she looked down at him, her eyes were clear and deadly serious.

"I've helped to unleash a monster on the world, Remo," Amanda insisted. "And as far as I can tell, you and Chiun are the only two people who might be able to stop it."

Across the deck, the tone of Chiun's snoring changed. It grew slightly softer. Remo noted the difference.

"You've got to make sure every last one of those seeds is destroyed," she continued. "You can't let him plant them in that valley or anywhere else. They'll spread like weeds. You can't be weighed down with worrying about me. Not when the whole world is at stake."

"Someone's always saying it's the end of the world," Remo said. "Someday it'll be the real thing. Tomorrow, a million years from tomorrow. Somebody will have to be there to see it. Whoop-de-do if it's us."

Somewhere in the distance he heard the sound of a helicopter rattling over the jungle.

"Remo, the *whole world*. Everything. *Gone*." She shook her head. "You can't be so blasé."

The helicopter noise melted into the other night sounds. Remo rolled his gaze to Amanda.

"My whole world is that little pain in the neck making a racket up there," he said. With his chin he pointed to the front of the boat where, unseen, the Master of Sinanju continued his incessant snoring.

"You don't act like he means that much to you," Amanda said. "The two of you seem to fight a lot."

"That's because he's irritating as hell," Remo said.

The snoring stopped.

Remo knew it. The old coot was listening.

"And he's a nasty-tempered, racist old nuisance," he added.

He pitched his voice low so that only Chiun could hear. "Mind your own business," he whispered.

"In that case, stop shouting," came the disembodied reply, so soft that Amanda failed to hear it. "And if you try coupling with that female, listen for the splash, for I will be hurling myself overboard."

The snoring resumed.

"The piranhas will spit you out, you bag of bones," Remo muttered.

"What?" Amanda asked.

He hadn't realized he'd spoken aloud. "Nothing," he said.

Amanda didn't seem to care. She was staring across the river. The nearer shoreline was a smear of black.

"I guess you've got a different way of showing your affection," she said, her voice faraway. "In my family it was a big breakthrough in communication if Mother and Daddy abused the butler together." She sat next to him on the deck, hugging her knees to her chin.

For the first time Remo wasn't really bothered by her presence.

"I guess," Remo admitted with a heavy sigh. "Actually, for a pint-sized pest, he casts a big shadow."

"I don't have that with my family," Amanda said. "I was raised one way. The Lifton way. I think it blinded me to anything beyond the end of my nose." She shook her head bitterly. "I should have seen that Hubert was up to something with those trees."

She had grown more angry with herself as she talked. Lying on his back, Remo looked up at her. She had pulled her knees tighter to her chin. Vacant eyes stared at the night.

Seeing the look of worry and regret on her beautiful face, Remo felt an old stirring.

Reaching out with his left hand, he tapped the inside of Amanda's left wrist. She sucked in a little gasp of air.

It was the first of the twenty-seven steps designed to bring a woman to sexual ecstasy. He hadn't used it in a while, and he was afraid he might be a little rusty. He needn't have worried. As he continued tapping in rhythm to her quickening heartbeat, Amanda let out a contented purr.

The sound beat all to hell her usual blubbering. Or

the way she was always prattling on about her father. In fact, with her mouth shut, Remo was finally noticing just how attractive Amanda Lifton was.

He switched to her right wrist, and she arched her back in delight.

What the hell, Remo thought. It had been a long time. Besides, there was the romantic backdrop of the warm Brazilian night, the soothing rush of water and a tapestry of a million stars flickering overhead. Not to mention the impending Apocalypse.

By the time he'd worked his way to step four, she had rolled over to him. One breast pressed against his shoulder.

She smelled good.

By step six she was wriggling out of her khaki shorts and pink panties. Shaking fingers undid her blouse. Massive firm twin mounds exploded from the fabric.

For a moment the snoring stopped across the deck. There came a snort of disapproval. With a honk the snoring resumed.

Amanda had been lowering herself to Remo. Quivering in her desire, she hesitated at the sound.

"Do you think we should?" she whispered huskily.

Remo smiled up at her. "Hey, you rather the world end with a whimper or a bang?"

He pulled her down to him.

"I AM NOT ANGRY at you, Remo."

This did the Master of Sinanju announce at daybreak. He stood at the front of the boat. Remo had just come up to join him, leaving Amanda sleeping back behind the cabin.

Day broke bright and hot around the wizened form of the old Korean. Hands clasped behind his back, he surveyed the awakening Amazon.

"Great," Remo said. "Good. That makes two of us, 'cause I'm not angry at you, either. You see a Dunkin' Donuts anywhere?"

Chiun's brow lowered and he turned his attention from the jungle. "As usual you are babbling," he said. "I said that I was not angry at you."

"And I said right back at you," Remo said. "I think it's more humid than yesterday."

He breathed deep. The Amazon smelled muddy, but it was a clean kind of muddy. The current had grown stronger in the early hours before dawn. The boat weaved in long, lazy arcs to avoid half-submerged rocks.

"I am not angry at you for several reasons," Chiun persisted. "Would you like me to list them?"

"Not really."

It was as if he didn't hear. "First, I am not angry at you for whatever disgusting things you did last night. Although if there is a baby, it is your responsibility. You will not take advantage of me like other grandparents."

Remo sighed. Chiun had a knack for taking all the fun out of fun. "Next," he said.

"The second reason I am not angry at you is for calling me racist. Although I should be angry at you for this, Remo, I am not."

"Fine," Remo said. "And since you shouldn't have been listening in the first place, I'll be magnanimous and not be ticked at you for eavesdropping and voyeurism."

Chiun raised an instructive finger. "This is not about me," he insisted. "This is about you and the reasons that I am not angry with you, even though I clearly am justified in being so. Do you want to know the third reason?"

"No."

"You are white," Chiun said. He held up a staying hand, warding off any argument. "Yes, there is a speck of Koreanness in you, for which we should all be eternally grateful. Yet you are white in appearance, in attitude and in your barnyard habits. I have decided, Remo, that I can no longer hold this against you. You are what you are and it was wrong for me to conceal the truth, lo these many years. Once we have completed this task for Emperor Smith, I will sit down and dutifully record the truth of your heritage in the Sinanju histories. Let the accusations of fraud fall where they may."

Remo saw the look of sad resolve on his teacher's face. Even though he didn't agree with all the wringing of hands over race that had been going on, he could see that the decision had been a difficult one for Chiun to make.

"What brought this on?" Remo asked.

"It was becoming clear that there was no other alternative," Chiun said. "I know you would not keep silent. I will just set it to paper with no attempt to make it anything other than crystal clear."

"Thanks. I think."

"I am, however, nearly angry about one thing. That you would refer to the only one who ever bestowed anything of value upon you as a pint-sized pest. *Pest* I could live with. It is the diminutive *pint-sized* that I would find offensive. That is, if I were angry at you. Which I almost am but am not."

"If your ears are so good, you also heard me say you matter a lot to me," Remo said.

Chiun shook his aged head. "That, I didn't hear," he admitted. "This boatman you hired snores so loudly all the words were not clear."

Remo didn't mention that there was only one person on board who snored at all, and it wasn't Chim'bor.

"You got a pretty good list there, Little Father," Remo said. "In the old days you could have kept all four plates spinning for a month. Any particular reason why you're letting me off the hook?"

The old man directed his gaze far ahead. For a lingering moment he was looking beyond the river, beyond the jungle. His hazel eyes saw a world far away.

"Because winter has arrived for me," the old man said softly. "Soon it will no longer be my time." He sensed the tension that suddenly gripped his pupil. "You don't see it now, Remo," Chiun said, "because you are in the summer of your own life, with years of promise stretching out before you. But with age comes acceptance. I forgive you all these sins against me now because I do not want death to forever rob me of the chance.''

In spite of the heat, Remo felt his blood grow cold.

"Little Father, you're dying like the sun is dying," he grumbled, clearly uncomfortable with this topic of conversation. "A hundred years from now, you'll both still be here, so knock it off.''

He didn't realize how angry his own face had grown as he stared at the water.

"Perhaps," Chiun admitted. "If you never fulfill the tradition of Master Nik, you cannot assume the title of Reigning Master. In that case I would be forced to stay on, with you as my perpetual apprentice. At that point my shame would be so great I would rather live forever than die and face the ridicule of my ancestors.''

"Master Nik can go take a flying leap," Remo grumbled. "So sue me for not finding the one person in six billion who I should do something nice for.''

He continued to stare at the water. Chiun saw the heavy weight that had settled on his pupil's shoulders.

"The sun will someday lose its brightness, Remo," the Master of Sinanju said quietly. He didn't pull his eyes from the river. "It is the nature of all things.''

Remo said nothing. The last thing he wanted to think about was the Master of Sinanju's mortality.

Together they watched the rushing waves break white against the prow of the boat.

THE AMAZON WIDENED to a basin where the Tapajos River broke south. By noon the small charter boat was steering into the basin. The small-boat traffic grew thick. They wound their way between the other boats.

The area was as big as a lake. Several ocean liners were docked at both shores. Tourists in loud clothes scoured kiosks in open-air markets for authentic South American trinkets that had been made in China.

Amanda was awake. She sat in the shade of the cabin, away from the punishing sun.

There were too many other boats heading in every direction for them to cut straight across. It took Chim'bor three hours to break through to the other side. Even when they'd left the basin and returned to the Amazon proper, the distance from shore to shore remained great. The river was still as wide as a lake.

The water was so deep ocean liners could travel as far again as Remo and the others had already come. There was another cruise ship anchored beyond the Tapajos–Amazon basin. Remo noted much activity on the deck. People were streaming from shore and up the gangplank. Several big freighters were anchored all around.

The jungle beyond the boats had been clear-cut. One line of trees had been left near shore. Peeking over them was the big domed shell of some kind of outdoor amphitheater.

"What's that?" Remo asked.

Chiun crinkled his nose in displeasure. "I do not know," he said.

Amanda stepped out of the cabin. She shaded her eyes with her hand. "It must be the stadium they built for the Pan Brazil Eco-Fest," she said. "It looks like they cut down a lot of trees to build it."

"If that's where Prick's gonna be singing, I hope they recycled them into earmuffs," Remo said. "Hey, Chim'bor, step on the gas."

In addition to the departing cruise-ship passengers, there were other people hurrying around the docks and shore. Men carried cameras and heavy equipment from one of the freighters. Wires ran everywhere, connected to huge generators that were nestled in gouges of earth where plants once grew.

Remo had grown bored with the activity onshore. "Chiun, let's see that map again," he said.

The Master of Sinanju produced the map from his sleeve. He watched as Remo spread it out on a rusted tool chest.

"We're here, right?" Remo asked.

As the two men looked at the map, Amanda continued to watch the shore. "That's odd," she said all at once. Her face tightened in puzzlement.

"What is?" Remo asked without looking up.

"There's someone on that dock," she said. "I think he's waving to us."

"Does he have a Hair Club for Men suture weave and a crummy singing voice?" Remo asked, hoping for a moment that Prick was preparing to drown himself.

"No," Amanda replied. "He seems pretty agitated. I don't blame him. Who wears a three-piece suit in weather like this? Hello?" she called questioningly as she waved to the stranger on the dock.

Remo had already felt the telltale waves of interest from someone onshore. At Amanda's description, he raised his eyes slowly from the map.

Standing at the end of a distant dock was a familiar gaunt figure.

Harold W. Smith's omnipresent briefcase was at his ankle. He waved at their passing boat with one hand, trying desperately not to be to conspicuous. A pointless exercise, given his choice of attire.

"Remo," Smith mouthed once he had the attention of CURE's enforcement arm. Worry flushed his ashen cheeks.

Smith's presence alone was evidence enough that things had somehow gotten worse. Remo turned to the others.

"Who's for sailing right by and pretending we didn't see him?" he suggested. "C'mon, show of hands."

To his great disappointment, after a quick count his was the only hand raised.

23

"Remo, thank God," Smith breathed as the boat chugged to a stop next to the dock.

The CURE director took the tossed bow line, quickly knotting it into an expert clove hitch which he tied to a rusted cleat at the dock's edge.

"I wasn't certain I'd find you at all," he continued as Remo and the others climbed up to the dock. "I had to make a rough guess at speed and distance based on your likely departure time from Macapa and your mode of transportation. When you didn't pass by ten minutes ago as I had estimated, I began to worry." He offered a crisp nod to the Master of Sinanju. "Master Chiun."

Chiun gave an informal bow. "Emperor Smith."

"Smith?" Amanda asked Remo. "This is your boss?"

"In the monochromatic flesh," Remo replied.

Amanda looked Smith up and down.

"No offense," she said, "but your firm must have a great reputation, because my father certainly didn't hire any of you for your looks."

Remo noted that for the first time she didn't refer to her father as Daddy.

"Er, yes," Smith admitted uncomfortably. "Remo, we need to discuss something alone. Perhaps Dr. Lifton would care to take a tour of the concert site. From what I could see on my way in, it's quite impressive. Master Chiun, could you please look after the doctor?"

"My heart soars to do your bidding, Emperor," the old Korean said. "Come, temptress."

Taking Amanda by the elbow, he led her down the dock to shore.

"How'd you get here, Smitty?" Remo asked when Amanda was out of earshot.

"A military flight straight to Macapa. I rented a helicopter there," Smith answered. "And that is irrelevant. The situation with St. Clair and the CCS has changed."

"Tell me about it," Remo said. "We had a boatload of those clown-suited cowpats attack us last night. I'm still picking corduroy from under my fingernails. We didn't get that big grease stain St. Clair."

Smith's expression grew hopeful. "What of the seeds?"

Remo shook his head. "He transferred them to the last boat. We know where he's going with them, though. Here, take a look."

He ushered Smith down to the boat. Chim'bor was in the back tinkering with the motor. Remo showed the CURE director the map they'd collected from the

CCS jet. It was still spread wide across the tool chest. He had told Smith about it when he called from the hotel back in Macapa.

"X marks the garden spot," Remo said, tapping the encircled region of jungle with his finger.

"Yes," Smith said. "When you called you suspected that he was taking the seeds to that valley for planting, and I concurred. However, that has now changed. This is part of why I came down here."

He quickly went on to tell Remo about the satellite surveillance photographs, as well as the course of action for dealing with the *C. dioxa* situation that had been recommended to the President.

"You think he'd really nuke Brazil?" Remo asked once the CURE director was through.

Smith nodded. "Given what is at stake, if it becomes necessary, yes," he said with unemotional certainty. "When this President makes a decision, he sticks with it, whether it is the politically popular thing to do or not."

"Great," Remo groused. "I must've dodged a hundred nukes from a hundred tinhorn foreign jackalopes since I've come to work for this outfit, and the one that's gonna finally dust me gets dropped by my own team. Well, ain't that just a kick in the keister. When you talk to Mr. Integrity, tell him he just lost my reelection vote."

"That is part of why I was forced to come down," Smith said. "To relay information to the President during the crisis. You know, Remo, things would be easier for all of us if you would just carry a cell phone.''

"Don't like gadgets," Remo said, shaking his head. "They throw off the body's rhythms. And if all you needed was a spear carrier, you should've sent Bonny Prince Mark down instead of coming yourself. What good's the twerp if you can't use him for the scut work?"

Smith hesitated. "Mark is not feeling well," he admitted cautiously. "Given that fact, I thought it best to leave him in charge at Folcroft rather than commit him to the field at such a sensitive time."

Remo noticed the odd undertone in the older man's voice.

"Yeah, he was looking kind of green around the gills last I saw him," Remo said slowly. "Besides, I've seen him at work in the real world before. That twitchy Don Knotts stuff he does is only funny if he winds up dead." His eyes narrowed. "Is there something up with the kid, Smitty?"

Smith shook his head. "I don't think so," he said. "I believe he's feeling some work-related stress, that's all. It is nothing that a few days off can't cure."

Remo arched an eyebrow. "You're giving Junior a vacation? I figured you'd just chain him to the boiler like the rest of the galley slaves in that nuthouse."

"I am as generous with time off as the law requires," Smith said. He changed the subject from Mark Howard. "We should go," he insisted, setting his briefcase to the deck. "If it is as you say, St. Clair's boat is weighed down. At full speed perhaps we can overtake him before he reaches the valley. If that is indeed his ultimate destination.''

"And assuming we don't get zapped by that nutty German who's after us," Remo said. "By the way, I don't think he was behind those guys last night."

"It is likely he was not," Smith said. "His name is Olivier Hahn. According to the information I uncovered, he rarely hires out. He prefers to work alone."

"Olivier?" Remo asked. "That sounds French."

"It is," Smith said. "Although his father was Swiss German, he was raised by his mother, who was Swiss French."

"He stunk German, not French," Remo said, puzzled.

"That I cannot explain," Smith said absently as he looked around for a clean place to sit. He chose a life preserver that was lying on a tackle box. "By the sound of it, he never even met his father. However, I am certain that Hahn is your attacker. He has had a covert relationship with the CCS as far back as the days of Sage Carlin. It has continued under Hubert St. Clair's regime. Now, I must check in with Mark. Please collect Master Chiun and Dr. Lifton."

Smith took his phone from his briefcase.

"Hmm," Remo mused to himself as the CURE director began dialing. "Smelled like a typical knockwurst-breath to me." He shrugged. "Oh, well. I'll be right back."

Leaving Smith to place a call to his assistant, Remo scampered up the ladder to the dock and headed off toward the domed concert hall.

24

"Nothing new to report from here, Dr. Smith."

The old-fashioned blue phone felt clunky in his hand. Everything about the CURE director's office felt strange.

Mark Howard's own office was much smaller than Smith's. He hadn't realized how used he had gotten to the cramped space. He was uncomfortable enough working at his employer's desk. The size of the room merely added to his discomfort.

"I've been trying to locate him via satellite," Howard continued. "But boat traffic is hard to track on the Amazon. It's so heavy it's like a needle in a haystack. The jungle overgrowth doesn't help, either."

"Very well," Smith replied over the scrambled line. "Continue to monitor the situation in Washington and report back to me if there are any changes."

With a beep, Smith was gone.

Mark hung up the special contact phone. When he leaned forward in Smith's chair, the springs squeaked. With a frown, he pressed the office intercom.

"Mrs. Mikulka, could you do me a favor and get someone up here from the custodial staff?"

"Right away, Mr. Howard," Eileen Mikulka replied efficiently.

Releasing the button, Mark pushed the seat back. It squeaked again. He leaned forward. Another squeak.

He was surprised Dr. Smith would let something like that go. Mark had heard the squeak many times over the past year. It was likely Smith didn't even notice it.

He'd do his boss this simple favor. From his first job as a stock boy at a local supermarket to his days as a CIA analyst, Mark Howard's work ethic made him always want to leave things in better shape than he'd found them.

Mark pressed the concealed button beneath the edge of Smith's desk. The buried computer monitor winked out.

His cell phone was tied into the CURE system. It would alert him if the basement mainframes pulled any relevant information on the South American situation.

He had realized something the other day when Smith sent him to the previously unknown attic to retrieve Remo and Chiun. He didn't know Folcroft as well as he thought.

There seemed to be a lull now. Time to complete the tour he apparently hadn't finished when he first came aboard.

Leaving the computer behind, he stepped out of the office. Mrs. Mikulka glanced up from her desk.

"A custodian is on his way up, Mr. Howard," she offered helpfully.

"Thanks, Mrs. M.," Mark said. "There's a squeak in Dr. Smith's chair. See if they can find it and kill it."

Mrs. Mikulka returned his smile. Mr. Howard was always so nice. Dr. Smith was a good boss and a fine man, mind you, but Mr. Howard was just, well, different. There was a lightness to his attitude that was unusual for stodgy old Folcroft. He was like a breath of fresh air.

"Yes, sir," she said. "Are you going out?"

"No," Howard said. "I'm just going to take a look around the building. I'll be right back."

He was heading for the door when he felt something brush the backs of his hands. It was like needles of prickly cold water. When he looked down, he stopped dead in his tracks.

There were red specks all over his hands. The blood from his dream. Splashed up from the bay with the dead body.

But that was impossible. Stunned, he drew his fingertips across it. It left a smeared trail of red.

He had to have made some kind of noise, because Mrs. Mikulka was saying something to him. She seemed concerned.

"I'm sorry, what?" he asked, blinking amazement.

"I asked if there was something wrong, Mr. Howard," the woman asked worriedly.

He rubbed his hands. They were warm again. When he glanced down he found them dry and clean.

"No," he said, clearing his throat. "No, nothing's wrong. I'll be back in a little while."

Staring at his own hands as if he were seeing them for the first time, Mark Howard stepped woodenly from the office.

25

The Pan Brazil Eco-Fest was a joint venture sponsored by the Brazilian government and an American soft-drink company. To make room for stages, seating and parking areas, more than twenty acres of pristine jungle had been scythed, hacked, chopped, chainsawed, chipped and burned into oblivion.

Asphalt roads were built on tons of dumped sand and gravel. Amazon tributaries were dammed, with resultant flooding that devastated the ecology of a region thirty miles above the concert site.

An outdoor shell, designed after the Hollywood Bowl, was built into the soft embankment of the Amazon. The plan was to use the second-longest river in the world as backdrop to the eco-conscious musical acts that would grace the stage. But the embankment proved too soft.

The first bowl had tipped out of the mud into the river. It floated downstream, where it jammed into the mouth of a small stream. When the water backed up, the river overflowed its southern bank, flooding miles of jungle. Fifty thousand old-growth trees gave their lives for the cause.

The new stage was to be built back from the river's bank, secured by steel rods in bedrock. The first day of drilling, crews struck an underground river. It erupted into the concert area, washing most of the native workmen, as well as all of the seats up to the mezzanine out into the Amazon.

Fortunately for the concert's organizers, by the time all of the imported construction workers, masons, electricians, plumbers and carpenters had come down with malaria, nearly everything had finally been put in order. As Remo entered the concert site, he passed dozens of ill workmen who were shivering and sweating under blankets while glueing up Loco-Cola posters and hanging officially licensed Prick merchandise.

Remo caught up with Chiun and Amanda near the stage.

Chiun was a few yards away from Amanda. Although there wasn't a musical performer to be seen, the old Korean had found something far more entertaining. On the stage a malaria-ravaged workman was chasing a monkey with a broom. He tried to hit the creature, but his broom got tangled in his blanket. He tripped and fell and the monkey bounded away.

Away from the Master of Sinanju, Amanda was talking to a haggard young man in a green suit. His shirt was open at the neck, and his pale skin was covered in a blotchy red rash. He sat in a corner seat in the front row of the concert site. Remo noted as he approached that it was the only occupied seat in the entire empty stadium.

Beside the man, a high fence acted as a security barrier next to the stage. When the performers were through, they would be ushered down the side behind the fence, this to keep them safe from the crowds. But from what Remo could see, there was no threat of even a small crowd. On his way in, he'd seen part of the parking area. Acres of asphalt were left empty to bake in the hot sun. Other than the concert workers themselves, no one had yet arrived for the Pan Brazil Eco-Fest.

"Oh, Remo," Amanda said when she saw him coming down the aisle. "I was just asking around to see if anyone had seen Hubert. Are you ready to go?"

Remo nodded. "Smitty agrees we can catch him if we hurry," he said. He nodded to the sweating man. "Who's he?"

The young man looked up. His dark-rimmed eyes were filled with dread. "Chuck Parkasian," he groaned. "And I *used* to be in the promotions department of Loco-Cola."

Remo had seen a hundred of the soft-drink company's famous signs plastered everywhere on his way inside.

"You're the guys behind this?" he asked. "Maybe you know better than I do about this stuff, but this doesn't seem like the best spot for a concert."

The promoter had a briefcase balanced on his lap. He hugged it close to his chest. "Where were you eight months ago?" Parkasian moaned.

Remo glanced at Amanda.

"Things aren't going exactly as they'd planned," she whispered.

"Why? When does the concert start?" Remo asked.

Parkasian looked at his watch. "Three hours ago," the promoter lamented.

Remo frowned. "Where is everybody?"

The man clutched his briefcase tight to his belly. It looked as if he was going to vomit on his dress shoes.

"There's no one here yet," Amanda explained, keeping her voice low so as not to upset the promoter any more than he already was. "It doesn't look like anyone's coming."

"What about that cruise ship?" Remo asked. "There were a lot of people running back there."

"That was a singles cruise," the promoter complained. "No one over thirty on board. When they heard Prick was the headliner they left. Some of them hadn't even heard of him. The rest said they'd rather not stay for music their grandparents would listen to."

Remo hummed thoughtfully. "Gives you some small hope for the younger generation," he said. He turned his attention to the Master of Sinanju. "Chiun, we're going."

The old man was standing directly in front of the stage, his attention still drawn to the activity at the back.

Two monkeys were now chattering on the stage. They were trying to scale the side fence while the sickly workman smacked at them with his broom.

Screeching angrily, the animals finally jumped down from the fence.

Hopping from the stage, the monkeys circled through a gap in the fence, disappearing from sight. The workman went after them. A native with a stick ran in after him.

By the sound of it, there were even more monkeys beyond the fence. They shrieked furiously as the native hollered curses at them.

Remo's brow lowered. "Have all the monkeys gone nuts around here?" he asked.

"They were not following me this time," Chiun pointed out.

"I thought they weren't following you last time."

"They were not," the old man sniffed. "And they are following me even less this time than they weren't before."

He turned on his heel and padded up the aisle. Amanda went with him.

Lingering for a moment, Remo leaned around the fence.

He saw the tail and one sagging rotor blade of a helicopter sticking out from behind the rear wall of the stage. The shivering workman had sunk to the ground, clutching his blanket to his chest. A few natives ran around the helicopter, swatting and kicking at a swarm of angry monkeys.

Remo turned to Chuck Parkasian. The promoter was still sitting alone in his seat. Moaning softly, he was rocking back and forth as he clutched his briefcase.

"You wanna fill this place, I'd trade the monkey you've got headlining now and sign up the big brown one," Remo suggested, aiming a thumb over his shoulder.

Leaving the Loco-Cola executive alone in the big, empty stadium, Remo headed up the aisle.

26

By the time he pushed open the door to the stairwell, Mark Howard had largely shaken off the aftereffects of the strange event outside Dr. Smith's office.

He had no doubt now that the blood specks were real. Or, rather, were a projection of something real.

They had to be some new variation on the unique ability Mark possessed. While it made him uncomfortable to think of his special insight as paranormal, it remained an intuitive gift that allowed him to see things that others might miss.

The blood spots on his hand were just a projection of something lurking in his mind. When his mind finally finished toying with him, it would tell him what this was all about. That was the way the Feeling had always worked.

He forced all thoughts of his strange waking dreams from his mind as he headed down the stairs.

Something had suddenly occurred to him as he made his way around Folcroft. When Mark had first come to work there, Dr. Smith mentioned something about showing him the special CURE security wing of the sanitarium. But then Smith got busy and Mark took his own tour. When his employer failed to mention it again, Mark assumed he had already seen the special corridor. He figured it was one of the empty halls on the west side of the building. They never discussed it again.

Mark realized now that he had been mistaken. It had to have slipped Dr. Smith's mind.

He went back and asked Mrs. Mikulka if there was a part of the building where Dr. Smith kept patients with unique care needs. She directed him downstairs.

Mark was two floors down from the executive offices of Folcroft. He pushed open the door at the bottom of the stairs and stepped out into the hall.

He wasn't surprised now that he'd missed it first time around. The hallway that led to the security corridor was at the far end of the main hall. The way it cut around the corner made it easy to miss at first glance. Even as he approached the hall, he had a hard time seeing it until he was practically right on top of it.

The instant Mark turned down the corridor, he stopped dead in his tracks. He felt his heart quicken.

He had seen the hallway before.

The angles weren't twisted. The walls weren't warped. Sun streamed in from barred windows to the left. But it was the same. The hallway of his dreams.

A cold shiver touched the base of his spine.

For a moment he just stood there.

He knew he shouldn't go on. Should wait for Dr. Smith.

He took a step back. But he did not turn.

A year's worth of nightmares...a year's worth of unanswered questions...

The *same hallway*.

Before he knew it, he was taking one step. Then another.

The walls remained solid. Painted in the same drab hospital grays and greens as the rest of the sanitarium.

There was the same window he had seen a hundred times.

Yet not the same. The tree was there. Just beyond the glass. The branches now waving gently in the breeze. No longer grasping witch's claws. The owl that had perched in it for almost a year was gone.

Yes, that was right. It had flown away. Flown away the last time he had been in this corridor.

He reached the door at the end.

It wasn't a patient's door. It was another ordinary fire door, this one with a security panel attached to the wall. But Mark didn't know the code.

Apparently, he didn't have to. His hand was moving before he even knew it, his finger operating on some level he couldn't comprehend. It punched out the six-digit code for him. The tiny red light on the panel winked out and a small green one blinked on.

Mark pulled open the door, stepping woodenly inside.

The corridor continued. An exit sign at the far end. In between the hall was lined on one side with patients' rooms.

Mark continued walking, unmindful of the growing humming inside his own head.

A voice whispered to him. He couldn't understand the words. Through eyes that now seemed trapped between what was real and some fuzzy dreamworld, he walked past the first few rooms.

A comatose male patient was in the first room. A young female in the second. Although the girl's eyes were open, she was staring vacantly at the ceiling. When Mark walked by the open second door, he caught a faint whiff of something that smelled almost like rotten eggs.

He approached the next room on feet of lead.

It was the one in his dream. It had the same wire-mesh window. The door was there. Beyond it lurked the Beast.

But this time the door was open. Not even a simple chain to secure the monster that lurked inside.

He knew that he should turn and run. Yet some compulsion he did not understand forced him to go on.

There was a clear plastic tab on the door. Beneath it had been slipped a rectangle of cardboard. On it, the patient's name was printed in neat block letters. Almost as if it had been typed. Dr. Smith's printing.

Mark read the name. John Doe.

He knew that wasn't right.

In his earliest versions of the dream, he would have felt blind terror at this point. A moment of awful anticipation just before the Beast sprang. But there was no terror this time. No night sweats or pounding heart. In fact, as he rounded into the room, any small fear that he had felt bled away.

There was a patient lying in the bed. Mark recognized him from his last version of the recurring dream. Not a beast at all. Just a pale, blond-haired man. Lying alone and forgotten in a corner basement room in Folcroft.

There was a nurse standing next to the bed tapping air from a needle. When Mark entered, she looked up. She seemed surprised to see the assistant director of the sanitarium.

"Oh," the nurse said. "Hello, Mr. Howard."

Mark didn't answer. Face blank, he crossed over to the bottom of the bed. The patient's chart hung on a clipboard.

Picking up the clipboard, Mark pulled a pen from his breast pocket. He drew a few black strokes through some of the handwritten lines on the chart. Initialing the changes, he hung the chart back up. Without a glance at the puzzled nurse, he headed back out the door.

The nurse followed him with her eyes until he was gone. Putting down the needle, she went to retrieve the chart.

The nurse frowned. Chart in hand, she hurried out into the hallway. Assistant Director Howard was already at the fire doors at the end of the corridor.

"Mr. Howard, do you realize that you've canceled this patient's sedatives?" the nurse called.

At the door, Howard paused. When he looked back at the nurse, his eyes burned bright. If she had known him better, the nurse would have realized that something was a little off. The assistant director's eyes were ordinarily a brownish green. At the moment they were electric blue.

Mark Howard smiled a smile that was not his own. "It's time," he said softly.

And that was all. He pushed through the door and was gone.

The confused nurse didn't quite know what to make of all this. But Mr. Howard was in charge. He had to have consulted with Dr. Smith about the change. So that was it. With a stroke of a pen they had canceled the standing order of sedatives that had been administered to this particular patient for the past ten years. And for so long now Dr. Smith had been adamant that the injections be administered at precise intervals without fail. Probably some new type of experimental treatment.

Shaking her head in confusion, the Folcroft nurse went back to retrieve her unused syringe.

27

The straps from the harness bit into his shoulders. Hubert St. Clair stuck his thumbs beneath them, trying to hike them up into a more comfortable position while shrugging the tanks up higher on his back. Almost immediately, they began sliding back down to settle in the lumbar curve of his lower back.

He hated the tanks. To a man with his fear of technology, it was like strapping canisters of poison to his body. But, thank heavens, this was one of the last times.

St. Clair grunted at the heavy burden. The sound was muffled by the rubber mouthpiece clamped between his teeth.

It would be over soon. He'd never have to worry about the tanks or anything like them again.

He was at home in the middle of his *C. dioxa* forest. Except for his breathing, all was silent.

The beautiful blue trees that stretched up to the sky were big and full and tightly packed, not like the carefully spaced rows of trees back at the CCS greenhouse in Geneva. These woods were an oxygen vacuum.

Even the leaves that had fallen to the ground didn't rot.

St. Clair looked up at the towering *C. dioxas*. Gentle breezes tugged the uppermost branches. And as the leaves danced in the soft wind, the oxygen drained away.

It was amazing. In the wild they'd grown much faster than any of the ones back in Switzerland.

This was the future. A future of quiet contemplation, away from the menace of technology that had been choking the globe in its mechanical claws. Of course, Hubert St. Clair was one of the only living things on the planet that would live to see Earth's simpler future.

Without even realizing it, St. Clair smiled. Pure oxygen hissed out around his rubber mouthpiece. Clamping his lips back down around the black rubber, he hurried on.

Stepping into the center of the tangled forest, he came upon the abandoned Quonset huts that had been a part of the early operation. The scientists on the CCS board to whom St. Clair had brought seeds and shoots had manned a small lab at the center of the forest until the trees grew too large.

St. Clair passed empty huts, benches and tables. He ducked into the woods just beyond the old work site.

In a small clearing was a circular glass dome that bubbled up from the earth. Standing next to it was an upright enclosed box that looked like an extra large telephone booth.

With the tip of one shaking work glove, Hubert St.

Clair pressed a security code into the pad on the side of the box. A door hissed open with chillingly mechanical precision, and St. Clair stepped inside. When the door closed, he closed his eyes and held his breath.

An awful few seconds passed while fresh air hissed into the closed chamber through floor vents. Once the airtight chamber was filled, an inner door slid open, revealing a set of curving stairs.

St. Clair was tearing the oxygen tanks from his back and tugging the mouthpiece from between his lips even as he was descending the stairs. He dumped them onto a sofa.

The living room where the CCS elite would live out their days in peaceful contemplation was big and round. The dome that had been part of the forest floor outside became the ceiling inside. When Hubert looked up, he saw a powder-blue sky framed all around with *C. dioxas.*

The subterranean chamber was a marvel. Both vast and functional, it had everything that the last men on Earth would need for decades to come. There was a small garden, goats and some cows for milk, sleeping quarters, a kitchen and library. And, best of all, aside from the obvious recurring need to recycle and extract oxygen, there would be virtually no technology employed in the shelter whatsoever.

At the moment there was only one other man from the CCS board in the whole valley. The rest were on the two supply boats. For some reason the men he had ordered to intercept Amanda Lifton and her bodyguards hadn't called in. It was just as well. In the past few days he had used his phone more times than he had in the past two years.

St. Clair had wanted to spend this time alone. But there was someone waiting for him in the living room.

The CCS head was surprised. He had been here several hours already and hadn't seen the man arrive.

Olivier Hahn stood quietly in the door to the hallway that led to the storage rooms. The portly Swiss assassin had a serious look on his wide face.

"They are on their way," Hahn said. "Perhaps you would feel safer somewhere else until I have dealt with them."

St. Clair waved his hand. "I'm snug as an anaerobic bug," he dismissed. "They're not coming."

Hahn shook his head. "There is not a lot known of these men," he said. "But I am certain they will not give up."

"They haven't a choice." St. Clair sighed. "I didn't tell you this before, but I had some of my men set a trap for them on the river last night. They're dead."

Hahn seemed skeptical. "These men of yours. Have you heard from them?"

"Well, no," St. Clair admitted. "But I'm sure they must have succeeded. I mean, they couldn't have failed. There were nine of them. And they had a gun."

Hahn gave the CCS head a very French look of impatience. "Nine men or ninety would not matter.

They are coming. And I alone will be the one to stop them.''

Without another word he turned and walked with certainty back into the long shadows of the storage corridor.

28

They traveled another hundred miles downriver from the Pan Brazil Eco-Fest. Chiun sat in a lotus position at the front of the boat. Remo watched as Smith and Amanda studied the map. At one point the CURE director brought the map into the cabin with him. As soon as their boat pilot caught a glimpse of the circled valley, he began babbling fearfully in a language even the Master of Sinanju didn't understand.

"What did you do to him?" Remo asked Smith as the older man exited the cabin.

Chim'bor was still chattering to himself in fear.

"I suspect he is from the area," Smith said as he neatly refolded the map. His gray face was worried. "It seems he is concerned about what is in the valley."

"I'm a little concerned myself," Remo said. "Shouldn't we have caught up with that seed boat by now?"

Smith nodded. "Several hours ago, according to my calculations. That is, assuming they didn't veer off onto a tributary. It is also possible that they light-ened their load by jettisoning some of the supplies they had with them.''

''Or unloaded some of the seeds,'' Remo pointed out.

Neither man wanted to consider what that might mean.

They sailed on.

The boat left the Amazon an hour later. Using the map as guide, they followed a much narrower river that sliced through the thick jungle.

Chim'bor grew more panicked the farther they traveled. To ward off evil spirits, he made a special magic symbol with his hand that had been brought to the Rsual by white missionaries.

Out of the corner of his eye, Remo caught the native repeating his magic ritual for the eighth time in as many minutes.

''I'd feel a lot better if he'd stop making the sign of the cross,'' Remo grumbled.

The jungle canopy grew dense above their heads. Shafts of sunlight broke through the thick overhang of branches, illuminating steaming water. The mist didn't cool. The river seemed almost stagnant—more a slime-coated swamp.

The heat finally became too much even for Smith. The CURE director stripped off his suit coat and vest, hanging them neatly on a rusted hook at the back of the cabin. Still, he didn't loosen his tie or roll up his sleeves.

''Humidity's pretty high,'' Remo commented.

''The rain forest is a perfect outdoor greenhouse,''

Amanda said tensely. She sat in the front of the boat, periodically swatting flies on her bare legs. Her blouse was soaked through.

Thanks to his Sinanju training, Remo rarely perspired. He was able to regulate his body heat in extreme temperatures. Short of an actual inferno, he and Chiun would be okay. He glanced at the Master of Sinanju.

Chiun stood unmoving in the prow next to Remo. When Remo got a good look at his teacher, he almost couldn't keep his jaw from dropping.

Sweat had broken out across the old man's forehead. Not a lot. Just a thin, glistening sheen. Remo couldn't ever remember seeing the old man perspire.

"Are you okay, Little Father?" Remo asked, his voice stretched tight with concern.

The old man nodded. "I am fine," he insisted.

Remo tuned his hearing to the Master of Sinanju's heartbeat. It sounded fine. Stronger than any man's. His breathing seemed normal, too.

It had to be the result of Chiun's age. At over one hundred years, the jungle temperature was having a greater effect on him than on Remo.

There was no way to escape the heat. Feeling his concern for the world contract once more into the tiny space occupied by the frail ninety-pound figure beside him, Remo returned his attention to the river.

Above their heads, squirrel monkeys darted from tree branch to tree branch, chattering curiously. Weak branches bent low and the animals scurried up to safety. At the tops of the trees, they turned and screeched at the passing boat.

The boat was cutting through a ravine of black rock when they heard a splash behind them. When they looked back, they saw Chim'bor swimming back for shore. Once on land, he stripped off his T-shirt and ran into the jungle. As he disappeared, he was still making the sign of the cross.

"There goes his tip," Remo said.

Smith hurried into the cabin and took the wheel.

The ravine walls grew higher. After a few miles, they split off in either direction, forming the rough contours of the valley.

"This is the edge of the CCS valley," Smith called from the cabin. "There should be some sort of desert up ahead. The experts have not yet determined what it is. Have you any idea, Dr. Lifton?"

"I'm sorry, no," Amanda admitted, distracted. She was squirming where she sat. "This might sound crazy, but does anyone else feel a draft?"

She glanced up at Remo and Chiun. When she saw their shared look of silent concern, Amanda felt an involuntary shiver.

Both Masters of Sinanju were focused on a bend in the river up ahead. A frown had settled deep in the lines of Chiun's wrinkled face.

Looking forward, Remo saw angled sunlight shining out across the water's curving path. That meant a break in the jungle canopy. Ordinarily, it would mean mild relief from the locked-in heat. But as Remo trained his senses directly ahead, he felt something else in addition to the vastness of Smith's desert. Something cold.

"Little Father?" Remo questioned quietly.

Chiun's frown had deepened. "I do not know," the old Korean admitted.

"What is it?" Amanda asked, coming to stand with them.

Remo's voice was steady. "If I'm right, something that definitely shouldn't be here," he said somberly.

They were coming around the curve. A soft breeze pushed downriver, and Amanda felt another unexpected chill.

The river picked up speed around the turn. Smith tried to slow the boat at the bend, cutting the wheel. They were slipping around the turn when the CURE director felt something hard slam the bow. The boat rolled to one side and then righted itself as it continued on.

"What the devil?" Smith complained. "Did we hit a rock?" he called out to the others.

"Um, not exactly, Smitty," Remo called back.

Smith leaned out of the cabin. There were large chunks of some sort of white material floating down alongside the boat.

"Remo, this looks like..."

The CURE director's words died in his parched throat.

The boat finally broke free of the jungle. The high walls of the valley stretched up all around them, casting shadows on the land beneath. The vast plain of the valley floor stretched out to the north, a sheet of smooth white.

Where sunlight struck the plain, it sparkled like scattered diamonds.

Smith cut the engine and dropped the anchor. "Sweet mother of mercy," the CURE director said, stepping lifelessly from the cabin.

Amanda blinked in disbelief. She was looking at a mirage. She *had* to be. But when the vision before her stubbornly refused to disappear, she turned to Remo.

"This can't be," Amanda insisted. "It's—"

"A glacier," Smith supplied, stepping up beside them.

The ice field looked as if it had been transplanted to Brazil from the South Pole. It covered nearly the entire valley floor. Water trickled away in thin blue streams buried beneath the hard-packed white surface, drizzling into the river. As they watched, a chunk of ice broke away, floating off downstream.

"Okay," Remo said evenly. "So we're all seeing the same thing. That means I'm not going crazy. So how the hell did that get here?"

"Snow induction is possible, I suppose," Amanda said slowly. "Even in this climate."

"Amanda," Remo said. "This is Brazil, not Switzerland. It doesn't even get cold here, let alone snow."

"That isn't true," Smith volunteered. His initial amazement was already wearing off. "While in most parts of the country the weather does not change with the seasons, cold waves have appeared on occasion. It is not even unheard-of for it to snow in the southern part of the country.''

The CURE director felt a chill from the breeze blowing across the plain. Tearing his eyes from the ice field, he went to retrieve his jacket.

''You've heard of cloud-seeding?'' Amanda said to Remo. ''It's possible to do it with snow. That's what must have been done here. Orographic clouds are laced with silver iodine. The mountains would hem in the heavy clouds.''

''According to old satellite images, there was a thick cloud cover here for more than a year,'' Smith said as he buttoned up his vest. ''Most likely from burning. The carbon black could have aided in the creation of this.''

''Carbon black?'' Remo asked.

''Soot,'' Amanda explained. ''Science is coming to realize that carbon black from controlled burns in forests or volcanic eruptions is likely more responsible for atmospheric changes than the burning of fossil fuels. There were eruptions back in 1816 that caused such severe weather changes that there were ice and sleet storms in the United States as far south as South Carolina. He's artificially done the same thing here.''

''And there is no shortage of natural precipitation,'' Smith pointed out. ''Dr. St. Clair has created a firn by repetitively seeding the clouds. Possibly in conjunction with the types of snow-making equipment used at ski resorts.''

''With the river as a water source,'' Amanda said.

"Precisely." Smith nodded.

"I see no ferns," the Master of Sinanju said as he peered suspiciously across the ice field. "Nor any other plant."

"Not ferns, Master Chiun," Smith explained. "*Firn*. It's another term for 'glacier.'"

"Ah, yes," the old Korean said, nodding wisely. "Ferns that are not ferns at all. I see." To Remo, he said in Korean, "More white insanity. If they mean glacier, why do they not say glacier? This, Remo, *this* is the race you're so proud of. A race of nonsense jabberers."

"I'm not proud or ashamed, Little Father," Remo said. "I'm just me."

Smith and Amanda were chatting excitedly between themselves, both marveling at the technological ingenuity that would have been required to create such a thing.

"There have been cases recently of Magellanic penguins washing up on beaches near Rio de Janeiro," Smith was saying excitedly.

Amanda picked up his thread. "You don't mean?"

"Exactly," Smith said, nodding.

"What's wrong now?" Remo asked suspiciously.

"Don't you see, Remo?" Smith said. "Scientists were baffled why the Magellanic penguins were washing up on Brazilian shores. They feared cold shifts in ocean currents, since the penguins are ordinarily found near the Antarctic."

"But maybe it was something else," Amanda completed. "Maybe they sensed this inland. Maybe through air currents or some other means."

Remo shook his head. "Three cheers for you and the penguins," he said. "Geez, two seconds with you, Smitty, and you make her as boring as you are. The two of you can write a paper about it when we're done. Assuming you can make paper from those trees that are going to wipe us all out."

"Oh," Smith said. For a moment he'd forgotten about the *C. dioxas*. "Oh, yes. Of course."

There was a dock fifty yards upriver. Another boat similar to their own was moored there. Smith returned to the cabin and drew up the anchor. Starting the engine, he headed for the dock.

As they moved parallel to the shore, Remo kept his eyes trained on a distant spot in the valley. A dirt hill rose from the center of the glacier. It was capped in blue.

Amanda could not yet see the *C. dioxa* forest. She was watching the glacier as they chugged past.

"This fits the pattern," she said. "It's the ice age the CCS predicted."

Remo looked out over the field, stretching for miles. The trunks of dead trees jutted along the edge near the river. The short stretch of jungle they'd passed through on entering the valley was brown and withered for a few dozen yards, the result of its proximity to the glacier.

Remo shrugged. "Ice is ice," he said. "I'll take it over acid rain any day of the week."

Smith pulled up to the dock and the four of them

got out. Trotting over, Remo made a quick inspection of the other boat.

There were five bodies on board. One looked to have been the boat pilot; the others appeared to be natives. They had been shot and stacked in the boat's cabin. There were no supplies on board.

"No seeds," Remo said grimly, returning to the others. "Must have brought them there."

Smith was shading his eyes as he looked inland. Amanda had just seen the man-made hill. Her face held a look bordering on dread. Given the glare off the glacier, she wasn't sure of what she was seeing.

"It can't be," Amanda said, her voice trembling. She pointed to the distant hill. "Can any of you see what's up there?"

"It is a stand of *C. dioxas*," the CURE director said.

Amanda couldn't believe the calm in his voice.

"It can't be," she insisted. "Those are bigger than any of the ones we had growing at the greenhouse. Judging from the size, they'd have to be at least three years old."

"How long until those plants mature enough to develop seeds?" Smith asked.

"If they're part of the earliest generation of trees we engineered? Less than a year."

Smith's face tightened. "Then St. Clair likely has even more seeds at his disposal. With luck they will be contained to this valley."

Amanda was frowning deeply. She seemed about to say something more, but Smith was distracted by the two Masters of Sinanju. Remo and Chiun had gone to the very edge of the dock near the shore. They were both peering intently across the bright surface of the glacier.

"There," Chiun announced imperiously as he aimed a bony finger across the ice field.

Remo nodded agreement. "A bunch more over there," he said.

Smith hustled up to them. "What's wrong?" he asked.

"Take a look at this," Remo said.

With the heel of his loafer, he cracked off a fat chunk of ice from the glacier's edge. Drawing his arm back, he hurled it a quarter of a mile inland. When it struck the surface, the ice exploded.

There was a flash of brilliant yellow-orange. The dock rocked beneath their feet and pebbles of ice splashed the river. Amanda shielded her head from the hail.

"Mines," Remo explained, dusting off his hands. "Looks like the place is loaded with them."

He and Chiun could see the faint outlines of hundreds of the devices buried in the ice. They stretched far inland.

"How did St. Clair get the seeds in?" Amanda asked.

"He knows where they aren't," Remo said. "He might have gone around to the mountains. Could be a clear path around the back of the valley."

"We do not have time to search," Smith said firmly.

"Of course we don't," Remo muttered. He turned to the Master of Sinanju. "We could get in okay. Leave Smitty to watch Amanda."

"Do that," Amanda insisted. "Stopping Hubert is more important than anything."

Chiun had turned his attention from the glacier to the river. There was a small rowboat tied to the dock.

"Given the level of attacks against us, it is not safe to leave them," the old Korean said. "Fortunately, there is another alternative."

Stooping at the edge of the dock, he took hold of the rowboat. Dripping water along the way, he carried it up to the dock, setting it at the edge of the glacier.

"I don't understand," Smith said, brow dropping in confusion.

Remo had gathered what the Master of Sinanju was up to.

"Trust me, Smitty, you're better off not knowing," he said. "And I hope your insurance is paid up."

With an outstretched hand he ushered the CURE director and Amanda Lifton into the old wooden boat.

29

The vice president and the CIA director were waiting anxiously next to the fax machine in the West Wing office of the vice president. Since the start of the crisis, spy satellites over South America had been relaying images to the Central Intelligence Agency on a continuous basis. They in turn were sent to the White House. Every minute a new image would spit out of the vice president's corner fax.

Over the past hour the photos had gotten more disturbing as the human activity around the *C. dioxa* forest increased.

"Something's happening," the CIA director said when the frozen black blur of a helicopter appeared over the blue blob of trees. His voice was tight with concern.

The next fax that rolled off the machine showed a close-up of the helicopter. It had landed near two others. Some sort of metallic arms had been fixed to the underside of the aircraft.

The vice president, who at one time had served as secretary of defense, knew immediately that the old West German Messerschmitt had been tampered with.

The fact that the aircraft had been altered sparked fresh concern.

"We'd better show him these," he said.

He and the CIA director gathered up the photos and hurried down to the Oval Office. The President was there with a few of his national security advisers.

As the President and his advisers gathered around, the vice president and CIA head lined the satellite photographs up in a neat row on the coffee table. The vice president brought their attention to the helicopter in particular.

"There has been an increase in activity around the valley," the vice president explained. "The boat carrying the *C. dioxa* seeds arrived not long ago."

He pointed to a photo. Little blurs of men dragged bundles across the white desert that rimmed the valley.

"Have you figured out what that is yet?" the President asked, indicating the desert region.

The CIA man and the vice president glanced uncomfortably at each other.

"It appears to be ice, sir," the CIA director said.

All eyes in the room looked slowly up at the CIA head. The men weren't sure they had heard right.

"Did you say ice?" the President asked flatly.

"I've had experts looking into the archived satellite photos of that area," the CIA director explained. "There was a dense cloud cover over that valley for almost thirteen months. More than likely man-made from burning the indigenous flora. The surrounding mountains held the smoke in, like smog in L.A. By the looks of it, they've altered the normal climate of that isolated area. Those plants of theirs don't photosynthesize, so they wouldn't have been affected.''

"These people are insane," the President said, more to himself than to the others in the Oval Office.

''All the more reason to assume they're capable of anything," the vice president said. "I hate the thought of it, Mr. President, but it might be time to take decisive action. Before the threat expands to a point where it can't be stopped.''

The President gazed down across the photos. "No," he said quietly.

"I can understand your reservations, sir," the CIA director said. "But it's not like we could get Brazil to do it themselves, even if they had nuclear capability. It has come down to that small valley or the entire world.''

The President chewed the inside of his cheek. It was an old habit he'd been trying to break.

"We have to wait a little longer," America's chief executive insisted.

The NSC chairman cleared his throat. "Mr. President, we've had people researching the genetic alterations that were made to the plants. The projections you were shown are accurate. Those plants will grow like weeds.''

The President looked up. All of the faces in the room were staring expectantly at him.

"Dammit, I can't," he said, shaking his head. "We have...people down there.''

No one else in the Oval Office was aware of any

agents who had been sent to the region. The nation's top national security advisers—the very men who would commit such agents—glanced at one another in confusion.

"What people?" asked the CIA director.

The President seemed reluctant to even discuss the subject. "I can't say," he insisted. "But there are people there that I trust."

"Whoever they are, they are expendable, sir," said the vice president.

The President looked over at his vice president.

During their time campaigning, the two had become good friends. Since assuming office, the older man had become the President's most trusted adviser.

"Believe me," the President said, his voice strong and level, "these men might not be." He held up a hand, staying all arguments. "But in spite of that, I promise all of you that I'll do what I have to when the time comes. Until then, excuse me, gentlemen."

And that brought their meeting to an abrupt end.

He offered the confused men a few encouraging nods as he ushered the group of advisers out the door. The vice president was last to leave. The President caught the older man by the arm, holding him back from the pack.

"You think he's going to use that helicopter to spread the seeds?" the President asked once the rest were gone.

"I believe so, sir," the vice president replied.

The President nodded somberly. "This is just between us," he said, careful to keep his voice low.

"Get the Chairman of the Joint Chiefs of Staff on the phone. I want a plane scrambled and above that area within the hour. Tell him he's authorized to drop whatever's necessary to neutralize those plants. Have him call me for the codes."

The vice president felt a tightening in his chest.

"Yes, Mr. President," he said.

The President saw the wan look that had settled on his vice president's face.

"We're not doing this yet," the chief executive assured the older man. "But we need to be ready for the worst. I want you on top of this. Keep me informed. The minute you see that helicopter taking off, I'll give the order."

The vice president nodded. "Yes, sir," he said. He hesitated a moment. "But can I ask you, sir, why are we waiting? Who exactly is it we have down there?"

The President offered a lopsided smile. It was a smile devoid of mirth. "If I told you who they were, they'd have to kill you," the leader of the free world said, his tone serious. "Now, if you'll excuse me, I have to go figure out what I'm gonna tell those Clymers in the press about why I had to go and blow up half of Brazil."

Shoulders sinking wearily, he shut the Oval Office door on the sickly face of the vice president.

30

They left the river far behind. The rowboat raced across the glistening surface of the glacier.

Cold wind bit Smith's and Amanda's skin and stung their eyes. They barely noticed. They were too busy gripping their seats for dear life.

Chiun sat behind them. He used delicate nudges to keep them from flipping out of the boat with every wild turn.

Remo was standing in the very back of the boat. He was using an oar to propel them forward at breakneck speed. Any time they seemed to be slowing, the tip of the oar would gouge the surface of the ice and they'd be whipping forward once more.

"See, the trick here is pretty simple," Remo instructed. "We go fast enough that we're not so much on the surface as we are above it. Mines don't feel us, mines don't go boom."

Another tap from the oar. Chips of ice scattered in their wake.

Smith's glasses bit back into the bridge of his nose.

The g-forces pulled his thin lips back in a pained smile.

Unseen by Amanda and Smith, between shoving off, Remo was tapping the paddle against the glacier's surface. The vibrations that came back to him gave him a rough sense where the most mines were buried.

Another subtle course alteration. Smith nearly launched from his seat. A weathered hand guided him back to the wooden bench.

"There is something up ahead," the Master of Sinanju observed as he helped the CURE director settle back down.

Remo had noted it, too. There was some sort of dip beyond the end of the ice field. It rimmed the *C. dioxa* hill like a moat.

"I can't see it from here," Remo said from where he stood in the back of the boat. "But judging from all the surveillance equipment, I smell a German rat."

There were no mechanical vibrations coming from the hilltop. All they could see as they approached were the rotor blades of three dormant helicopters drooping at the edge of the forest. The long-range surveillance devices they were sensing had been positioned around the mountaintops that rimmed the valley.

"Why do I get the feeling we're being lured into the spider's web?" Remo grumbled to himself.

Digging his paddle in deep, he propelled them like a wooden bullet toward the base of the hill.

WHEN THE FEAR BEGAN this time, there was no naughty thrill to it.

Olivier Hahn couldn't believe his eyes.

The Swiss assassin was hunched over a single glowing monitor in the bowels of the CCS bunker. It was the only computer St. Clair had allowed in his underground haven.

The storage room was filled with barnyard smells. Around his small computer table, sacks of wheat and rice were piled high. Somewhere in one of the nearer rooms, a goat bleated. Herr Hahn barely heard it. He was busy watching the two Masters of Sinanju as they raced across the glacier.

It shouldn't have been possible. According to his equipment they were passing directly over hundreds of mines. Yet they failed to set a single one off.

This was his last stand. Although he'd had setbacks with these two before, Herr Hahn *knew* to the marrow of his German bones that he would succeed here.

Hubert St. Clair had gone back to the surface. When he saw the boat coming in across the ice, the frightened little technophobe had ordered his pilot to start his helicopter. St. Clair intended to use the special hoppers Herr Hahn had designed to spread his blue seeds beyond the valley. Seeing Amanda Lifton arrive with her two bodyguards and another man, the CCS head was afraid that the valley was no longer safe.

But it *was* safe.

Hahn had designed this entire valley for the Congress of Concerned Scientists. It was his undeniable masterpiece. The engineering and technical skills that had gone into creating the firn, the hill, the *C. dioxa* forest and the subterranean chambers were sheer genius.

Hahn didn't know what Hubert St. Clair's ultimate plans were. Something to do with those blue trees of his. As long as the money was good, Herr Hahn hadn't cared. Hahn had started for the money and, with the introduction of the Sinanju Masters to the mix, had remained for the thrill.

But the thrill was long gone, and he couldn't spend his millions of CCS dollars if he was dead.

The mines *should* have exploded.

Remo stood in the back of the rowboat like a gondolier. The boat flashed over the hard-packed ice.

He was flying in too fast and changing course abruptly. There was no way for Hahn to track the small boat. No way to set off a mine directly beneath. But he could still set off the mines manually. There was a chance he might get them.

And after the ice field there was still one last line of defense. Maybe Hahn wouldn't need it. Maybe by sheer luck, he could get them before they left the glacier.

As his frightened eyes watched the boat zoom in, Herr Hahn's thick fingers fumbled at his keyboard.

THE FIRST EXPLOSION flashed bright orange to the right. It ripped through glacial ice, launching white chips over the speeding boat.

"I didn't do that," Remo called.

A second mine exploded, this one dead ahead. Remo had to twist and hop the boat over the smoking crater. Chiun kept Smith and Amanda from being flung to the glacier.

"I guess he couldn't wait for us to hit one," Remo said.

"We have another concern," the old Korean replied.

Tracking the Master of Sinanju's gaze up to the hilltop, Remo saw one of the helicopters had spluttered to life. The rotor blades were rapidly picking up speed.

"That could be Hubert," Amanda said. "He might be trying to escape with the seeds."

"One catastrophe at a time," Remo answered.

Through his tapping oar, he felt a metallic click. Another mine blew, this one a hair after they'd passed over it. It was only their great speed that kept them from being blown to bits. The boat pitched, and Amanda was thrown from her seat. Chiun grabbed her by the waist and settled her back to the bench.

The explosions became more frantic. It was as if whoever was controlling them had finally panicked. Mines exploded near and far. The path they were taking blazed to life with blast after blast. And then it didn't matter anymore because they were through the glacier and over to the other side. The ice pitched down, and the boat slid to the bottom of a short embankment. It came to a stop in a patch of soft mud.

Remo helped Amanda to her feet while Chiun saw to Smith.

The CURE director was rattled but unharmed. His knuckles were white around the handle of his briefcase. Bits of ice melted down the lenses of his glasses. Panting as he stood in the mud, Smith looked up to the hill. He spied a figure getting on board the helicopter.

"That's St. Clair," Smith said urgently. "Remo, you *must* stop him."

"Can do, Smitty," Remo said. "Let's go, Chiun."

The glacier's edge ended at a hundred-yard-wide stretch of sand that encircled the artificial hill. It was only muddy at the periphery, where melting water seeped into earth. Remo and Chiun had ventured only a few yards out into the sand when Remo noticed something rising up before them.

It was small and black and reminded Remo of the cap from an underground sprinkler system. Two others rose out of the sand on either side. More beyond these. Another row came into view beyond until the entire plain of sand was peppered with little black nozzles. They encircled the plateau, disappearing in wide arcs in either direction.

Remo and Chiun stopped at a cautious distance beyond the first row of nozzles. The caps were hissing.

Smith and Amanda were coming up behind them.

"Why have you stopped?" Smith demanded. The helicopter was just lifting off.

"We've got trouble," Remo said. "Both of you get back."

"Why?" Amanda asked. She sniffed the air. "Do I smell gas?"

She had barely gotten the question out before the air before them turned to flame.

The natural gas that had been seeping from the nozzles ignited in a flash of orange so brilliant it put to shame the midday sun. Spouts of fire spit up from underground like dragon's breath, forming an impenetrable wall of overlapping flames to the base of the broad mesa.

The heat beat them back. The four of them hurried back to where they'd abandoned the rowboat.

"He must have tapped into a natural-gas source," Amanda panted. "An ice age and global warming in the same valley."

The distance from fire to hill was far enough that the trees were unaffected by the spouts of flame. Safe, too, was the helicopter, which was lifting high over the fifty-foot spouts of flame.

"He's getting away," Smith said tightly.

Remo was glancing rapidly around the area. He found what he was after buried in the hill at the edge of the ice field. Just visible beneath the surface was a faint blue circle.

Racing over, he sent a fist cracking through the ice. Flashing fingers caught the triggering mechanism just before it went off. Extracting the mine whole, he brought it back to the muddy edge of the sandy plain.

The helicopter was clearing the flame and angling toward the mountains and the jungle beyond.

"Cover your ears," Remo suggested.

Hauling back, he let the land mine fly.

HUBERT ST. CLAIR WAS in his happy place.

It was one of the tricks he'd learned as a way of dealing with his fear of technology. When the panic of having to climb into a car or train or plane became too great, he'd think of that calming blue spot in his mind that was the world of tomorrow. The world where he lived in a bubble underground and could look up at a sky free of planes and satellites and, well, birds. But they'd come back one day. And the world would be better and it would be all Hubert St. Clair's doing. Thinking of this happy place, he felt calm in spite of the helicopter that rattled and shook all around him.

The seeds were in the back. They had been poured into the steel hopper that would funnel them through the floor and into retractable seeding arms. Over the jungle, he'd simply dump them. Spread them for miles and let nature take over.

The helicopter bounced as the pilot flew up over the spouts of flame. St. Clair's breath caught.

"Happy place, happy place, happy place," he repeated.

He saw the *C. dioxa* forest. Small from the air compared to the ice sheet of the valley. Around the hill, fire. The gas flames wouldn't harm his precious plants. Nothing could harm them.

Movement at the inner edge of the glacier. From the corner of his eye he saw the man on the ice.

Amanda Lifton's young bodyguard. He came from the glacier holding something in his hand. He reached back, and then the something in his hand was no longer in his hand, but in the air, and it was flying at the fleeing helicopter.

"Happy place, happy place," Hubert St. Clair blurted just before the mine exploded against the underside of the helicopter.

The world turned upside down.

It was the nightmare Hubert St. Clair had always envisioned. Strapped and helpless inside one of humanity's manufactured death traps.

The pilot fought to regain control. Trailing smoke, the helicopter flew back through the spurts of flame. It was a moment in Hell, with fire all around. St. Clair screamed even as he fumbled with his seat belt.

Somehow he kicked the door open. He was out in the empty air before he knew what was happening. When he hit the ground, the superheated sand burned and blistered his hands and face.

The helicopter was too low now. Tail section spinning out of control, it flew back into the wall of orange flame. It emerged on fire. When the explosion came, it was already scraping the surface of the glacier. It crashed in the narrowest band of ice near the jungle-covered mountains.

As the smoke kissed the sky, St. Clair was stumbling to his feet, cradling his burned hands under his armpits. A wall of fire still separated him from Amanda Lifton's bodyguards. He needed a haven. He needed his happy place.

Turning from the spouts of flame, Hubert St. Clair ran for all he was worth for his precious forest.

A TERRIBLE MISCALCULATION. Of a kind he had never made before in his well-ordered life.

But how could he have known? There had been Benson Dilkes's warning, but why—*why* would Herr Hahn have listened?

Sinanju. What were they? Legends. Mere men who killed with their hands. They were no match for the modern age, for a clever technical mind whose skills were far greater than mere kicks and punches.

And yet they had succeeded. And were about to succeed again.

Hahn's flaccid face was lifeless as he watched his monitor. The young Sinanju Master had just downed Hubert St. Clair's helicopter. The CCS head was crawling pathetically up the hill to the forest as Remo returned to the glacier to harvest two more mines.

Hahn didn't even try to detonate them. He'd tried it the first time, with the mine the American had used on the helicopter. The Sinanju Master had been too fast.

A mistake. Herr Hahn didn't make mistakes. He planned for every contingency. Even now.

He switched off his monitor. Hahn didn't need it anymore. It was inevitable. It was only a matter of time before they got through.

In the storage room of the Congress of Concerned Scientists' bunker, Herr Hahn walked woodenly over to a supply shelf. He pulled it from the wall. It rolled away easily, revealing a long, dark tunnel beyond.

He always planned for every little thing. Except for the one thing that would be coming for him. He understood that now. Now that it was too late.

Herr Olivier Hahn stepped into the tunnel, drawing the door shut behind him.

REMO CAME to a sliding stop at the mountain's edge, an unexploded mine in each hand. His thumbs held down the triggering mechanisms.

Amanda and Smith were picking their careful way around the crashed helicopter. It had landed near the edge of the ice field at the base of a mountain. Jungle stretched up to the mountaintop.

"This can't be all the seeds," Amanda announced worriedly as she examined the spilled contents of the hopper.

"The rest of them must be up there," Remo said.

Through the wall of shimmering flames, they could see St. Clair clambering up the side of the hill.

"Chiun, take care of them," Remo instructed. "This is gonna be one big boom."

The Master of Sinanju had Amanda and Smith lie flat on the ground behind the smoking helicopter. Over their prone bodies he placed the upended rowboat, which they'd used once more to get over to the helicopter. Once they were covered, the old Korean flounced over to Remo's side.

"Do you have any idea what you are doing?" Chiun asked.

"Course I do," Remo said as he brought one mine up to his chest. "I'm praying. And in a minute I'll be running like hell."

With a snap of his wrist, he let the mine fly. The second mine followed a millisecond later, whistling over the ice and out across the sandy plain. They were drawn like magnets to a pair of distant flaming spouts.

As the mines soared into the inferno, Remo and Chiun were already racing around the back of the helicopter. When the explosion came, they were planted in the ground behind the upended rowboat.

The explosion was huge. The ground buckled and twisted beneath them. Sheets of glacial ice as big as buses crashed to the jungle foliage in the mountains around the valley. When it was over and the shock waves had receded, a blackened crater gaped wide across the sandy plain. It was so large it had collapsed part of the *C. dioxa* plateau.

When they helped Amanda to her feet, she was shaken but unharmed.

Inspecting the plain, Smith nodded in satisfaction. The fires were all out. Remo had disrupted the flow of natural gas. Shading his eyes, he looked up the hill.

"I don't see St. Clair," the CURE director said.

Remo's face was cold. "He's hiding with the rest of the weeds."

With a look of doom on his cruel face, he raced for the hill.

31

Hubert St. Clair stumbled and fell, sprawling at the top of the hill.

Hands grabbed for him, pulling him to his feet.

"Dr. St. Clair, are you all right? What happened?"

It was one of the CCS board members. The last CCS member in the valley. The ground was still shaking from the gas explosion. The man seemed terrified. St. Clair shoved him out of his way. He lurched forward, falling into one of the temporary structures at the edge of the forest.

There were oxygen tanks inside.

The fear of technology was gone, replaced by a more urgent fear for survival itself.

He shrugged on the tanks. His hands were almost worthless as he tried to buckle the belt.

Limping and in pain, St. Clair headed for the primordial safety of the dense blue forest.

REMO AND CHIUN crested the hill a moment later.

The frightened CCS board member was startled by their sudden appearance.

"St. Clair," Remo snapped. "Where is he?"

"Um," the man said, glancing at the *C. dioxa* forest.

Amanda had just come over the hill. She helped Smith up, pulling him by one arm.

"He went into the woods," Remo told her. "I thought no one could breathe in there."

Amanda spied the rows of oxygen tanks through the open door of the shed.

"The tanks," she said, running to grab a set. "You'll need them to follow him."

"No, thanks," Remo insisted. He saw a set of goggles hanging with one of the tank sets. "These'll be enough. Chiun, watch the store. I'll be right back."

Pulling on the goggles, he ran into the forest.

THE AMMONIA BURNED his open sores.

St. Clair stumbled blindly for a time. Every tree looked alike. Every space between them looked like the path. He was lost for what seemed like an eternity.

Panic gripped his lungs. The rubber mouthpiece hissed in time with his erratic breathing.

St. Clair found what he thought was the path.

Yes! Yes, it was. Stumbling once more, he tripped up it. A moment later he was staggering into the original science campsite in the center of the forest.

He was almost there. He could lock himself safely away in his technology-free womb.

St. Clair staggered and fell. His burned palms slid across the ground. He wanted to cry out in pain.

He stumbled back to his feet. His goggles were fogging over. Tripping over his own feet, he made it through the abandoned camp.

Up ahead the arch of his underground hideaway rose from the forest floor.

He'd made it. He lurched for the air lock. He was reaching for the door when something strange happened.

The door vanished.

Not just the door, but the entire telephone-booth-sized unit. He caught a brief glimpse of it sailing through the air. It was a dark blur as it crashed through the domed ceiling of the place where Hubert St. Clair was supposed to sit and watch Earth's dying days.

St. Clair wheeled around.

Amanda Lifton's younger bodyguard stood beside him, a hard look on his cruel face.

St. Clair tried to turn, tried to run, but a thick-wristed hand was already reaching out, grabbing hold of the rubberized oxygen line that fed from the back of his tanks.

Remo mouthed a single word.

When St. Clair realized what he was saying, he felt his blood run cold.

"Timber," Remo said.

And he pulled the hissing line from the back of Hubert St. Clair's tanks.

32

Remo heard the helicopter rattling to life even before he'd made it back out of the *C. dioxa* forest. He assumed someone else was trying to escape, but when he broke into the open he found Chiun standing guard next to the helicopter.

The CCS man they'd found at the top of the hill was now sitting in the pilot's seat. Whirling rotor blades attacked the humid air.

Smith was in the process of snapping his cell phone shut and placing it in his briefcase. He and Amanda hurried over to Remo.

"Did you find St. Clair?" the CURE director asked as Remo ran up to them.

"He's taking a breather," Remo said tightly.

Smith nodded, understanding Remo's meaning. "That is at least some small satisfaction," he said grimly. "Although I fear we'll be joining him soon. I just got off the phone. There is a B-1 bomber en route. The President has ordered a strike on the area."

"What, is he nuts?" Remo snapped. "Get him to call it off."

Smith shook his head. "It is the only way to insure containment. I had Chiun commandeer that helicopter before I knew how little time was left to us. You are welcome to try escaping. Without my added weight, perhaps you will make it out of the blast zone in time." His tone didn't reflect the optimism of his words.

"We took care of everything, Smitty," Remo said. "The rest of the seeds are stashed here somewhere."

"No, Remo," Amanda insisted. "I checked the sheds. There were only about half as many seeds on Hubert's helicopter as there should have been. That's why we didn't catch his boat. He unloaded them somewhere on his way here."

"What about him?" Remo asked. He jerked a thumb to the CCS man in the helicopter. "Let's ask him where they are."

"He doesn't know, Remo," Smith said. "Chiun already helped me question him. The rest of the seeds are in the region, but since we don't know specifically where, we are left with only one alternative."

"There's some kind of underground hideout in the woods," Remo offered. "Maybe they're there."

Amanda shook her head. "He said he saw all the seeds Hubert brought here," she said. "There weren't any more than the ones we saw. They aren't here, Remo."

She seemed so calm. Her back was rigid, her face composed. As if she'd already accepted her fate.

Remo's eyes darted around in frustration.

He couldn't believe it. To come this far only to fail.

St. Clair was dead. He'd be no help locating the missing seeds. The worst thing of all was that his last vision in life before the end came would be of Hubert St. Clair's artificial ice field.

Remo's eyes alighted on the crashed CCS helicopter. The twisted wreckage lay near the edge of the glacier. Something was picking its careful way down from the jungle walls to the still-smoking helicopter.

A monkey. Another came out after it, then another. They began picking the ground around the crash site.

And then it hit Remo. He wheeled on Smith.

"Cancel the bombing, Smitty," he snapped.

The older man had been watching the sky, awaiting the bomber's arrival.

"But the seeds," the CURE director said.

"Are right where St. Clair left them," Remo said excitedly as he ran for the helicopter. "And I know just the monkey he's got guarding them."

33

When they started passing out the blame for all this—and, oh, don't think they wouldn't—there was no way they were going to drop any of it at the feet of the man whose name had once been Albert Snowden.

Prick was pacing back and forth past the barrier beside the stage at the Pan Brazil Eco-Fest. The former English teacher was absolutely, utterly and completely pissed.

The concert had been a disaster.

The Loco-Cola people had tried to make it work. They'd literally beat the bushes, rounding up locals and sticking them in officially licensed *Loco-Cola, Proud Sponsors Of The Pan Brazil Eco-Fest, Presents Prick* T-shirts. The result was pathetic. Scrubby native headhunters spitting poison darts at one another during the warm-up act, all wearing one hundred percent cotton Ts with Prick's face emblazoned across the fronts.

Prick had refused to go on, twenty natives had been poisoned and dragged into the bushes, and Chuck Parkasian, the promotions man from Loco, had locked himself in a Sani-John and was refusing to come out.

A complete and utter disaster.

"It's not my bloody fault," Prick muttered. "I packed them in in Buenos Aires last year."

As he paced behind the stage, he felt eyes tracking him. When he glanced up, he saw his two natives standing quietly off to one side. Watching him.

It was their knife-and-fork look. He was used to it by now. He'd been catching them giving him that same look ever since their album had been consigned to the Columbia House $1.99 bargain bin.

"You wanna eat someone?" Prick snapped at them. "Go and bloody eat the guy hiding in the plastic toilet. You have my blessing. Bon appetit."

As the two natives raced away on bare feet, Prick glanced at his watch.

"Where is he?" he demanded, looking up into the open pilot's door of the helicopter.

The scientist inside shook his head. "I can't raise the other helicopter at all."

Planting his hands on his hips, Prick glanced angrily around. There were now monkey-proof barricades around the helipad. Beyond the chain-link fences capped with razor wire, dozens of the animals chattered furiously.

Something inside Prick snapped.

He'd had enough of the Amazon rain forest. Leave it all to strip miners and Agent Orange for all he cared. He just wanted to get out of this jungle with its smelly monkeys and go back home to his Sussex estate.

He looked back through the open helicopter door at the silver tureen. It was filled with seeds. Some sort of environmental terrorism for the CCS. He wasn't certain what they were for exactly. And right now he really didn't care.

"I've had enough of this," Prick snarled. He climbed in next to the pilot. "Let's get on with it."

As the monkeys hopped and screeched, the helicopter began lifting slowly off the ground.

"ARE YOU CERTAIN of this, Remo?" Smith shouted over the roar of the rotor blades.

They were sweeping low over the jungle canopy. Up ahead, the silver shell of the outdoor concert hall rose up out of the trees.

"Just hold them off a couple more minutes, Smitty," Remo insisted. "If I'm wrong, they can blow up all of South America."

The helicopter screamed down before the dome of the concert hall. Cutting sharply over rows of empty seats, it swept up toward the stage, throwing up a cloud of angry dust.

The Master of Sinanju was pressed in the back with Amanda and Remo.

"There!" the old Korean announced. A slender finger unfurled, pointing dead ahead.

Looking forward, Amanda and Smith saw the rotor

blades of another helicopter rising beyond the barrier at the side of the stage.

"It's a CCS helicopter," Smith said tightly when the markings appeared.

He glanced over his shoulder at Remo and Chiun.

They were no longer there. Amanda Lifton looked around, surprised to find she was now alone.

Dust whirled in through the open rear doors.

WHEN THEY JUMPED down to the aisle from the helicopter, they hit the ground running.

Their legs and arms pumped in perfect harmony as the two Masters of Sinanju swept through the cloud of churned-up dust to the empty stage.

No communication was necessary. They vaulted to the stage. Clearing it in a few great strides, they flew at the side barricade. Up and over, they landed out back.

Squirrel monkeys parted before their flying feet, chattering angrily as the two men raced for the tall hurricane fence.

The helicopter was rising beyond it. It had cleared the fence and was rising higher. The nose dipped and it began to fly off.

One chance before it was out of reach.

Dust flew in their faces as they raced to the fence. Leg muscles coiling, they sprang to the top of the chain link. The razor wire was pulled taut. Avoiding the barbs, they used the wire as a spring. They launched like loosed arrows for the fleeing helicopter.

The helicopter was sweeping toward the jungle when Remo and Chiun reached the skids. Each grabbed one, clambering quickly up.

Inside the helicopter, the pilot felt a sudden increase in weight. Assuming it was a downdraft from the concert dome, he compensated. The chopper righted itself and soared out across the jungle behind the stage.

Hot wind whipped Remo's hair. On the other skid, the Master of Sinanju's wisps of hair blew crazily around his parchment face.

Even as they were reaching for opposite door handles, Remo heard a noise from the belly of the helicopter.

Two long silver arms extended from either side of the helicopter, identical to the ones on the helicopter that had crashed in the CCS valley.

Over the roar of wind and the scream of the rotors, Remo heard something rattling down the long, hollow pipes. Before he and Chiun had even opened the doors, tiny blue seeds began falling from holes in the metal arms.

Remo's reaction was immediate. Hooking his legs around the landing gear, he swung under the helicopter. From the other side, Chiun did the same.

They each grabbed a fat metal pipe, crushing them solid. The seeds clogged in the collapsed tubes.

Swinging back out, Remo and Chiun reached for the doors once more.

By now the CCS pilot knew something was wrong.

He was flying crazily, tipping from side to side and flying in close to the trees in an attempt to knock off the unwanted passengers.

The silver dome of the Pan Brazil Eco-Fest stadium raced toward them. The pilot was bouncing off the treetops when the door beside Prick popped open.

"You fly like he sings," Remo said coldly. "Bad."

Chiun popped the door next to the pilot.

Prick had been grabbing for something on the floor. He was pulling up a silver handle as the doors sprang open.

Remo heard a new sound from the belly of the helicopter. The handle Prick pulled had opened a door beneath the steel hopper. From where he stood, Remo could see thousands of blue *C. dioxa* seeds pouring from the underside of the helicopter. They pelted the concert site like blue hail.

Prick grinned triumphantly. "St. Clair said someone might try to interfere with whatever it is we're doing here." He leaned to Remo, lowering his voice. "By the way, what is it we're doing here, mate?"

Remo's face was hard. "You?" he asked, reaching out and grabbing Prick by the scruff of the neck. "You're falling." He tossed the singer out the open door.

They were above the trees once more. There was a lot of crashing and cursing and breaking of branches as Prick fell the long way to the ground.

The last of the seeds had been dumped out over

the concert site. The stainless-steel container was empty.

"Are you through?" Chiun called impatiently from the other open door.

Remo was looking down at the jungle. So big, so green. Now, thanks to their failure, its days—as well as those of the entire planet—were numbered.

"I think the whole world is," he muttered.

"I worry about you first," the Master of Sinanju sniffed. A long nail flashed out, snipping the pilot's carotid artery. "The world may take care of itself."

As the pilot grabbed at his throat with both frantic hands, Chiun dropped from sight.

There was nothing more Remo could do. His feet slipped from the skid, and he dropped from the helicopter.

As the aircraft screamed off, Remo soft-landed on the dense jungle canopy. Chiun was perched on a high branch in another tree, eyes directed at the helicopter.

The aircraft flew in a straight line for a few long seconds before lunging suddenly down. Tipping to one side—rotors chopping and flinging up chunks of green foliage—it slammed into the trunk of a fat tropical balsa tree. It exploded on impact.

From where they sat half a mile away, Remo and Chiun watched the ball of orange flame and black smoke rise up from the jungle. The flames died quickly, leaving behind just a thin curl of smoke.

"I guess that's it, Little Father," Remo called over

to the Master of Sinanju from his treetop. "We didn't make it. The bombing starts in five minutes."

Remo heard whimpering from somewhere far below.

When he looked down through a gap in the trees, he saw Prick lying on the jungle floor. The trees had apparently broken his fall. The singer looked dazed but intact. The two natives he had kidnapped from the rain forest stood above him. They were poking him with sticks and carefully pinching his thighs and chest like fussy housewives at the butcher shop. Satisfied with their selection, they each took a leg and dragged the semiconscious pop singer off into the bushes.

"I hope they've got a mighty big microwave," Remo commented as Prick's hairplugged head disappeared, "because lunch is gonna be cut short today."

"Yes," Chiun called over. "It is a shame, Remo. Do you realize that you will be the first Master since the time of Nik to not honor his tradition?"

"Too bad," Remo said. "But I guess none of that matters now. We should go hook up with Smitty, I guess. Wait for the end together."

He tipped from where he was treading the treetop, swinging down to a lower branch.

Chiun was scampering down his own tree. "There is still a way," the old man called slyly.

"Chiun, that helicopter dumped its seeds and Uncle Sam will be nuking the rain forest any minute now. There isn't time. Unless you think being nice means

I have to go rescue Prick from the jungle brunch buffet because, trust me, that ain't happening.''

"There is someone else you could do something nice for,'' the old Korean suggested. ''Someone who has been wrestling with a very difficult problem. Someone to whom you owe all and who is thus infinitely deserving of this one, final act of kindness.''

Remo had climbed about halfway down the tree. He stopped, looking over to the Master of Sinanju. There was a look of great optimism on the old man's face.

"What the hell,'' Remo said. ''We're toast anyway. Chiun, I give you my greatest solemn promise as Transitional Reigning Master of Sinanju that I will not for the rest of my life ever mention the fact that I am white in any way at all so that it might become known to future generations of Masters of Sinanju, including in the Sinanju Scrolls, which I will never get a chance to even write a single entry in because we're both about to die. There. Happy? Enjoy it while you can, 'cause you've got about two minutes left.''

Across the chasm that separated the two trees, the Master of Sinanju smiled craftily.

"Do not be so certain,'' the old Korean said knowingly.

He resumed scurrying down the tree.

Remo felt a sinking feeling in his gut. He wasn't sure how, but he knew somehow he'd just been had.

Frowning, he followed Chiun down.

From out the thick jungle came the chattering chorus of hundreds of happy monkeys.

34

It took Remo and Chiun twenty minutes to hike through the jungle back to the concert site. By the time they got there, Remo was scowling like a man who'd been hornswoggled.

Hundreds of spider monkeys were scurrying around the seats and over the stage. They were devouring the seeds that had been dumped by the CCS helicopter.

Smith and Amanda hurried to meet the two Masters of Sinanju as they came down the aisle of the outdoor theater. The CURE director was on his briefcase phone.

"Remo!" Amanda cried excitedly. "Can you believe it? It's a miracle!"

"No kidding," Remo said glumly. "We just saw the same thing in the jungle on the way back here. They're eating all the ones that fell out back there, too."

"It must be the smell," Amanda said. "They're attracted to the smell. There must be some olfactory trigger buried in that ammonia scent that's drawing them in like a beacon. Something we didn't even know was there when we were engineering the plants. Do you know what this means, Remo?''

Remo eyed the Master of Sinanju. The old man's wrinkled face held a look of placid innocence.

''Yeah, I know,'' Remo muttered.

She pressed on as if she hadn't heard him. ''It means that even if the monkeys don't get all the seeds, they'll get the saplings before they mature. The *C. dioxas* emit the same odor throughout their entire life cycle. It's over.''

Amanda skipped off to watch the monkeys gobbling up the pile of blue seeds that had landed on the stage. As she left, Smith was clicking his phone shut.

''I have just spoken to the President,'' the CURE director said, relief evident on his lemony face. ''The bomber has been recalled. The crisis is over.''

''What about those trees back in the valley?'' Remo asked.

''I discussed them with Dr. Lifton. She believes them to be an earlier strain of the *C. dioxas*. While they have many of the properties of the later plants engineered by the CCS, the seed coats were too tough. They would not germinate without human intervention. She has agreed to remain here to oversee the complete destruction of St. Clair's forest.''

Remo glanced over his shoulder. Amanda was standing back from the monkeys as they feasted on the seeds. A broad smile was plastered across her beaming face.

"Looks like Daddy's girl has found a purpose in life other than blubbering," he said.

"About Dr. Lifton," Smith said, his voice low. "She has seen and heard more than she should. Given the earlier circumstances, I assumed it no longer mattered. But now…"

"No problem, Smitty," Remo assured him. "She'll forget all about you and the President conspiring to nuke Brazil."

Smith allowed a rare smile. "Good," he said. He was digging in his worn briefcase. "Now I must arrange our transportation back home. I tried to call Mark to have him make the arrangements, but for some reason he is not answering the Folcroft line."

Pulling out his laptop, he took a seat nearby, balancing the computer on his bony knees.

As the CURE director began typing at his portable keyboard, Remo turned his attention to the Master of Sinanju. The very picture of tranquillity, the old Asian was watching a pair of monkeys battling over a fat blue seed.

"I want to take back what I said before," Remo said.

"You cannot," Chiun warned, "for you gave your word as Transitional Reigning Master. For the rest of your life. That is what you said. I intend to hold you to that, Remo Williams."

"No fair. That's when I thought the rest of my life was about ten seconds. Now you've roped me into carrying your 'Remo the Pale' cover-up clear through another generation.''

"Not a cover-up," Chiun insisted. "A selective omission." He tipped his head. "Now we need only involve your pupil and, perhaps, his pupil. All future Masters beyond that time need never know your great shame. Oh, my son, you have made an old man very happy."

When he saw the look of joy on the his teacher's upturned face, Remo's own harsh features melted.

It was in that moment that he realized he had fulfilled the decree of Master Nik after all. He had done something nice for the one person on Earth he most wanted to do something nice for. And it made Remo feel good.

"You're still an ugly old racist," Remo pointed out.

"Not according to the Sacred Scrolls," Chiun replied.

There was a scratching near Remo's foot. Looking down, he found a single monkey clawing to get past him. It pulled a blue seed from beneath one of the stadium seats. Clambering up to the top of the fence, it began chewing contentedly.

"And when I finally do read your bogus account of how civilization was saved today, I better not read the word 'Remo' and the word 'monkey' anywhere near each other," Remo warned.

Looking up at his pupil, Chiun raised a single eyebrow.

"There is limited space in the Sinanju Scrolls," the old Korean said, puzzled. "Why would I clutter up the scrolls with two words that mean exactly the same thing?"

He returned his innocent attention to the cavorting monkeys.

35

Thomas Urindangabo of the Zimbabwe government postal service stopped his Jeep near the tidy mailbox. The box was a scale model of the big clapboard house that sat in the heat at the end of the crooked little path.

Climbing down to the dirt road, he went to the cute little dollhouse. Opening the tiny front door, he slid a handful of mail inside.

He made this five-hour trek twice a week. Other people in the rural parts of the country were lucky if they got their mail once a year. But this was a special case.

Thomas climbed back into his jeep. Taking a silver whistle from his pocket, he placed it between his broad lips. Careful not to exhale too soon, he first started the Jeep back up and slipped it into drive. He kept one foot on the gas, the other on the brake.

Taking a deep breath, he blew hard. The whistle shrieked loud and shrill even as he stomped down on the gas pedal. The Jeep lurched forward and quickly disappeared down the road in a cloud of tossed-up dust.

As the Jeep raced away, Benson Dilkes came around from the back of the house, a pair of silver pruning shears in his hand. He walked under the shade of his climbing rosebushes, down the short front path to the road.

He found the mail where Thomas Urindangabo's shaking hands had put it. Dilkes took the envelopes out and began sorting through them.

His retirement five years ago had put an end to any interesting mail. Sometimes he'd get a note from his elderly father back in Florida or a postcard here and there from a former associate. Mostly it was junk.

When he came to the last envelope in the stack, his brow lowered. But only for an instant.

All at once, the dark tan seemed to drain down from his face, leaving behind a mask of chalky white.

The pruning shears slipped from his fingers, dropping to the dust. From the other hand, the clean white envelopes slipped, one by one, until only one remained.

The last envelope wasn't like the rest. Instead of white, it was silver. And in the upper left hand corner where the return address would go, was a simple symbol.

A small trapezoid bisected by a vertical line.

"Oh, no," said the man whom all in rural Zimbabwe had come to know and fear. "It's true." His voice was small.

With a sickly expression, he dropped back against his mailbox. Clutching the envelope tight in his hand, Benson Dilkes sank slowly to the dirt road.

36

Olivier Hahn had built an unassailable fortress in the half canton of Basel Stadt in northern Switzerland. The land mines were thick around the small cabin, which was tucked away beneath a rock overhang in the Jura mountain range. Crisscrossing trip wires were secreted for acres all around. Motion and sound detectors ringed an even wider area. A mosquito couldn't get within ten miles without Herr Hahn knowing it.

He came here after the disaster in South America. He had been hiding on the Swiss side of the Alpine system for five days. His eyes were weary and red-rimmed from the sleepless hours he had spent staring at the thermal monitors.

Five days. If they truly wanted to find him, wouldn't the Masters of Sinanju have found him before five days?

Maybe they weren't coming at all.

This was his own fault. He should have taken the advice of Benson Dilkes. His mentor had known. But how could Hahn have possibly known? After all, they looked so ordinary. And then there was the dirty thrill of fear.

Hahn had never felt fear before. Reveling in the new emotion had gone hand in hand with the challenge of trying to eliminate the vaunted Masters of Sinanju. But he had failed. Over and over until the giddy thrill of fear was all gone, replaced by the terrible realization that they would not stop until he was dead. Or would they?

Five days. Maybe he was safe.

Herr Hahn had tried to call Benson Dilkes many times over the past few days. The older man had some insight into the Masters of Sinanju. He might know how fanatical they were about tying up every little loose end.

Dilkes hadn't answered his phone.

Hahn knew that Dilkes didn't leave his home for so many days in a row any longer.

Maybe something had happened to Dilkes. Maybe they were using him to get to Hahn.

And then there was the final ironic twist in this sorry string of events. It had been waiting for him at his post office box when he returned to Switzerland. He could scarcely believe it, given the circumstances.

Herr Hahn glanced over at his butcher block table. Sitting on the place mat in the middle was a single envelope. The timing of its arrival would have been funny if the events of the past few days had turned out differently.

He was tearing his eyes from the envelope when he heard a sound at the front of his isolated cabin.

Herr Hahn couldn't believe his ears. Someone was knocking at his front door.

It was impossible. No one could have gotten through his defenses. Alarms would have sounded. Mines would have blown half the Alps to kingdom come. Hahn wheeled to the thermal monitors even as the knock came again.

"Avon calling," a familiar American voice called from the front porch. And the door exploded into the cabin.

When the two Masters of Sinanju slipped inside his home, Herr Hahn was already moving. There was no art now. No tricks, no gadgets. Hahn grabbed up a Luger from his computer table. Hand shaking, he spun on the two intruders.

Chiun was sniffing the fetid air of the cabin.

"No wonder we thought this one was a Hun," the Master of Sinanju said, nose crinkling in disgust. "He is attempting to mask his true self by gorging on German pastry and meat. In these confines I can smell the Frenchness in him."

"Smitty says he's a Swiss Frenchman. Or a French Swissman. Who knows with this screwy country? Anyway, he's Swiss and French and has a real bug up his ass about it."

"This is worse than I thought," Chiun said. "The French are public cowards while the Swiss hide their cowardice behind the skirts of neutrality. And he is both? No wonder he cowers behind machines and kills at a distance.''

Herr Hahn's hand was shaking like mad. He leveled the Luger on the Master of Sinanju's belly and fired.

At only ten feet away, the bullet somehow missed. A smoking hole appeared in the cabin's wall.

"Yeah," Remo agreed. "Smitty says he's only half French. The other half's German. I guess he didn't get much from that except for the name."

"That is because there is no such thing as being half French," Chiun sniffed. "It is like being half pregnant."

"Shut up! Shut up!" Herr Hahn shouted.

He fired twice more. Two more bullet holes erupted in the wall behind the Master of Sinanju. Hahn saw the ghostly twirling flutter of the old man's silk kimono.

"He even sounds French," Chiun pronounced.

"No kidding." Remo laughed, hearing Hahn speak for the first time. "Buddy, with an accent like that, you should open up a baguette-and-beret shop in the Eiffel Tower."

Sweating profusely now, Hahn wheeled on Remo. "I am German!" he yelled in an accent so French it should have had subtitles. He began firing wildly.

"Well, yippee-do for you," Remo said, shaking his head. He walked over to Hahn, pulling the gun from his hand even as the fat man continued firing at him.

The killer's pudgy finger continued to squeeze

empty air. Herr Hahn's frightened eyes darted dumbly from Remo to Chiun.

"I had to do this thing, Master of Sinanju," he pleaded with the old man. "If not now, soon." He pointed a flabby quivering arm at the kitchen table.

Remo's brow dropped suspiciously. "What the hell are you talking about, Maurice Chevalier?"

The Swiss assassin never had time to respond.

Like a curl of angry, whirling wind, the Master of Sinanju flew over to the trembling killer. A bony hand snatched the back of Olivier Hahn's shirt collar and the old Korean delivered the assassin's head through the screen of his thermal monitor. The device continued to spark even after Herr Hahn's brain no longer did.

"What was that all about?" Remo demanded, jumping back from the shattering glass and collapsing body. "How did he know who you were?" He glanced to the table where Hahn had pointed. His face fell. "Wait a second..."

But Chiun was already on the move. Whirling to the butcher-block table, the old man snatched up the lone envelope that Herr Hahn had left there.

"I have waited enough in this nation that is afraid to commit to cowardice," he insisted. "I wish to go home."

In a swirl of kimono skirts, he headed for the door.

"That was one of them, wasn't it?" Remo called after him. "He had one of those goddamn silver envelopes you've been stuffing inside those gold envelopes these past few months. I *know* it. The way you just jumped on it, I just know it.'' He shook his head, shoulders sagging. ''So is this something I'm gonna live to regret?''

At the cabin door, Chiun paused. When he turned, his parchment face was drawn in lines of deep reflection.

''Perhaps,'' he admitted. There was a mischievous glint in his hazel eyes. ''If you are lucky.''

And like a silent whisper, the old Korean slipped out into the cold mountain air.

James Axler

OUTLANDERS®

PRODIGAL CHALICE

The warriors, who dare to expose the deadly truth of mankind's destiny, discover a new gateway in Central America—one that could lead them deeper into the conspiracy that has doomed Earth. Here they encounter a most unusual baron struggling to control the vast oil resources of the region. Uncertain if this charismatic leader is friend or foe, Kane is lured into a search for an ancient relic of mythic proportions that may promise a better future…or plunge humanity back into the dark ages.

In the Outlands,
the shocking truth is humanity's last hope.

Take
2 explosive books
plus a
mystery bonus
FREE